The Thirteenth Child

J.L. O'Faolain

Dreamspinner Press

Published by
Dreamspinner Press
4760 Preston Road
Suite 244-149
Frisco, TX 75034
http://www.dreamspinnerpress.com/

The Thirteenth Child
Copyright © 2011 by J.L. O'Faolain

Cover Art by Paul Richmond   http://www.paulrichmondstudio.com

ISBN: 978-1-61372-003-5

Printed in the United States of America
First Edition
May 2011

eBook edition available
eBook ISBN: 978-1-61372-004-2

To Paula Stokes

Who was there from the beginning,
even when I wanted to give up.
Consider this the first of many.

Chapter *One*

IT WAS far too cold to be working outside today.

Cole took in the dozen or so thugs standing around him with an irritated glare of contempt. If the money for this job hadn't been as good as it was, he'd be back in his loft curled up underneath a nice, thick blanket enjoying a replay of his old copy of Blood Omen right now. As it was, the rent was due. Katalina had already reminded him of that twice this week. The first gust of New Year air had nearly been enough to make him turn around and go back inside. Only the fact that Awar the troll paid good money made him keep going. Now, he was lurking underneath a trash-strewn bridge that reeked of raw sewage as members of the attacking gang closed in on him.

Cole took half a step backward, crouching down slightly as the red-hot end of his double-headed blade, Aed Deigh, extended out from the hilt. The thug that was nearest caught a swipe across his abdomen as Cole feinted forward, and then turned into a sweeping spin that caught two more with the opposite end, the one endowed with the power of arctic cold. There was perhaps a half-second where nothing occurred, as though his attacks had missed. His first target, however, suddenly clutched his belly in pain as fire exploded all over his skinny frame, incinerating him in an instant. The others went rigid at the same time as ice crawled like ravenous spiders all over their skin.

Cole never let up, even as the remaining members of the gang began having second thoughts. Two more found themselves the victims of spontaneous combustion as Cole drove his twin-bladed weapon with the hilt in the middle down into the chest of the boy who he assumed was their leader. The shocked expression on the man-child was actually somewhat comical. Cole withdrew his blade as the ice claimed him, then tipped the frosted statue over with his finger and smirked at the remaining few thugs as it shattered on the ground. The head wound up rolling down the incline and stopped at his feet. Cole placed the heel of his boot atop it and stared his audience down.

No one blinked. They were all too terrified to move.

Smart.

"I was asked by a friend to ensure none of you harass him any further," Cole said, standing with a practiced ease. "This can go one of two ways. Either I slaughter the lot of you and walk off without breaking a sweat, or you can all go back to wherever it is you came from, and leave the nice troll alone so he can finish his homework and get over his head cold in peace."

"This is our hood," one bravely spoke up, yet Cole could distinctly hear the rapid beating of his heart. "Freaks like dat should stay da fuck away."

A handful nodded their affirmation. "He kind ain't welcome here no mo'."

Cole was on the speaker in the blink of an eye. "Would you prefer to be frozen, or burned to a little pile of ash?" he whispered in the young man's ear. "I'd be happy to oblige with either."

There was the unmistakable sound of a hammer being drawn back from a gun. Cole waited, waited until he knew the shooter was about to pull the trigger, then moved. At the same time, he jerked the boy in front of him forward slightly, putting him directly in line of the bullet as it left the chamber with what sounded like a thunderclap. Had it been rush hour, the sound would've been muffled by oncoming traffic. It was with his ears ringing that Cole released his grip just as the young man's head exploded. Turning around, he saw that the shooter was holding, of course, a .357 Magnum.

"Those things make such a mess," he muttered as blood and other things ruined his clothes. "My dry cleaning bill is going to be outrageous."

Everyone else was still taking in the sight of their spokesman crumbling to the ground with most of his head gone. Not one to miss an opportunity to finish a job quickly, Cole dashed forward and took out the one holding the gun first. It was made of metal, and given the decidedly high iron content, it would do the most damage to him. One swipe with the fire edge of his weapon reduced the bastard's arms to smoldering bones. Cole stabbed him with the ice edge for good measure, then carved a path through the scattering crowd as though he were the wind and they were caught in molasses. Less than a minute later, his job was finished. Ominous footsteps pounded the ground heading in his direction as he slowly stood upright.

"That should do it, then," he said, willing the blades back into their shared hilt. "I'd like to collect my pay now, if you don't mind."

"No problem," sniffed Awar, grunting from chest congestion as he fumbled around for the opening to his back trouser pocket. "Thanks for coming on such short notice."

"I hated to ask you to get out of bed given your current condition," said Cole, graciously accepting the bag of gold from him. "But I wanted to make sure they were indeed the ones harassing you. It would make me look bad if I'd murdered the wrong ones."

"It's no big deal," Awar assured him. "I'm feeling much better, but the runny nose is killing me. I've got a calculus final to study for, and my correspondence term paper for American History is tomorrow. All I wanted was some peace and quiet, but those little shits just wouldn't leave me alone. And it isn't like I can just phone in the police, not that it would do me much good…."

"No need to explain," Cole assured him, counting out the gold coins. "Go get some rest. You look like hell."

"I haven't been able to sleep because of this damned cold," he muttered weakly. "I'd love to have handled this myself, but this crud has sapped all my strength."

Cole nodded in professional sympathy as he resumed counting. Awar, meanwhile, turned his rather lumpy head to the side and let out an impressively loud sneeze, which caused the bridge overhead to shake. Dust and icy frost rained down on their heads, signaling to Cole that it was past time to go. "Here," he said, holding up three gold pieces. "You gave me three more than we agreed on."

"Keep it," Awar insisted, waving it away. Cole's long hair was swept up as Awar's hands inadvertently caused a small wind to kick up around them. "Consider it a tip for a job well done, since I wasn't up for handling things myself. I honestly thought you'd just come down here and scare the little bastards, but this works out much better. The lot of them should fit in my meat locker with a little extra cramming. I've got food for almost a month now, and the bones should scare away anyone else that tries to hassle me.

"Besides," he added, "I was getting sick of chicken soup. It gives me bad gas."

Cole accepted his tip and, with a wave over his shoulder, left the underside of the bridge very quickly.

A WHILE later, Cole climbed the stairs leading up to his loft, shaking his hair to remove the bits of snow that hadn't melted yet despite the warm temperature inside of the building. It was one of the many drawbacks to being a full-blooded sidhe living in New York. No matter how powerful he was, all the metal, glass, and man-made plastics hampered his abilities considerably. It was getting to the point where the changing temperatures really bothered him. Before long, he might even suffer from sinus problems like all the other red-nosed shoppers.

Shuddering at the thought, he waved a hand idly at the door and waited as the locks on the other side tumbled open. At the same time, the wards that had been placed years ago temporarily fell, allowing him passage. Shaking the rest of the snow off, Cole hung his coat on the rack and strode idly into his home. The place was quiet for the moment, which meant that Katalina had already left for class. Happy to have the place to himself for a few hours, Cole immediately stripped out of his clothes and stood naked in the living room for a moment, allowing the muted sunlight from the expanse of windows behind him to rake across his moonlight-colored skin. Sighing, he took a few steps over to the open kitchen area, grabbed a bottle of oak mead from the refrigerator, and downed its contents.

Having a roommate meant he was rarely able to go naked in his own home. The loft's rent was cheap, however, so it was a trade-off he accepted on good terms, mostly. Feeling a nice light buzz from his drink, Cole made himself a sandwich from some leftover turkey, then made tracks for the shower. The gold from the job Awar had given him was strewn across the counter. He would put it away after he'd gotten clean and, more importantly, warm. Katalina could take it to the exchange bank on her way to class tomorrow. For now, though, his only priority was to stand under a steady stream of hot water for as long as possible.

There was only one shower in the whole loft. Luckily for him, Katalina rarely left anything of hers lying around for him to step on. Today, however, he nearly fell flat on his face because of a stray bra getting tangled around both feet. Rising up, he swept his eyes across the counter top, which was loaded with makeup and used cotton pads. There were puddles of water near the edge of the shower, and a used towel hanging on the bar alongside a drawn-back curtain.

Apparently, Katalina had been in a hurry this morning.

Disregarding all of it, Cole marched into the shower and closed the curtain behind him before turning the hot water all the way to the left. Steam rose quickly up toward the rafters as the jets beat down on his backside. Cole groaned; if there was one upside to being affected by cold weather, it was warming up afterward. For years, he'd wondered why humans made such hype over things like hot chocolate and warm soup in the wintertime. Now it made perfect sense, though he still missed the warm climate of Avalon.

An image of it, long buried, rose up in his mind. Cole found himself thinking of the last time he'd stood on its shores, looked out at the expanse of trees and distant fairy mounds, and realized he would never be coming back. Through the decades of his time amongst humans, Cole had countered his sorrow with thoughts of not wanting to return and the memories of his last encounter with Lord Oberon. The thought of returning to Avalon now seemed almost like a joke, but that didn't stop him from crying. It didn't stop the tearing in his chest, like something vicious was trying to eat its way out of his heart. It didn't stop his head from swimming.

He must have been under the steam for too long. Even after Cole managed to get hold of his emotions, he still felt light-headed.

Tuulois MacColewyn....

Cole blinked and turned around in response. It had been a while since anyone had called him by that name, but hearing it seemingly out of thin air was especially odd.

Tuulois MacColewyn....

Oh, crap.

Cole looked around desperately for something to hold onto, or at the very least, something to cover himself with. The spell, however, had already taken effect, and he was being drawn out of the shower through the very air toward the one summoning him.

Tuulois MacColewyn!

Cole felt himself being forced through a sort of rubber tunnel, starting with his head. There was a loud splash as the water from the shower that had been teleported along with him came crashing down onto the head of Detective James Corhagen, who was conveniently kneeling at the edge of the chalk circle, directly in front of Cole's groin. A small cut from the detective's thumb indicated the blood he'd used to activate the summoning circle. The chalk, now soaking wet, was still clutched in his other hand.

Cole couldn't resist. "While you're down there...."

Immediately, Detective Corhagen rose up to his feet. Noticing that Cole was severely naked at this point, he darted his eyes heavenward at the same time that his head snapped sharply to the left. "Ouch!" he grunted. "Warn me next time, won't you?"

"You could have called first," Cole pointed out, not bothering to cover himself. "It isn't my fault your bad timing persists even when you're using that spell I taught you."

"I am sorry," he groaned. "I guess I caught you at a bad time. Are you busy right now?"

Cole rolled his eyes at the question, but Corhagen didn't notice as he'd just covered his eyes with the hand that had the bleeding thumb. The sight of his former friend stumbling around slightly trying to regain his sense of direction with both eyes covered was enough to make Cole snicker privately to himself. It was only then that he began to notice his surroundings, and realize that the place where they both stood was unfamiliar to him.

"Where are we?" he asked, gazing around at what appeared to be someone's bedroom. "Have we been here before?"

"Huh?" Corhagen asked, turning almost too fast to keep his eyes covered. "Oh, no. This is a crime scene. The murder that took place occurred in the baby's room on the other side of that wall." Corhagen pointed just behind Cole at the carefully made bed. "I think that's the right direction, anyway."

"You could take your hand off your eyes," Cole suggested coyly.

"No, thank you. This was the victim's bedroom, anyway. Her name was Susan Brown. She worked as a cleaning lady at some subsidiary company of Microsoft. At approximately 12:01 last night, her heart somehow managed to explode out of her chest and splatter into pieces against the refrigerator. The babysitter discovered the body this morning when she showed up to look after the woman's daughter while Mrs. Brown was at work. We've got her in the living room right now."

"I thought you said the woman was murdered in the child's bedroom?" Cole interrupted, confused.

"That was where the...." Detective Corhagen fumbled for a moment. "Where the 'incident', I guess, took place. Her heart somehow achieved escape velocity after exploding from her chest, sailed out the open bedroom door, and then splattered into pieces against the fridge."

"Ah." Cole nodded. "Now I understand. Please, continue."

"That's about it," the detective finished. "Except that the baby is also missing, and this is the third case of such an incident happening. The chief is breathing down my neck, most of my department thinks we've got some kind of serial murderer-slash-kidnapper on our hands, except for the fact that all three crime scenes have been swept thoroughly with a fine-toothed comb, and nobody can come up with so much as a fingerprint. There's no signs of forced entry, no sign of a struggle at all, unless you count the mess the victims made in their last few seconds before becoming an *Aliens* stunt double. So I've got a murderer who can make themselves undetectable to all forms of modern forensics, even down to DNA sampling, and people are turning to me like the answers are supposed to just come flying out of my ass."

Cole studied his former friend for a moment. "You quit smoking again, didn't you?"

"What?"

"You're always this cranky when you stop smoking," he clarified. "It makes you stressed out. So, why did you summon me here?"

"You have to ask? I need help here, Cole. This is some serious shit going down, and I don't know what to do about it."

The bedroom door eased open just then. Both Cole and Detective Corhagen turned to find a very small woman look directly at James. "Sir, they've questioned the babysitter. She had a spare key to the apartment that was given to her by…."

The woman's eyes finally took in Cole and widened. James turned around to face him, received another eyeful, and quickly jerked away. "Um," he stammered, thinking fast. "Thank you, Officer Morrison. This is my… old friend, Cole. He and I used to work on some cases together. He's a police consultant who specializes in…."

Corhagen snapped his fingers quickly.

"Unusual cases," Cole finished for him.

"Unusual cases! That's it." Corhagen was blushing now, which Cole had to admit was fun watching. "I asked him to come down here and have a look at the crime scene. He might spot something the other forensics guys missed."

"How do you do, m'lady?" Cole bowed slightly, giving her a full view of his package. "Forgive my present state. I was in the shower when the detective called."

Cole gave the detective a knowing look, and he promptly blushed red. "He got here really fast," Corhagen tried, feebly.

Officer Morrison had been unable to tear her eyes off Cole during the whole exchange. Cole himself doubted the poor woman had absorbed anything that was said the entire time. "I'm very efficient," Cole went on, deciding that he might as well enjoy himself. "As Detective Corhagen himself knows very well."

"Could we maybe get the nice police consultant a pass so that he could examine the crime scene, Officer?" Corhagen pressed, his face turning redder. "And perhaps a towel, to hide his shame?"

"What shame?" Cole teased, as the door slammed shut. "I don't feel any shame."

Corhagen ignored him in favor of staring daggers at the opposite wall. A moment later, the door opened again just wide enough to allow a police pass entry. The plastic-coated tag sailed through the air and smacked the detective upside the head. A second later, one mauve-colored towel crossed the barrier forming the summoning circle, breaking it. Cole caught the towel and began drying himself off at his leisure. Officer Morrison eyed him for a second more through the tiny crack, then quietly slid the door shut.

"A very dedicated policewoman you've got there," Cole remarked, taking longer than necessary to dry his balls. "I'd hold onto that one if I were you."

Corhagen thrust the pass back behind him as he adamantly continued to avoid looking anywhere near Cole. Cole finished drying off, then wrapped the towel securely around his waist and took the pass from him. This one had a clip on it, so he fastened it to his towel just to the left of where his treasure trail ended. Corhagen risked a quick peek and sighed.

"Will you take the case?" he pleaded. "I could really use your help."

"It's obvious you need it," Cole replied, avoiding his gaze now. "Why else would you have used that spell after so long?"

The weight of that sentence hung in the air between them. "I think I'd like to go home now," Cole finished dryly. "And resume my shower. Do you think Officer Morrison would be willing to call a cab for me?"

"I'll pay you double," Corhagen spat out before Cole could step out of the circle.

"What?" Cole was sure he hadn't heard right.

"If I have to pay you myself, I will," he added emphatically. "Chances are, though, the chief would rather cough up the extra cash than risk letting shit like this continue. And that's really saying something, if you'd just stop for a second and remember what a tightwad he's always been. Things on the force have been sour since… well, for a year now. It's not getting better, and since no one wants to admit what's really going on, the problem just gets worse and worse. I've managed to get a few people at my precinct to come over to my way of thinking."

It was impossible for Cole to mask his surprise.

"I know," Corhagen said, nodding. "Believe me, I know. It wasn't easy, but some of them have had bad experiences themselves that they couldn't explain afterward, or just didn't feel other people would believe. None of us know what to do about it yet, but we're trying. The chief wants this case taken care of yesterday, though. It's way too messy and would be a tabloid reporter's wet dream. Imagine what would happen if word of this got out to the press. It wouldn't be an outright panic, but the end result…."

Cole thought of Awar living under his bridge, thinking that all was peaceful now that the punks that'd been hassling him were dead.

"If I have to, I'll strong-arm the chief into paying it," James finished. "But we need you on this one. I haven't been having the dreams yet, but I can feel it. It's going to get a hell of a lot worse."

Cole nodded. "You'd better not squirm out of paying for me," he threatened lightly. "Or I'll have the goblins on your ass for it."

Corhagen laughed. "Right. So, where do we start?"

"Where else?" Cole replied, adjusting his towel as he headed for the door. "We talk to the victim. She probably knows a thing or two."

NONE of the other police officers at the crime scene were happy to see Cole. Though he didn't recognize many faces in the crowd of discontent stares, Cole had gained something of an infamous reputation among Corhagen's fellow officers. He supposed word about Lieutenant Heisen's sudden bout of erectile difficultly had spread very fast. That had been the last time he'd set foot in James's precinct, so it was natural, he supposed, that people were less than thrilled by his return.

Fortunately, it didn't take long for Corhagen to clear the room. Most of the police officers on the scene were male, despite the fact that humans today liked to think of themselves as equals. No one seemed in any big hurry to do more than glare reproachfully at him one last time before making tracks for the door. Once they were gone, Cole turned to his former friend and smirked.

"Nice bunch. Very people-skills oriented."

"It's your own fault, you know," James reproved him. "Heisen didn't deserve anything like what you put him through. His wife left him after a while."

"I'm sure it had everything to do with his impotency and not the numerous times he'd cheated on her in plain sight." Cole looked down at the body. "Funny, but I always imagined an ejected heart would make a much larger mess than this."

Corhagen looked down. "What do you mean? There's blood everywhere."

"Just on the body," Cole clarified. "I always pictured the whole floor soaked with blood stains. I thought there'd be splashes on the walls, but other than ruining a perfectly nice bathrobe, this is a relatively neat piece of black magic. Who knew a murderer could be so obsessive-compulsive?"

Corhagen looked repulsed. "Do you just sit around when there's nothing on television and imagine different ways of destroying a human life with magic?"

"Not really," Cole replied. "I don't watch much TV."

Cole extended his left hand without another word and drew forth his power. The Hand of Cold Death began its work at once, causing the body at their feet to stir and twitch. In a moment, the eyes fluttered. None of the officers had bothered to close them. The pupils rolled back and forth, glancing around sharply as Susan Brown's corpse lifted itself up off the floor and hovered for a second in the air before its feet touched the floor.

"Susan Brown," Cole said in a clear, distinctive voice. "We were wondering if you'd mind answering a few questions for us about how you died."

The corpse, still pale and a little sallow in the cheekbones, turned to stare emptily at Cole for a moment. "It was late, and the baby had just woken up from a nightmare. I was rocking her back to sleep when I thought I heard a noise. It was coming from the living room, so I thought it might be a burglar, so I grabbed the gun out of the nightstand."

"She kept a gun in the same room as her baby?" Corhagen interrupted.

Cole put a finger to his lips and shushed him.

"I went to the living room, but there was no one there. The same sound came out of the kitchen area, but I could see it was empty, so I assumed it must have been a rat. I've had problems with rats before. I put the gun back into the nightstand and picked Cheslia up again. She never stopped crying the whole time. It wasn't a normal cry, more like she was scared of something. It was midnight, and I was exhausted. I had a long day ahead of me tomorrow and needed sleep. I put her back in her crib and turned...."

For the first time, the corpse of Susan Brown showed real emotion. Everything before had been like listening to a tape recording of someone reading dialogue. Cole steeled himself in case she began to cry. He hated seeing a dead body cry.

"Something was wrong," it whispered. "My chest hurt, like I was having a heart attack. I was just thinking that, if I died, who would take care of Cheslia? Then, something happened. I thought I heard something pop, like a balloon being stuck with a needle underwater. It was so loud, my ears rang. Something went 'splat' in the kitchen, and I was just wondering whether I should go and see what it was. Then I looked down, and...."

Cole quickly lowered his hand, bringing her body back down to the floor.

"My poor Cheslia. Who's going to take care of Cheslia?"

Corhagen didn't look well. Cole sighed and led his friend out of the room toward the kitchen. After a minute of searching, he found a clean glass in one of the cabinets and poured a glass of water. Holding it up, he surveyed the frozen, stoic expression on the detective's face.

Without a word, he tossed the water straight at him.

Corhagen sputtered. "What the hell, Loose!"

"Don't ever call me that," he replied, putting the glass down. "And snap out of it. You're the one who called me here, remember? You've got a job to do and I need to get paid, so let's figure this out so we can both get back to our old lives. How does that sound?"

"Sorry," Corhagen apologized. "I…. She was worried about her daughter. I can relate."

The heavy, awkward silence from before was back in spades. "How are the kids?" Cole reluctantly probed. "You're on, what? Two now?"

"Three," James corrected. "Or we will be. Sarah is pregnant again."

Cole very much wanted to comment, but he managed to avoid it by biting down on his tongue. With the taste of blood in his mouth, he instead replayed what the deceased body of Susan Brown had told them. "She talked about hearing something in the living room," he said thoughtfully. "And then in the kitchen. I don't think for a second it was a rat. She hears a strange noise in her own home, and then dies rather spectacularly a minute or two later?"

"You're right," James agreed, mopping his forehead with a handkerchief. "It's too much of a coincidence. Could the spell caster have been in the apartment with her?"

"You said before that there were two other incidents like this," Cole pressed. "And that forensics hadn't found any signs of the murderer being anywhere near the scene of the crime. I doubt the perp… it is still 'perp', isn't it?"

Corhagen nodded.

"Right, thanks. I have such a hard time keeping up with slang. Anyway, I don't think the perp in question would break pattern just to sneak a peek at his handiwork. He or she has too good of a thing going. Whatever their motive, the method of murder ensures that they're nowhere near the crime when it occurs. It's a serial killer's ideal situation, assuming they don't want to be caught."

"Then how come there aren't more crimes being committed like this?" Corhagen wondered. "Not that I'm complaining, mind you."

"This is black magic, James," Cole stated, obviously. "Spells such as these are very complex, requiring years worth of focus and concentration as well as a great deal of magical energy to power them. It's not as though one could simply wave one's wand and make something like this happen. Such spells are nearly always powered by rituals. These can go on for days or even weeks, depending on the skill and abilities of the user."

"So we're dealing with someone with fey ancestry?" James considered. "Or a renegade sidhe, like you?"

"Possibly," Cole admitted. "But something like this feels too human. Most sidhe wouldn't consider dabbling in spells like this. They're considered crude and unimaginative."

"Exploding someone's heart out of their chest shows a lack of imagination?"

Cole smiled. "The sidhe are immortal. We've had eons to perfect artful execution. Yes, a spell such as this would be lowbrow for much of the fey. I imagine the goblins, or perhaps the hobs, would get a kick out of watching it happen, but that's more akin to reality TV. Fun to watch, but few would actively participate. Goblins prefer a hands-on approach to their victims, anyway. No, I imagine this was done by a human, maybe a human with some magical ancestry in their veins. Either way, we're dealing with a human criminal here."

Corhagen was silent for a long time.

"What's wrong?" Cole wondered. "I expected you to be thrilled. For once, there's a case involving magic with a perpetrator you can actually arrest."

"Assuming we can prove the perp in question did it," he pointed out. "Either way, this has to stop."

There was silence for a moment, then James leaned back away from the counter. "I'm going to bring everyone back in here," he said, heading for the door. "Her body isn't going to do any funny tricks, or get up and dance in the middle of an autopsy, is it?"

"You still ask me things like that," said Cole, deeply offended. "When has that ever happened?"

"With you, I can never be too careful."

The underlying meaning of that struck home. Cole waited until James's hand was on the doorknob before asking, "Does she still put out?"

James froze. "What?" he asked, turning around.

"Sarah," he clarified. "Does she still put out for you?"

The look in Corhagen's eyes was worth the anger stretched taut over his face. "She's pregnant, isn't she?" he replied defensively.

"Yeah." Cole nodded. The implication hung in the air between them worse than the deceased remains of the apartment's former tenant.

"I'm going," James uttered, turning away.

"I'll be right behind you, after I check one or two more things."

The door slammed shut before Cole could finish. Looking around, he scanned the kitchen for a moment, taking in several deep breaths through his nose. His senses told him nothing, yet Cole had the distinct feeling he had missed something obvious. Something tangible.

His search of the kitchen was brief. Cole wanted to finish before the police came back, so he scanned through the living room quickly before moving on to the baby's crib. At first, it seemed as though he were on a wild goose chase of sorts. But then, just as he was about to give up, his eyes landed on something. Behind the baby's pillow, a stray hair protruded out against the soft pink spread. Cole snatched it up quickly as the front door to the apartment banged open. Fumbling, he cursed himself and the man who thought that towels would never need pockets. With few options left, he killed the lights and backed off into the shadows as the sounds of heavy footsteps approached. The glamour he wove around himself affixed itself to his flesh just in time as the police reentered the room.

Moving while under the concealment of magic was next to impossible. Simple glamours like what he used to stay out of sight would usually break after a nice hard jolt, but since everyone's attention was focused on the dead body in the room, Cole dropped his disguise and instead focused on keeping their eyes on it instead. Once he was out of the room, he made a gesture with his hand, and Officer Morrison took a sudden fascination with a young man who was changing in the building across the street. No one else was present, including Corhagen, so Cole was able to slip away undetected.

He could have asked Corhagen to send him back to his apartment via the circle in the other room, but Cole suspected he would have a difficult time getting the detective to agree while he was clutching the hair sample. The police could be very anal retentive when it came to removing evidence from a crime scene, and Cole was sadly lacking pockets at the moment. Though his suspicions hadn't been confirmed yet, Cole maintained the belief that there was more to the case than met the eye. That, and he wanted to get home and change. The towel was getting scratchy.

Chapter Two

THE cab driver kept looking back at Cole the whole way home. The backseat was sticky, and it smelled as though someone had been working their stick shift all over the upholstery. Finally, after getting sick of watching the bearded guy up front trying to peek back discreetly and nearly running the car up on the sidewalk, Cole removed his towel and sat his ass back down on the grimy seat, fully exposing himself.

"Happy now?" he asked pointedly.

Luckily, they weren't too far from his loft. Cole managed to fix his towel back on and give the bastard the finger before being forcibly ejected from the cab. It was going to be a cold walk back, and he was barefoot to boot, but it turned out the asshole wasn't finished yet. Several discriminating swear words pertaining to his gender, orientation, and manhood later, Cole realized his wallet was still up in his loft several blocks farther down. He had no cash with which to pay the driver, who was screaming more by the second and pointing at the meter beside his steering wheel. After a moment of that, to which even the more jaded pedestrians were beginning to take notice, Cole finally threw his hands up in surrender. With a slight twist of his fingers, he brought the man's eyes toward his and made contact.

The asshole's face went slack suddenly, as though he'd just been hit with some heavy tranquilizers. Once Cole was sure the mortal's mind was fully ensnared by his web of glamour, he extended a hand as though to pass the bastard something. The man's hand closed around thin air, grasping it as if it were as real as solid matter, and nodded blankly. Cole gave the gentleman an imaginary tip of his hat to top off the gesture, then calmly walked away. A few seconds later, the cab pulled out into traffic, nearly causing a rear-end collision, and swerved on its way. Cole realized as he continued his trek amidst some rather bemused people that, if he were human, he might feel guilty for such a thing.

Which, in the end, just went to prove that it didn't pay to be human. Furthermore, the driver had more than earned it. There had been a time at one point in Cole's life when he would've charged for such prize-viewing. As it was, the people on his street were getting way too much of a show at the moment.

Katalina was waiting for him when he entered the loft. "Why did you leave the shower running?" she demanded. "I wanted to get cleaned up, and there's no hot water left."

Her eyes drifted over him for a second. "And why did you go outside in freakin' January weather with only a towel on?"

"I didn't," he replied dryly. "Is there any hot chocolate left? I need something to get this creeping chill off my skin, since a shower's not an option anymore. Honestly, I don't know how the rest of you handle this sort of thing. It feels like my skin is being peeled off."

"You're sidhe," Katalina scoffed as he strode into the kitchen. "Goosebumps are the worst you'll ever have to worry about when it comes to negative wind chill."

"The Goddess favored my kind and not yours," he smirked, pulling down a clean coffee cup from the cabinet. "Not my fault."

"Asshole."

Cole busied himself with putting some water on to boil, then dug out the box of chocolate mix. "Only two left," he noted, grunting. "Gonna need to go shopping again soon."

"Add it to the list," she said, pointing at the pad lying beside the flour can. "And don't change the subject."

"Right," he said, nodding. "Now, what were we talking about?"

"You were being a dick about how Danu preferred to grant your race with the ability to withstand zero degree weather instead of mine," she recounted. "And you were also going to explain yourself as far as why the shower was left running, and there's no hot water. And, why you're still wearing a towel that doesn't appear to be one of ours?"

"Oh, right. Actually, that's nothing at all like how it really happened. The part about humans being denied that ability, I mean. There's a whole lot more to it than that, but if I say anything else on the subject, your head will probably explode and your soul will most likely be tossed into the Abyss of Eternal Despair for good measure. Just to make an example out of you. Besides, if the whole 'weather tolerance' thing is bothering you, I might have some bad news. Living here in the city for so long seems to be affecting my natural immunity to climate changes. If this keeps up, I may be moving to the country. Less metal and plastic there."

"Oh," Katalina said, sounding rather shocked. "When will this happen?"

"Not right away," he assured her while pouring hot water into the cup of powdered chocolate mix. "Probably not for another thirty or forty years. I still have people in this town who owe me a few favors, and it would be harder to collect on them after I've moved."

"Ah," she said with a smile. "I'll make sure to mark my calendar, then. Now, what about the shower?"

"It wasn't my fault," Cole stated firmly before taking a sip of his hot chocolate. "You remember Detective Corhagen, right?"

"It's so not fair that you can drink hot chocolate so soon after it's been mixed," she scowled. "It always burns my throat. And yes, what about the little bastard?"

Cole smiled. Katalina had moved to the loft at a time when he and the detective had been on speaking terms. She'd also been the one to call him out on being a spineless coward and a fraud when their friendship had soured. It was one of the many moments that had endeared the human to Cole. Well, part-human, as it were. Katalina had a fair amount of feyish ancestry in her blood; an odd melting pot of demi-fey, pixie, brownie, and trow had been mixed into her human bloodline, to the point where she'd gained some rather interesting abilities. Katalina fancied herself a budding enchantress; she refused outright to call herself a witch, preferring to rely on such tools as potions and alchemy to help aid her in spell casting.

Cole realized he'd been quiet for longer than was considered normal in the human world. "He summoned me earlier today to have a look at a crime scene."

"Out of the shower?"

Cole nodded.

"Directly *from* the shower?" she pressed.

Again, he nodded, feeling a smile tug at his lips. "Totally naked," he added for good measure before drinking more of his chocolate.

Katalina burst out laughing. "Oh, I wish I could have been there to see that. The look on his face must have been priceless. Please tell me his eyes were bulging out of their sockets."

"Quite," he informed her. "He was still kneeling on the floor when the spell brought me to him, along with a surprising amount of water from the shower."

Cole waited patiently for Katalina to stop rolling on the floor laughing. When she was finally able to pick herself up, he saw that there were tears in her eyes. "That's too precious," she gasped, wiping them away. "I only wish someone else could have been in the room with him, but even Corhagen knows better than to do something like that in front of witnesses."

"He does, surprisingly, but an officer opened the door almost immediately afterward and caught us both standing there." Cole finished off his hot chocolate as Katalina fell down to the floor again. "She was the one who loaned me the towel, by the way. I guess maybe I should've left it behind, but it would've been even harder to get a cab, then."

Katalina still hadn't gotten up off the floor. "Whenever you're finished," he said, stretching the tone of his voice just a bit, "I was wondering if you could have a look at something I found while I was there."

"Aha!" she gasped, standing up at once. "You found a clue before the clueless detective did!"

"I found a hair in the baby's crib." Cole quickly explained what had happened at the murder scene, including his raising of the corpse so that it could be questioned, and finished off by explaining about the missing child. "It may be nothing. I mean, human babies are prone to disappearing all the time, as I understand it."

Katalina took the hair from him. "It doesn't happen quite like that," she corrected. "But the missing baby girl is a funny coincidence, and you know how I feel about those."

"Right." Cole nodded. "There was also a weird smell coming from the apartment. I couldn't put my finger on it; it was almost as though the scent had been masked. But the hair itself doesn't feel totally human. I sense fey magic coming from it."

"And whatever took the baby might've left this behind by accident." Katalina nodded. "I'll run some tests, but it'll have to wait until later. I have to meet someone on my computer. I was going to shower first, but since that's no longer an option, he'll just have to put up with me being less than presentable this time."

"He?" Cole pressed curiously.

Katalina stuck her tongue out at him as she dashed off toward her bedroom. "I'll tell you just as soon as you've managed to get in Detective Corhagen's pants again."

The phone began to ring just as Katalina's door slammed shut. "Don't answer it!" he called out, heading for his own room. "That's probably Corhagen, wanting to know where I disappeared to and why I'm not there to bail his ass out of trouble."

Katalina's door cracked open slightly as he passed it. "Check your email," she commanded. "You've got another hit on the website."

Cole entered his room and shucked the towel before gleefully darting over to his computer desk. With the advent of modern convenience in the last few years, people were ironically becoming more open-minded about the idea that elves and witches lived right in their own backyard. Though he couldn't quite figure out how that worked, it was nonetheless a good thing for business. The problem was letting people know that the supernatural was in fact readily available at their fingertips. Katalina had given him the idea of making a website for himself. Most humans regarded it as a joke, and it was a chore just sorting through the hate mail and snide comments left behind by skeptics. Fortunately, though, humans weren't the only ones making use of the Internet these days.

With a few keystrokes and a click or two of his mouse, Cole had the message folder opened. The request was brief and looked as though it might have been typed by a four-year-old. To Cole, however, this meant it was most likely somebody whose hands were not the right size to use a keyboard.

PixiEs in pARk.

mEan GoBLins uNder bRidge. PlEaSe RespOnD by pIzzA guY.

SilVeR payMEnT.

"Silver payment" meant that they were most likely willing to pay in silver. Pixies were notorious about finding things and could slip in and out of the most unlikely places without anyone else being the wiser. Even many of the sidhe didn't give them much notice. Cole had used this to his advantage once before and had learned that it paid to keep the smaller fey in his good graces.

The problem was, this message left him with no means of contacting them. More to the point, there was little indication of which park they were referring to, or which bridge said goblins were lurking under. The pizza-guy part he was totally lost on. Cole could only assume a pizza delivery was somewhere nearby. Most, if not all, delivery boys knew better than to take shortcuts through city parks, though.

Cole thought about it for a bit. Going out again wasn't on his to-do list for the day, and the gold Awar had given him covered all the rent, with a bit left over for a few frivolities. He didn't need the cash right away, but there was always the next month to consider. That, and he didn't have anything else going on at the moment. When the phone rang again, this time sounding more shrill than usual, it made up Cole's mind for him. Getting dressed quickly, he snatched up his wallet and Aed Deigh, then wheeled his bike out the door.

The most obvious place to look was Central Park. Most New Yorkers thought of it when they thought of the word "park." A pixie would likely take that to the next level by immediately assuming that everyone knew it was *the* park to be at. With this in mind, Cole pedaled down the street, weaving around the occasional straggler still out walking at this time of the day. He was dressed for mild spring weather. Everyone else looked as though they were getting ready to build igloos. Cole smiled at this thought and did a nice little wheelie past a magazine stand, which didn't even make the guy behind it flinch. Onward, Cole pedaled through the streets and back alleyways. He'd been this way many times before and was less concerned about being assaulted than some other people might. As a member of the highest order of fey, his body was quite durable even amid the labyrinth of metal buildings.

That, and he could punch holes through car doors if the situation merited it. Muggers were the least of his worries. Being unemployed and homeless ranked much farther up the line, in his opinion.

Cole took a long lap around the outskirts of Central Park once he'd arrived. There were several pizza parlors not far away, if the delicious fumes were any indication. Cole mused over this as he turned into the park itself and started pedaling idly down one of the designated paths. At this time of the day, with the weather being as cold as it was, very few people occupied the frigid expanse. Cole only felt a mild sense of cold as he moved along, keeping his eyes sharp. So far, he hadn't seen anything to suggest pixies lived in the area. Idly, he thought about James Corhagen's promise to pay him double his consulting rate and wondered what he could do with the sudden windfall fortune had so unexpectedly tossed his way.

Cole dodged a patch of ice on the concrete path and continued past a homeless man lying underneath an empty park bench. Sidhe or not, hitting the frozen ice would've sent him tumbling out of control. Much as he hated to admit it, Cole knew he was distracted. Getting out of the loft had been more about clearing his head than escaping a mundane afternoon full of Corhagen's constant phone calls. There was something about the detective's recent case that troubled him most severely. Cole couldn't put his finger on it, but it nagged at him with each push of the bike pedals. He could no more escape it than he could outrun the icy wind at his back.

His maudlin temperament notwithstanding, the ride through the park cleared his thoughts up a bit. As he neared one of the water fountains, Cole thought he spotted a figure racing urgently over the frostbitten grass toward a small pond in the distance. A second glance told him that the young man in question was wearing a Pizza Prince jacket. Cole put two and two together, whipped his bike around with the finesse of a champion X-Gamer, and rode off after his target as quietly as he could. There was no need to glamour himself. At the speed he was going, it wouldn't have been worth trying. Besides, the delivery boy seemed far too interested in where he was going to bother looking back.

At the lake, the delivery boy knelt down near the frozen edge beside what looked like a sewer drain. Cole waited patiently behind a cluster of withered bushes as the pizza boy glanced around cautiously, then pulled out a small squeeze bottle of honey from inside one of his jacket pockets. Letting a few drops land down the drain, the boy then leaned forward and whispered something at the opening. After a moment's silence, he nodded with a smile, as though something had happened, and pulled a total of four large pizza boxes out from his warmer. Nodding to himself in understanding, Cole waited as the boy set them down, then stood up and walked off.

Sure enough, a moment later, the area was swarming with tiny flickers of winged light. Cole snickered to himself and got down off his bike as the boxes were thrown open and their contents savagely attacked by what looked like a platoon of two-and three-inch tall humans with butterfly wings. No sooner had he moved than Cole detected another scent in the air. Turning, he spotted a single figure in the brush not far away. The scent was unmistakable, and Cole had about a second or two to consider before he reacted. As the squat figure in the brush leaped out, Cole darted across the gap between them and elbowed the creature in the face.

The pixies scattered. Cole seized the goblin by the collar of his ragged Giants jacket that was two sizes too large. Cole tightened his hold and gave the gruff, hairy creature a good, hard shaking. "It's okay," he called out, looking around slightly. "You can all come out now. I've got him."

Slowly, the pixies began emerging from their hiding places, some out from under bits of trash left strewn about. "You gots 'em!" one cheered, gleefully. "You gots the bad goblins!"

"So I did," he said with a nod. "I take it you were the pixies that hired me?"

"Yush'ums!" the larger one said. "We pay you in silver to take care of 'em good. Will you kill them for us?"

"Maybe," said Cole, considering the situation. "Has he been

eating any of your troupe?"

"No us, no. Mean goblins just...."

"They take our pizza!" one screamed righteously. "They comes each time to take our rightful boon from us!"

A rousing chorus of *"Yeah!"* echoed around him. "I see," Cole said. "Not that this is any of my business, but how is it that all of you are able to get pizza delivered out here?"

"The pizza man's sire knows of us," the larger one answered, pausing in the middle of making faces at the goblin to look at Cole again. "Has known for many years now. He pay us in pizza each week to help protect his place of trade. For many years now, the Pizza Prince has been one of the only places where nasty bandits cannot get in to raid and smash the sacred sauce pan. He and the Lord of Donuts both know of our people and strive to remain in our favor by paying tribute."

"But the goblin brothers try and take our tribute for themselves," finished another, between bites of extra cheese. "This tribute is payment to us for our service, not theirs."

"Brothers?" Cole had barely finished the word when something small but surprisingly heavy landed on his head. Sharp claws dug into his scalp as a drooling mess of fangs bit into his hair. Cole withstood the assault for a moment, then unceremoniously shook his attacker free with a toss of his head.

The moment the second goblin hit the ground, Cole had him pinned to it under the heel of his boot. "Brothers," he said, at what looked like the older one. "Got it."

"Gerroff me!" the goblin snarled, trying to force Cole's boot off him by doing a push-up, only to fall flat on his face. "I said, getoff!" he spat. "Ya no-account bastard courtspawn sidhe."

Cole's boot drove his face farther into the ground. "Watch your mouth," he warned, digging the heel into the back of the goblin's head. "And where did you get that Mets jacket?"

"Nunna yar business," he growled. "Lemme up, already. I've got grass stuck between my teeth."

"Not my problem," replied Cole, snatching him up off the ground. "Why don't we leave the nice pixies alone so that they can enjoy their meal in peace? I'd like to have a word with the two of you in private. I think your home is this way."

Cole gestured toward the bridge in the distance as the pixies cheered behind him. "And I haven't forgotten about that silver," he warned, looking back.

For the second time that day, Cole found himself heading for the underside of a bridge. This one, however, was much lower to the ground than the one Awar had taken up residence under. Seeing this, Cole stood just outside of it and dropped both goblins down into the melted slush at the shoreline.

"Stupid li'l crapsacks," the older one mumbled, spitting out grass. "That's the last time any ah them get ta use my computer."

"Your computer?" Cole asked, comprehension dawning. "Wait, you let the pixies you'd been stealing food from use your computer to send a request for me to come and kill you on their behalf?"

"Li'l shit said she was just checkin' her email!"

Cole shook his head. "Right. You know, I don't think I'll even bother asking where you keep this alleged computer. And how come your little brother there is being so quiet? What's the matter with him? Doesn't he talk at all?"

"Can't," the older one shrugged. "Doesn't have a voice box. Either that, or 'is tongue's too big. We weren't sure, really."

Both of them were extremely hairy and might have been mistaken for some sort of bizarre cross between a very small bear and a bipedal fox, except for the two horns coming up out of their heads and the incredibly long claws. Cole couldn't imagine anyone typing with those, but he decided not to delve into the subject. Instead, he took in the sight of them for a moment. They really did look a lot alike.

"Your names?" he insisted flatly.

"Like I'd tell ya," the older one snorted. "Whadaya think I am, stoopid or summin?"

The fire blade from Aed Deigh extended out from the hilt in answer and stopped just short of the goblin's nose. "Name?" he pressed again.

The older gulped. "Bugbear," he muttered. "Jus' Bugbear. And this is my younger brother, Bugaboo."

"Bugbear and Bugaboo," Cole repeated, committed both names to memory. "Well, guess what? You both work for me now. I want the two of you to keep your ears open, like that's going to be hard, and see if you can learn anything about several murders going on where the victim's hearts were blown right out of their chests by black magic."

"Sounds delicious," Bugbear said with a grin. "The part where the hearts are cummin' out, I meant. But why we gotta work for you?"

"I can pay you both in donuts."

Bugaboo's eyes widened, and his rather impressively large tongue rolled out to drip drool on the ground.

"Hey, Mikey, I think he likes it," Cole said. "A box of jelly donuts once a week for the two of you to be on my payroll. How does that sound?"

Bugbear eyed his little brother for a second, then grunted. "Sounds fair enough."

"And you leave the pixies alone from now on, got it?"

Bugbear snorted derisively, but nodded. "Got it. No more buggin' the little shites."

"I have your word?" he pressed, before glancing at Bugaboo. "Such as it were."

Bugaboo nodded, still drooling, while his older brother took longer to consider. "Yeah," he agreed. "Both ah ours."

"Good," Cole said, satisfied. "You'll get your first box of donuts when I get information. Start shaking down anyone you know who might have something to do with this or could lead me to whoever is behind it. Except for the pixies!"

Bugbear looked put out at that condition. "Whaddif they know summin', though?" Bugbear insisted. "How're we suppose to find out?"

"From the pixies?" Cole grinned. "That's easy. I'll just bribe them with more pizza."

Chapter
Three

COLE left the park feeling much better about his working situation. Occasionally, it was nice to have some hired help that could take care of the grunt work for him. Considering one goblin was only capable of grunting, this made things much easier. Nonetheless, it came as a shock to Cole when he exited the park to find a limousine waiting for him with the door held open. An elderly gentleman whom he hadn't laid eyes on in some time stood next to it, keeping his gaze locked on Cole as he came to a stop.

"Master Colewyn," Hagen spoke, sounding very pleased. "It's been such a long time. Mr. Bryne was wondering if you had a moment."

At once, as though on cue, two bruisers approached Cole from behind. Cole dismounted his bike and stood for a moment as each of them loomed over him, in what he was sure they believed to be an ominous fashion. Cole, meanwhile, ignored them and stared pointedly at Hagen.

"Someone will need to take care of my bike," he said. "I can't leave it out here on the street, and it won't fit in the trunk."

"The trunk is quite spacious, I assure you, sir," Hagen countered. "But, if you'd prefer, these two can return your cycle to the loft. You'll find it safely waiting for you there once your meeting with Mr. Bryne has concluded."

Cole smiled and could see the same grin tugging at Hagen's lips. "That would be fine," he said, rolling it back their way.

Both men scrambled suddenly as the bike threatened to tip over.

"Take care of her, boys," he called out, climbing into the waiting car. "She's real important to me."

It was only when they pulled out into the maw of traffic that Cole heard Hagen chuckling to himself. Cole joined right in as their eyes met in the rear-view mirror. "Are they always like that?" he questioned. "I always thought David preferred his hired muscle to be less uptight."

"They're new, Master Colewyn," Hagen answered, still snickering. "And eager to prove themselves, it would seem. I suspect the errand you sent them on will prove useful in the long run."

"You always were a flatterer. I just wanted to rub them the wrong way, not restart the whole 'wax on, wax off' teaching trend." Silence filled the limo as Cole gazed out at the passing vehicles. "It's been a while, hasn't it, Hagen? How is my godson?"

"Doing well, for the most part," the elderly man answered, though his eyes flashed for a moment, as if he was troubled by something. "He speaks very often of you."

"All bad, I hope."

"Nothing of the sort. On the contrary, he misses you a great deal, although I'm certain I was not supposed to inform you of that. You no doubt remember what a proud individual your godson is."

"It's the sidhe in him, I'd imagine," Cole muttered softly, observing his shoes. "How is his mother?"

"The same, sadly. Mr. Bryne remains convinced he can awaken her, though I fear his desire may have blinded him to other concerns recently."

Cole could tell what Hagen was asking him, though the man had yet to form the words. In some ways, Hagen was nearly as skilled as Cole was in the covert methods of communication that all fey employed to constantly one-up each other. It had caused Cole to question the man's background a few times, but in the end, it was all for nothing. Hagen was merely a mortal gifted with a silver tongue, however stealthily barbed. Cole had witnessed him in his younger years deliver subtle insults and criticisms in front of men who had just finished butchering an enemy without flinching. Even more surprising was how much respect it had gotten him. Had Cole's godson stayed in the "family business," Hagen would no doubt have been the consigliore right out of the *Godfather* movies. He'd seemed born for the role, even as a child when Cole had first met him.

The remainder of the limo ride was quiet, although not unpleasantly so. It was something of a brash gesture, sending a vehicle as opulent as a limo out to fetch him when David had surely known him to be close by. David had made his home atop one of the office buildings in Times Square. In a castle, no less.

Cole had been there to witness its construction. David had shipped over an actual castle from the Old Country stone by stone to be his new home. The fact that New York didn't have much in the way of space to offer such accommodations was hardly a setback for his godson. He'd had the place put back together and modernized for his convenience on top of a skyscraper that was in plain sight of nearly all.

It was, ironically, one of David Bryne's more subtle gestures.

Cole was allowed into the building without anyone so much as batting an eyelid at his presence. While his clothing would not have been out of place at a gothic renaissance fair, Cole was sure his attire might have elicited some icy stares, if not outright loathing, on sight had he not been expected. Everyone on the ground floor save for one or two employees kept their heads down with practiced ease. As a direct result, it was a simple matter to spot which ones were the newcomers. The ones who looked up immediately jerked their heads away fast enough to cause whiplash. One even looked panicked, as though he feared armed soldiers would swoop in and deliver retribution.

For once, Cole held himself in check as he strode quietly toward the elevator without doing anything that would draw further attention to himself. In his defense, he hadn't given a thought to paying his godchild a visit this morning, so everyone's reactions could hardly be called his fault. Smiling at the lady who pressed the button for him, he stood and waited while she blatantly took in his appearance. Unlike some others, however, her assessment was less critical and more an attempt to work out where he might be going. Just as the doors opened, Hagen came up behind him and addressed her.

"Good afternoon, Mrs. O'Brady," he said, smiling. "How are the children these days?"

Mrs. O'Brady looked back and forth between them, despite Cole walking into the elevator without a word. "Fine," she answered, clearly confused at the sight of them together. "And yourself?"

"Oh, I was just escorting Master Colewyn up to the top floor." Cole saw the twinkle in Hagen's eyes as he waved goodbye and climbed on board. "He has an appointment with his godson."

Cole waited until they were a few floors up before turning to face him. "She'll be trying to figure that out for weeks," he noted, shrewdly. "Well done, young man."

Hagen's mouth twitched. "I try."

The elevator stopped on the top floor, a maze of hallways and office doors that seemed to go on forever. Cole ignored them and followed Hagen up a flight of stairs, which ended in a locked door that the mortal nudged open after punching in a sequence of numbers on a pad next to it. Behind the door were even more stairs, leading up to the rooftop. Cole took in the scenery before following Hagen any further. The last time he'd laid eyes on this place, it was still under construction. The castle had been built, but the roof was still being converted into a lawn. David had renovated the entire roof of the building, remodeling it to add on another floor so that it would properly support his castle, as well as the level of dirt, concrete supports, and plumbing he planned to install. The result was a plush rectangle of greenery quite rare in the asphalt jungle of New York.

It even looked a bit like the old Emerald Isle, at least by the fairy tales' standards. It made Cole homesick just standing there gazing at it.

Looking away, Cole marched after Hagen, who'd been waiting patiently for him on the steps with the front door already open.

"I'll alert Mr. Bryne that you've arrived at once, Master Colewyn," he said once they'd stepped inside. "In the meanwhile, can I offer you something?"

"I'm fine," he dismissed. "Thank you anyway, Hagen. When you find my godson, tell him I'll be waiting for him in the drawing room. Don't worry, I remember where it is."

"Of course." Hagen bowed. "Mr. Bryne anticipated your preference and left something for you in there. I trust you'll find it without any inconvenience."

Now curious, Cole strode through the castle with familiar ease.

David had redecorated since his previous visit, and the old hardwood paneling suited the stone exterior. Cole admired the changes all the way down to the far end of the hallway, which turned to the left into the drawing room. There on the table, in front of the chair he'd sat in last time, was a single black suitcase marked with his name. Intrigued, he sat down and looked the case over for a moment, wondering what could be inside.

"You can open it now," a voice said from behind. "It's not going to explode."

Cole turned around in his chair to look at David. His godson wore the same cocky expression he'd always walked around with as a youth. In one hand, he clutched a glass of red wine, which was half-empty already. The thing that struck Cole as so amazing, however, was how young his godson still looked. "You cannot blame me for being cautious," Cole replied instead of commenting on that. "In your family, there's no such thing as 'too careful'."

"You're starting to sound like my old man," David said with a laugh, coming across to sit in the chair opposite him. "He was paranoid to the bitter end."

"Good." Cole nodded, approvingly. "He remembered what I taught your grandfather, then. You might want to take a page out of his book."

"I assure you, I'm quite cautious. I just enjoy a good adventure every so often." David took a slip from his glass. "I seem to remember you having quite a few adventures in your considerable lifespan."

"Trouble," Cole corrected. "Not adventures, David."

"You're splitting hairs," he countered. "Go on. Open up your gift, or I'll start thinking you don't trust me anymore."

Indeed. Cole eyed his godson for a moment, then hesitantly reached out and undid the clasps on the briefcase. "I found them on the black market a week ago," David explained, enjoying the wide-eyed look of shock on Cole's face as he slowly removed one of the twin guns. "I'm guessing Grandmother sold them after you left. It cost a pretty penny, but since they were always meant to be yours, I figured I'd better respect my elders and return them to you. I hope they still meet with your approval."

Cole felt his throat go dry. "I... had to leave back then, immediately. There was no time for me to pack anything, not even these."

The barrel of just one of the silver guns was as big as a grown man's forearm, and shaped like an old Colt M1900. The hammer, chamber, and cylinders, however, were more akin to those of a Schmidt M1882. They had been designed according to Cole's specifications back when he'd first started working for the mafia. David's grandfather had nearly spit out his meatball when he'd first laid eyes on them. Now, Cole's fingers slid into place as though he were touching the skin of old lovers. He could still smell the oil, alerting him to the fact that they'd recently been cleaned.

"Bandersnatch," he breathed, quoting from memory the names etched into the barrels. "And Jabberwock."

"Hagen cleaned them," David informed him, guessing his thoughts. "I think he did a good job, don't you?"

Cole was at a complete loss for words. "What do I owe you?"

David smiled. "You helped raise me. You saw potential in me when everyone else seemed to think I was little more than a lost cause."

"I wasn't around as much as I could have been."

David shook his head. "You were there," he said pointedly. "I owe you something, if not more. Take these with my compliments. They were always meant to be yours, anyway."

Smiling, unable to say how he felt, Cole raised both guns up and took aim with them. "You still think you can out-shoot me?"

COLE was feeling satisfied when he returned to his loft later that evening. True to their word, the goon squad had left his bike inside the door and just to the left, where it wouldn't injure him when he came inside. The consideration it showed left him smirking in surprise, but then he noticed the note that had been taped to it.

Two very large men told me that they'd been instructed to drop this off here.

I put it next to the wall where you would see it.

Incidentally, what the hell....?

Katalina

Tossing the note in the garbage, Cole retrieved a bottle of mead from the refrigerator and strolled toward his room. As he passed Katalina's room, he thought he heard noises coming from inside of it. Being nosy, he stuck an ear against the wood and listened. On the other side, a man's voice was speaking. Cole could just barely make out some of the soft words he whispered, though they had an oddly mechanical tinge to them. Just then, Katalina let out a deep moan, causing Cole to back away.

It really hadn't been any of his business to begin with.

Once in his room, Cole threw his shirt to the floor and stepped over to his computer. There were no new messages for him on his website, other than one jerk who'd posted a new flame about what a crackpot and loony he was. The dumbass had even used his real email address, as it turned out. One quick Google search later and Cole was in possession of the asshole's address and phone number. Making a note of them as he calmly sipped his mead, Cole brainstormed a few ideas as to what sort of hexes the poor bastard might find in his mailbox over the next couple of days.

It was getting late, and Cole realized he hadn't had anything in his system but mead and hot chocolate all afternoon. Moving his mouse around, Cole set a video to load on one of the free sites he liked to visit, then dashed off to the kitchen to make a sandwich. Finished, he returned just in time for his porn to start playing.

The sandwich felt good after having nothing in his stomach. Cole took his time as the movie continued to play on-screen. It was a rather long one, and the people who'd made it had tried to inject some semblance of a plot, though Cole was ambivalent as to their success. Idly, he munched on his sandwich while the movie cycled through the boring parts. He wasn't even sure why he liked this one all that much. It wasn't that he didn't find human women attractive. The girl in this was fair, by purely aesthetic standards, if slightly thinner than he preferred. But her groaning got old after a while, especially considering how obviously faked it was. Which didn't make much sense to him, as the guy who was currently feeling her up was obviously well equipped.

Cole finished his sandwich just as the man in question on-screen rose up, giving him a perfect view of his eyes. It amazed him how much their eyes looked alike, that man and James's. Sighing, Cole stretched back in his chair and closed the video as the memories of the year before last came back to haunt him.

It had been a mistake to tell Corhagen he would help with the murder case, especially since their friendship has been non-existent for over a year now. Corhagen hadn't said anything along the lines of never wanting to see Cole again, but at the time, it'd seemed pretty clear that they were through. The lack of contact for a year had certainly helped.

Angry with himself and feeling pissed off in general, Cole stretched out across his bed as the image of the last time they'd lain on this very bed together came unbidden. Corhagen hadn't had the benefit of oak-matured mead as an excuse to fall back on then. Cole, however, had been more than a little tipsy, almost like he was now. For some reason, the mead was really beginning to sock it to him, and he felt his shaft stirring in his tight leather pants. Opening his fly, Cole let the length of his sidhehood fall out and harden. His feelings for Corhagen had always been complicated. Now it felt like they were doing battle with one another inside his chest.

It hadn't started out that way, at least not for him.

Corhagen had come along at a time when Cole had needed a friend. He and Katalina had known one another a while beforehand, but she'd still been in high school and was more or less off-limits. She'd been one of the few people who'd recognized him as sidhe right off the bat. Her family, however, didn't approve and insisted he keep his distance. Cole had been down on his luck at the time, with work getting more difficult to come by. Corhagen had been the one to interrogate him after he was named a suspect in a murder involving the occult.

Apparently, he fit the description of a forty-six-year-old, married, *female* teacher that had been using powerful love potions to bewitch and seduce her students. One such tryst had ended in a killing, so Cole was forced to get involved as a means of clearing his name. It had taken him all of two hours total to work out what had happened. After that, Corhagen had treated him to some lousy, cheap beer as an apology.

It had started from there. When the things in the night that everybody, especially the police, claimed didn't exist needed help because of humans messing with magic, Corhagen gave him a ring. Between the two of them, they'd busted a sweatshop owner who'd enslaved a family of gnomes, ended an illegal fight club-slash-gambling ring where trolls were made to kill each other for the spectators' amusement, and even figured out why the donuts in the precinct lounge kept disappearing. That last one had been their saving grace, at least as far as Corhagen's supervisor was concerned. Nevertheless, thanks to Cole's involvement in Corhagen's life, a lot of funny rumors had begun to circulate. Not all of them had to do with the cases Corhagen had brought him in on, either.

One Lieutenant Heisen had made it personal. Whenever Cole entered the precinct, Heisen would be waiting to follow him around and made rude comments, along with suggestions that Corhagen was nuts and Cole was nothing more than a charlatan. Heisen had been a jerk, as well as a notorious philanderer. Finally, one afternoon after a particularly rough day of chasing a purse-snatching wood nymph, Cole decided he'd endured enough. The glamour spell he'd called forth left no doubt in Heisen's mind that Cole was the real thing. Every last doubt and insecurity the lieutenant had tried to run from was paraded right before his eyes, until he was left broken and sobbing on the locker room floor. As a final insult, Cole placed a subconscious suggestion in the back of the man's mind, rendering him unable to fully function sexually.

As Cole insisted earlier today, Lieutenant Heisen had been asking for it.

Cole had known the sort of havoc being involved in a mortal's life would bring. He'd experienced it more than once and had yet to learn his lesson. Before, he'd told himself that it was for a good cause and that after being on the wrong side of the human law since arriving from Avalon, it would be nice to do some "'good." In the end, however, it had all been because he'd needed a friend. He'd stuck with Corhagen despite his initial stubborn refusal to acknowledge the world around him because he'd offered Cole friendship in spite of the chaos that being around him inevitably caused.

And Cole, whether he'd acknowledged it then or not, had been lonely.

He wasn't sure when exactly his feelings for the mortal cop had changed, or if they'd ever really changed at all. The sidhe were a lusty breed to begin with, and feelings of affection from one sidhe to another inevitably became sexual at some point. That wasn't always a good thing, but it was a fact. Marriage was all about procreation, which was why no one among the sidhe ever exchanged vows until the female was with child. It was pointless to try unless the man and woman in question could prove they were capable of producing children. As part and parcel of being immortal, the fey in general didn't procreate much.

And then there was the whole problem of a sidhe falling in love with a mortal. When a mortal fell in love with one of the fey, it almost always ended badly for the mortal in question. When one of the fey fell in love, it most certainly ended poorly for the fey.

Cole couldn't accurately place where his feelings for Corhagen fell. He wasn't even sure he wanted the mortal for a friend anymore, especially considering how their conversation a year ago had ended. Cole felt a rush of heady anger and began furiously pumping himself in order to relieve the frustration. It'd been a while since he'd gotten himself off, and he was just starting to feel it when another familiar sensation crept in.

The exact same one he'd had in the shower this morning!

Cole jumped up off the bed, his pants still wide open, as the familiar voice rang out in his ears from all around.

Tuulois MacColewyn!

Tuulois MacColewyn!

Tuulois MacColewyn!

"Hold it, you son of a bitch!"

The sensation of being pulled through a tight rubber tube hit him again at full force. Magic, being driven by emotion, was more potent if the caster in question was feeling something particularly strong during the spell. In the case of summonings, the more urgent the caster felt, the faster the spell would work in bringing the object toward them. Cole didn't have time to reach for his guns or even his shirt before he found himself standing in a large storage closet with Detective James Corhagen standing off to the side. Apparently, he'd leaped away from the circle the moment his spell had taken effect. Every so often, he did demonstrate the capacity to learn, and going by the look on his face, he was proud of the fact.

Until he looked down and caught an eyeful of Cole's manhood standing even prouder and at full mast.

Cole sighed and tucked himself back in before zipping up. He was tempted to just leave his junk hanging out in the hopes that another lower-ranking officer came barging in. Staring down at the red-faced, German-born mortal, it was all he could do to keep from hauling himself back out and beating off in front of him.

Corhagen cleared his throat. "I guess I should just be glad you weren't in the shower this time."

"I'm not sure if there's any hot water for one just yet," Cole reminded him. "You did summon me from it before I could turn the water off. Katalina was pissed that she didn't get to clean up before her date."

"She had a date?" Corhagen sounded genuinely confused. "And it wasn't you?"

"She's a little young for me," he replied. "You know I don't go after women under forty. Now, where the hell did you bring me to this time?"

"The morgue," he answered. "And where is your shirt?"

"I was in my loft when you summoned me. I'm allowed to walk around shirtless there."

"Right." Corhagen nodded, glancing away again. "Well, you might as well come on out like that. After this morning, I don't think anyone will mind much."

"Wait just a moment," Cole said sharply, just as Corhagen reached for the door. "What the hell is going on? You've dragged me out of my home twice in the same day using a spell that you know burns up a hell of a lot of magic to use. You're not an accomplished spell caster or a wizard, and I know you haven't been practicing the meditation and breathing techniques I showed you so that you could use the spell correctly."

Corhagen turned back to look at him. "How'd you know?"

"You're aura's all fucked up to hell and back." Cole shook his head at the surprise on Corhagen's face. "You've pushed your body nearly to its limit just by doing that spell twice. How the hell can you expect to be on top of your game like this? Furthermore, what was wrong with just picking up the phone and calling?"

Corhagen didn't answer at first and wouldn't meet Cole's gaze. "Well?"

"I wasn't sure whether you'd come or not," he answered. "If I just called you, you could always hang up on me, and I needed you down here right now. They found another one."

"Another murder?"

"No, another free donut giveaway," Corhagen bit back. "Yes, another murder. A double murder this time, only it wasn't the same MO as the previous, so nobody believes it's the same case. They're trying to rule it as an accidental death, which would work fine if the two victims' lungs hadn't caught on fire."

"Lungs?" Cole repeated. "Their lungs burst into flames this time?"

"Yup," Corhagen said with a nod. "Coroner said he's never seen anything like it before. It looked to him like somebody just filled their lungs up with kerosene and shoved a lit box of matches down their throat. Also, it looked to him as though the fire was started from the inside. He couldn't find a trace of any chemicals, though, and the area that was burned was very localized."

"Meaning only the lungs were burned," Cole said, putting it together. "Very little else, and not the sort of thing you'd find in a case of ordinary fire."

Something dawned on Cole then. "Wait. There was already an autopsy?"

Corhagen sighed, and in that moment, he looked much older than his thirty-six years. "Thankfully, spontaneous lung combustion and Sudden Adult Chestburster Syndrome are still classified as unusual events. Because there wasn't an obvious cause of death, an autopsy was ordered at once. I think the police chief wanted it cleared up as to whether this was related to the other deaths, but since the lungs were burned instead of the victim's heart being blown out, they've decided to rule it an accidental death."

"Quite logical of them."

"Please, help me out here." Corhagen sounded pathetic, but more than that, he looked desperate. "You're still on retainer, and I'm still working on getting you double your pay. If you help me deal with this fast, it'll go a lot quicker."

Cole's eyes narrowed. "Call next time," he insisted. "I mean it. If not, then I'll shuck as many clothes as I can before the spell takes hold, then march out stark naked into whatever crime scene mess you've brought me to and begin describing in excruciating detail how your cock does that slightly curved thing when you're fully erect."

Corhagen marched for the door, looking both furious and embarrassed. "I'm leaving now."

"Right," Cole said, walking calmly after him. "Because exiting a storage closet in front of a half-naked, albino-haired man in leather pants won't look questionable at all."

James froze in his tracks, and then turned around. "I hate you. You know that, right?"

Cole just grinned. "Lead the way, Detective."

Now that he was aware of it, Cole could smell the formaldehyde. He could practically feel the artificial squeaky-cleanliness in the air, as well as sense the dead bodies in the room up ahead. Cole's left hand twitched every few seconds, the power held inside of it itching to be let loose. In the realm of faerie, death was more of a quaint notion, like the way humans observed old artwork of forgotten magical times, something that might be interesting to ponder but couldn't possibly exist. It was one of the reasons why Oberon had considered him such a weak specimen. That, and the fact Oberon could be a real dick most of the time.

Cole followed James into the main area of the morgue, a room of nothing but large metal drawers. Inside each of them was a dead body, one that his power ached to reach out to and fill. Cole inhaled, maintained a hard grip on his power, and walked over to where James was already standing with a young woman who looked a little too ruffled for it to be deliberate. The lab coat suggested she worked here, but going by the look on her face, she was new. Either that, or she wasn't too keen on getting a second look at a victim whose lungs were scorched.

Without a word, she opened the drawer all the way out so that they could see the body fully, then turned and left. Cole waited until the door clicked shut behind them before speaking.

"How long do we have?"

"Not long," James answered. "But hold off for just a second. We're waiting on someone else."

Cole's eyes widened considerably.

"Remember me telling you about some other people on the force that were coming around to how I saw things?" Corhagen pressed. "One of them wanted to be here for this. He won't whisper a word of this to anyone else, so you don't have to worry about him spilling your secrets or anything. He just wants to confirm with his own eyes."

Cole, meanwhile, was scowling with each word the detective said. "This isn't a carnival act," he growled. "And I'm not a performer for children's birthday parties."

Just then, the door swung open hard. Cole watched as a plain-clothes officer strolled in with a bagel clamped down between his square jaws. The first thing that Cole noticed about him was his eyes. They were the sharpest, most distinctive color of turquoise he had ever seen. More to the point, they were piercing. The man's eyes seemed to take in everything at once, even as his jaws munched idly on the cream cheese bagel in his mouth. The second thing Cole saw was the expanse of bald skin stretching over the top of his head. The back of his head had a thick mat of hair that hung down in curls from not being clipped regularly. It gave the impression that the gentleman was much older than he appeared, but Cole judged that he was roughly the same age as Corhagen, or maybe, a year or two older. He was also, going by the badge hanging on his belt, several ranks above the detective.

"Inspector Vallimun." Corhagen saluted respectfully.

Cole glanced between the two of them. "He's the one?"

James nodded. "He had a nasty encounter with a gang of drug dealers that'd been revived by a voodoo practitioner several years ago. Nobody would buy his story, but there was enough evidence of other dealings to get the witch put away for life."

When the inspector spoke after swallowing his bite of bagel, he actually sounded bored. "She was into human sacrifice. And voodoo religion doesn't have witches. I looked it up."

Vallimun's eyes went right for Cole's. "Corhagen here says you can raise the dead too."

"Not the same way that people who use voodoo do," Cole corrected, just in case the inspector got any strange ideas about him. "It's more of a natural gift. Corhagen has me use it mostly just to question murder victims."

Inspector Vallimun looked slightly impressed. "Every homicide cop's dream come true. So, let's see it."

Cole considered for a moment longer, then decided to trust the mortal. Holding his hand out, he willed power from it down into the body. Cole felt it stir long before the eyes fluttered open and gazed emptily at the ceiling. James actually jumped back a little when she rose up from the slab. Vallimun, however, didn't so much as flinch.

"What was her name?" Cole asked quickly.

"Melinda McKnight," Corhagen whispered. "Her husband is still in the coroner's lab."

"Melinda McKnight," Cole said in a calm voice. "We were wondering if you could …."

Cole was cut off by the sound of a horrifying screech coming from behind the rows of drawers. All three men turned at the same time to listen to the high-pitched, shrieking howl echoing through plaster, wood, and concrete to rebound off their rib cages and chill their blood. Cole's face, however, was perhaps the most shocked of the three. Without a word, Vallimun and Corhagen made a run for the door, with Cole coming up not far behind. In the background, there was the unmistakable thud of Mrs. McKnight's skull landing flat against the metal slab as the magic left her, broken by Cole's lack of concentration.

Cole chased after the men, praying for once that he was wrong. The sound was just as he'd remembered, just as it'd been hammered into his very soul years before. When they finally reached the coroner's lab, marked by the name and title etched into the door, Vallimun turned to the side and yanked it open, Corhagen already armed with his gun and ready.

The sight inside wasn't pretty.

The coroner, a Dr. Phil Hart, was sitting in the corner directly across from them. Even at a distance, Cole could see his eye sockets were nothing but empty holes. The man's bare hands were covered in blood, along with slimy mucus, all that remained of his eyeballs after he'd clawed them out. He was also wailing, but that wasn't the sound that'd drawn them there. This came from the nightflyer hovering dangerously overhead, sending things flying wildly around the room as its great, bat-like wings flapped every few seconds. The sluagh creature had a manta ray-shaped body with a nest of tentacles underneath and a stinger tail. Seeing them, it let out another wail that caused Corhagen to shudder violently and drop his gun.

Cole leaped in front of Vallimun. The inspector looked as though he was about to protest, but then Corhagen had the decency and good timing for once to collapse to the floor and start vomiting. Cole made a mental note to thank him for that later. Then, steeling his nerves, he leaped inside and slammed the door shut, where one of the foot soldiers of the sluagh was waiting along with the coroner, who'd gone mad just by looking at it.

It was turning out to be one of those days.

Chapter *Four*

THE nightflyer was just about to take the coroner's head off as Cole locked the door shut behind him. "Stop!" he cried out, putting as much force and command into the word as he could muster, for all the good it would do him. The sluagh, after all, obeyed the voice of only one, and Cole most certainly wasn't *that* entity.

The nightflyer, however, ceased its attack for a second. "Fallen noble of the sidhe," he addressed Cole in a surprisingly articulate tone. "What business do you have here?"

Cole attempted to reason with it. "The mortal has already lost his mind. What more does he have that you can take?"

"You care for this human man?"

Cole hesitated. "Well, no. Not really...."

The nightflyer snarled, causing Mr. McKnight's corpse to rattle on the table below.

"What purpose do you have here?" Cole pressed. "Since when do nightflyers travel solo?"

The nightflyer hesitated, then floated down to the slab. Its tail hung limply near the head of what remained of Mr. McKnight. The body was in terrible shape. It looked like some powerful force had literally torn its way out from the inside. Both halves of the rib cage were torn open and hanging off to the side, out of the body. That thought sent a jolt through Cole, and he glanced back and forth between the nightflyer and the whimpering Dr. Phil, who was now curled up on the floor in a fetal position.

"It was…. You're Melinda McKnight's husband?"

"Do not sound so surprised, young one," the nightflyer replied, offended. "These days, those who were exiled make do by living as they see fit. The old hunts are no more, and even if they were, I would certainly not be counted among their ranks now. The Erlking has seen to that."

He sounded angry, even reproachful. Cole took this into consideration before he spoke again. "I have to ask," he began, pointing at the carcass underneath it. "How did you manage…."

"A husk," Mr. McKnight said dismissively. "Merely a tool for traveling about among mortals."

"Ah."

"They were quite fashionable at one time," the nightflyer continued, glancing out the window. "I purchased one so that my human wife and I might live alongside her people unharassed. Things were going well until we discovered she was pregnant with my child."

"You had a child?"

"My son," he whispered, and the anguish in his voice was undeniable. "Taken from us, once the curse took effect. The caster stole my wife's life from her, and then sent minions to steal our child. Our only son. I would have followed, would have torn them to shreds, but the curse had weakened me."

Both he and Cole glanced down at the husk. "The curse still affected me, even if it was not in the manner the caster intended. I was weakened, too weak to claw myself free of it. The husk can serve as a cocoon, allowing its inhabitant to heal, but by then, the man over there…."

Mr. McKnight gestured with his tail at the eyeless coroner. "He was cutting into it with a blade, and attacked me when I tried to escape."

Cole used the silence that followed to think. Some things were beginning to make sense to him at last, but he was going to need more information from Corhagen to confirm his theory. Luckily, the nightflyer was low enough on the sluagh food chain that he didn't affect Cole. Corhagen had been made sick by the sight of it, so having him come in and interview it was clearly not an option. Then there was Inspector Vallimun, who apparently had enough fortitude not to claw his eyes out or lose his lunch, though the good inspector might've only gotten a glance.

As if on cue, there came a pounding on the door, which was knocked nearly off its hinges as someone kicked it in. Apparently, they hadn't been talking for very long, just long enough for Corhagen and the inspector to send for help. The minute their cavalry got a good look at what was going on, the humans did the predictable thing and started opening fire.

"Stop! Stop!" Cole screamed, ducking for cover. "Knock it off, you idiots! He's not the bad guy!"

"Hold your fire!" Inspector Vallimun commanded.

It was too late, though. The nightflyer had gone zooming around the room the minute the bullets started flying, and before the inspector could begin trying to restore order, Mr. McKnight dove straight for the glass window not far from where Dr. Phil was still huddled down on the floor, and flew out with an almighty crash.

Meanwhile, a handful of the heavily armed officers still hadn't stopped firing. From his vantage point behind the table, Cole considered it a blessing that they were all such horrible shots. Inspector Vallimun and Corhagen were each doing their best to disarm them without getting ventilated. The remaining officers on hand, however, didn't seem to mind that a few of their peers were firing shots wildly up in the air. Most of them looked dazed, as though they weren't sure what was going on. Cursing the fact that his precious handcrafted guns and his sword were both in his room back at the loft, Cole dove out from behind the table and tackled two of the gun-crazed cops at once. Before either of them could recover or do more than scream uncontrollably, Cole had snatched the guns from their hands and pistol-whipped them both into unconsciousness.

It wasn't pretty, but it worked. And best of all, he wasn't full of holes. It was really annoying when people tried to shoot him.

Looking around, Cole noticed the other officers were starting to come to, with varying degrees of success. Once the inspector was sure no one else would be opening fire on them, he stood up and pointed deliberately at Cole and Corhagen. "You two," he ordered. "My office. Now! The rest of you, see what you can do about Dr. Phil. Get him up to the hospital immediately."

For a moment, Cole considered running up to the inspector just long enough to send him the international symbol of friendship, then heading for the door. It was tempting, but he knew he couldn't. The inspector would send someone to look for him. Corhagen would be pissed, and Cole would most likely get taken off the investigation as a consultant, and that meant he wouldn't get a dime of pay.

So, somehow angry at Corhagen as though this were his fault, Cole followed after Inspector Vallimun and tried not to look too pissed. When he was angry, or feeling any particularly strong emotion, it tended to manifest in some way around him. Cole had once caused a tree to bloom out of season just by leaning on it when he'd been in an extraordinarily good mood for once. Another time, high winds had been summoned inside an obscenely small hallway of an office building all because he'd been furious. More to the point, his skin usually glowed whenever he felt strong emotions. Not like the way lights would shimmer around people in bad movies, but it literally glowed as if Cole had somehow ingested the moon. Mortals could become transfixed by it if he wasn't careful, and after the incident in the coroner's lab, Cole doubted the hospital could stand much more excitement.

As soon as he thought of it, the overhead lights flickered. They had just exited the stairs out into the ground floor waiting area. Cole could have kicked himself All three men looked up at the same time just as the whole building lost power.

What was more, the lights stayed off. "This isn't right," Cole muttered, noticing how close to dark it was getting outside. "There should be emergency power."

"It'll cut in sooner or later," Corhagen replied. Neither he nor Vallimun looked convinced. "We should...."

An alarm sounded. "What is that?" Cole asked above the noise.

"Emergency lockdown," Vallimun said as the doors leading into the waiting area sealed themselves. "If the hospital comes under quarantine, the entire building has to be sealed so that nothing gets out."

"Why now?" James wondered. The alarm, meanwhile, continued to sound, and it was giving Cole a headache. "And where is everybody? Can't they get someone to shut that thing off?"

Cole ignored the pounding in his head from the continuous, shrill cry as his eyes swept over the room. There were quite a few people in the waiting area. All of them remained perfectly still, as though the sound of the alarm didn't bother them. There was no one behind the counter, no security officers to reassure everyone. It was as if the room itself had somehow been held still in time. Once more, Cole's gaze drifted toward the settling dusk outside through the clear, sealed doors. He, more than anyone else there, knew of the things that could roam freely in the darkness. Many creatures of fey could not thrive, or even survive at all, under the harsh light of day. Come sundown, however, it was a different tale altogether. And many of the things that hunted liked to corner their prey.

No one in the waiting area moved, remaining inhumanly still.

"We need to leave," he said softly.

The alarm suddenly cut itself off as if the wires had been snipped. "What?" Corhagen asked.

"It's not safe here," he said, barely a whisper. "Something is not right. We need to find a way out."

They rose. All of them at once, as if by an unspoken command. Everyone in the waiting room stood at the exact same moment and turned to face them. Their bodies were concealed; only their outline gave away that they were humanoid. Cole felt nervous, but not afraid. Not yet, at least. He had been raised amongst the wild and the weird where the monsters that fueled humanity's nightmares were kept as pets and played with by sidhe children. Yet he was unarmed now, thanks to Corhagen's summoning and his own foolishness.

One after the other, their cloaks fell down to the floor. Corhagen gasped and raised his gun instinctively as the scarecrows turned to face him.

They were, indeed, scarecrows. Cole recognized them at once as being golems, creatures spawned by a magical craftsman to perform his dirty work. These were tall and lanky, stuffed with straw and dressed exactly like a scarecrow one might expect to find in a field of corn, though these were much thicker. They also had metal claws for hands, sharp ones that Cole could tell just by looking were made from cold iron. Pitchforks stuck out from their chests, making their marionette-like movements even more awkward. They didn't walk so much as hover just above the floor, their shoes lightly touching it.

Cole put a hand on Corhagen's arm to lower it. "That won't work on them," he said as the scarecrows shuffled toward them. "Start backing away now."

Corhagen raised his gun back up, as did the inspector, but neither man fired as they moved backward down a hallway leading farther into the hospital, with the scarecrows drifting after them. The closer they came, the faster all three men tried to move. Finally, Inspector Vallimun lowered his gun and turned.

"Fuck it. Run!"

Cole turned and ran after him. "Good idea!"

The three of them ran. It was quite possibly the most un-sidhe thing to do, but living to fight another day had always been a prerogative of Lord Oberon's, so Cole doubted the asshole would complain much. Cole's legs were longer, and he wasn't human, so he managed to take the lead with relative ease. When he reached the hallway intersection, he immediately swung right. Just as Corhagen and Vallimun caught up, however, he came flying back down in the opposite direction.

"You don't wanna go that way," he warned, motioning for them to follow. "Trust me!"

Two scarecrows were coming up the hall not far behind him, ready to join the mob already on their tails. Vallimun fired off a few shots as he backed away, but all this did was leave a few smoking holes where the scarecrows' lungs would have been were they human. One was close enough to take a swipe at the tail end of the inspector's coat as he gave up and ran after the others. He caught up with them as Cole was smashing the button for the elevator.

"The emergency power still hasn't cut on," Vallimun reminded him. "We have to find the stairs."

Cole punched the button in anger, pushing the metal slab into the sheet rock and leaving it cracked. Vallimun glared for a second, then looked up at him. "Why the hell are *you* running?"

"They've got pitchforks sticking out of their chests," Cole answered as they took off once more. "And their claws...."

"What about them?" Vallimun pressed, gasping. "I thought Corhagen said you were some kind of superhuman."

"I am sidhe," explained Cole, reaching the door to the stairs first and holding it open. "Cold iron is fatal to us. Whoever sent those things built them specifically for hunting down the fey. The question is, were they looking for me, or Mr. McKnight?"

"Why would anyone be hunting for you?" Corhagen wondered, taking the stairs three at a time. "What have you done this time?"

"Everybody hates me," he said, as they reached the second floor. "I'm just too beautiful to let live."

Vallimun groaned.

Just as they reached the second floor, more scarecrows came up from down below. Cole opened the door leading into the second floor hallway just in time to spot more approaching from the other end. Slamming it shut, he motioned for the men to follow him as he retreated farther up.

"They've split up," he said, running. "Trying to cut us off."

"I thought you said these things hunted fey," Corhagen pointed out, as they reached the third floor and kept going. "What do they want with us?"

"No idea," Cole retorted. "But feel free to turn around and ask one of them."

"No, thank you."

"Me, either," added Vallimun, firing a couple of shots behind them. "What does it take to stop these things?"

"They aren't alive." At the fourth floor, Cole checked the door and found it locked. One swift kick solved that problem, and he motioned the others through into the deserted corridor before slamming it shut. "We have to barricade it. It won't hold them off for long, but that at least will buy us some time until we figure out what to do."

"Here, help me with this." Corhagen was pointing to a rather large shelf inside somebody's open office. There were a number of books on it that Corhagen attempted to pull off, but Cole saved them both time by simply lifting it up with both hands and shuffling back out the door sideways.

"Oh, right," James said, looking embarrassed. "I'd forgotten."

"It's not much," Cole warned. "But it'll have to do for now. I don't suppose either of you has a good idea for getting the hell out of here?"

"I'm trying to get hold of my men," said Vallimun, giving his cell phone a frustrated shake. "Nobody's answering. They shouldn't still be down in the morgue."

"They're dead," Cole said, grimly. "Most likely, anyway. In case either of you didn't notice, we haven't run into a lot of people on our way up. Whoever is behind this either ordered the entire hospital to be killed, or has put them under some type of very subtle glamour so that they stay out of the way while we're all massacred."

"If they're doing glamour, can't you stop it?" Corhagen was breathing hard as his eyes fixed on Cole's naked chest. "That's your specialty, isn't it?"

Cole shook his head. "There were many others in Avalon more adept with glamour than I, and probably a few in New York, as well. I can disguise myself, or confuse people's minds, but on a much lower scale. Whoever is doing this has the power to cloud the minds of nearly everyone in the building. Which means they have a lot of power and, more importantly, they're willing to use it."

"So you can't break their spell, or whatever it is?" Vallimun didn't sound happy, which made Cole even more annoyed.

"Would it do any good to break it?" he asked pointedly. "Everyone else is safely out of the scarecrows' claws. Breaking the spell would mean putting them right along in their path. It would slow the scarecrows down but leave hundreds of people in the line of fire, waiting to be slaughtered. I was under the impression that the police took a vow to serve and protect."

The look on Vallimun's face was cold, unmoving, yet his eyes blazed with fury. Cole met that fury with a stare of seeming indifference, even as he felt his disgust and bitterness rise up to meet the man wearing the badge in front of him.

Corhagen looked back and forth between them, put his fingers between his lips like so many tourists tried to do when hailing a cab, and blew.

"Enough," he called out firmly. "We're all in this together, whether we like it or not. Cole is right in that breaking the spell would put other people's lives in danger. What we need is backup, and since you can't reach any of your men downstairs on the phone, how long do you think it would take for a squad to get here?"

"Not long," Vallimun said, looking at his phone. "If this damn thing were working, anyway. When I said I couldn't reach my men, it wasn't because they weren't answering. I can't seem to get through to anybody on this thing. It must be the... what did you call it?"

"Glamour," Cole and Corhagen both answered. "It's magical concealment."

"Which does work on cell phones and electronics," Cole finished. "Assuming the caster in question understands enough about them and how they work. Most of the sidhe are Old World types, and technology doesn't exactly agree with them, but a number of the lesser fey have become more modernized in the past few decades. One of them could've explained things."

Something slammed hard against the bookshelf. "They're coming," said Cole flatly. "To be honest, I'm surprised that bookshelf held them off this long."

"So backup isn't coming." For once, Corhagen didn't sound nervous. "Not for a while, at least. That means we're gonna have to fight."

"We can't fight them all off," Vallimun stated, matter-of-factly now. "And if we keep heading up, they'll have us cornered on the roof eventually."

"Fighting our way back down past them seems like the best bet,"

Corhagen agreed with a nod. The bookshelf against the door shuddered violently again, and pieces splintered off and went flying. "If only there were more than just the three of us."

Cole's eyes lit up. "Got it." He smiled confidently. "But we can't do it here. We have to move."

"What?" Vallimun demanded.

"This way," he commanded, racing down the dimly lit corridor. "They'll break through any second, and we don't have the tools needed to fight them off."

Cole slowed his pace enough to allow both men to catch up.

"Okay, so how do we fight these things?" Corhagen asked between breaths. "You seem to understand a lot about them."

"Not really, but while the principle behind creating them is complicated, it still uses fundamental principles of fey magic. Assuming the caster is a fey themselves, they would've had to reinforce the spells animating them with something physical in order to create so many. Either that, or have the innate ability to animate objects."

"You're babbling," Vallimun grumbled. "Get to the freakin' point."

"Fine," Cole said, cutting a sharp corner. "Would the sprinkler system still work in this place while the power is shut off?"

Cole shouldered open a nearby door leading into an empty patient's chamber and motioned the two to follow.

"Probably," Corhagen said, once they were in. "But why?"

"Flowing water grounds magic," he explained, shutting the window blinds. "It's where some of the stories about undead being incapable of crossing rivers comes from. Running water will ground the magic, keeping them animated. It might not stop those scarecrows, but if the sprinkler systems were turned on, the flowing water would wash away some of the spell."

"With the power off, we might not be able to turn all the sprinklers on, though," Vallimun pointed out. "We could probably find an emergency fire hose and spray them, but if it won't stop them completely, our best bet is probably just to burn the fuckers up with fire. I mean, they're made of straw, right?"

"I was hoping to avoid that because of how badly the fire could get out of hand," Cole replied. "Especially considering the hospital might still be full of people under an enchantment. The flowing water could break the glamour on them, as well, however. That would put them in danger, but it could also work to our advantage."

Corhagen stood up on the hospital bed and pulled out his cigarette lighter. "It's not working," he said, waving the lit lighter around the emergency sprinkler spigot. "Maybe we need a bigger fire?"

"Get down from there," Vallimun growled. "We're not starting a fire, and we can't endanger people's lives. And one of the evidence room girls told me you'd quit smoking!"

"I still carry around a lighter," Corhagen replied defensively. "You never know when you're going to need one."

"Give me that!" Cole ordered, waving him down. "I mean it. We can fight them off using the lighter."

Reluctantly, James climbed down off the bed and passed the lighter to Cole. "I never thought I'd say this," Cole said, grinning. "But you're a genius, James."

Vallimun watched as Cole quickly took the lighter from Corhagen. "What are you two...."

But the inspector never had the chance to finish his sentence, for Cole flicked the lighter on, and a jet of flames came rushing out from the tip. Cole caught them in his hand and formed a large ball out of them, the flames casting light across his pale face and hair. Looking across the room, he saw Vallimun watching the whole show with a bemused, wide-eyed expression.

"Um," he stammered, losing some of his composure. "Wow. You could take that act to Vegas."

Corhagen wasn't as impressed. "Lemme ask the same question he did a minute ago. Why have you been running all this time?"

"Because it's healthy," Cole ribbed. "And I didn't know you had the lighter with you. I can't summon flames out of thin air, but controlling them is a piece of cake."

"But I thought you were winter?" Corhagen fixed his eyes on the fiery ball in Cole's hand. "Or ice. Or whatever."

"On my father's side," Cole corrected, as a clamoring sound alerted them to the scarecrows' presence right outside the door. "My mother was aligned with the power over summer. I have her powers as well as my father's. It's not that complex."

The door to their room burst open, revealing a troop of scarecrows with their claws raised. "If you say so," Corhagen said, backing up. "Get crackin'!"

Cole gathered the power of summer into him, letting it accumulate in the ball of fire as the scarecrows swung forward into the room. Out of the corner of his eye, he saw Vallimun fling himself into a roll across the floor to the side and come up with his gun at the ready, emptying the clip into the first scarecrow that entered. Whoever had made these things had actually given them mouths, and then cross-stitched them back up. Taking aim, Cole sent the ball of fire out into the mob trying to swarm into the room, and clenched his right hand into a fist. There was a sound like a thunderclap going off. Cole concentrated hard, forcing the fire to expand no further into the room, but there was nothing he could do about the shock wave.

Or the noise.

The flames roared like a jet engine firing. Vallimun and Corhagen were both knocked right off their feet. Cole saw Vallimun's gun fly somewhere behind him and hit the wall, the thud swallowed by the noise of the fire. The scarecrows, meanwhile, staggered back in horror as their exteriors went up in smoke. Through the flames, Cole watched them with growing alarm as they stumbled into the hallway again. The ones that had been closest to the fireball when it'd gone off took the worst of it, and now that their bodies were encased in flames, he could see what lay inside.

The first thing that registered was the ribcage. It looked human, though Cole told himself it could've been anything. Then the straw covering their legs burned away, revealing more bones underneath. Soon, they were little more than skeletons with iron claws for hands flailing about helplessly. No sound came from their mouths, yet somehow, that made watching all the more horrible. Cole didn't turn away, however. He'd been the one to start this, so he would keep looking. The sidhe did not avert their eyes when terrible things happened. It was not their way.

Through his disgust, Cole recognized what was happening. Fire cleansed, purified. Nothing could withstand the power of fire's touch. A powerful fey might for a little while, but the longer the flames burned, the more they ate away bit by bit at the magic that powered the spell. The scarecrows were no exception, and with this many of them, Cole had the sneaking suspicion that their maker might have overtaxed himself just a tad by sending so many at one time. With his sidhe eyes, he watched as the spell disintegrated, revealing the nature of how the scarecrows had been animated. The pitchforks stabbed through the bridges of their ribcages glowed for a moment as the souls held prisoner inside them were released. With fire burning away their prison, they were free at last. Their jailer had entombed them inside the pitchforks, then run those through skeletons that'd been dressed up like dolls.

It was gruesome, and yet, somehow, beautiful.

"Hurry!" Cole called out back behind him. "More will be coming soon. We need to leave now!"

"What the hell?" Vallimun gasped as he and Corhagen stumbled out into the hall. "What are they?"

"No time. Move it."

Water poured down. It seemed that the fire eating away at the scarecrows' bodies and magic was sufficient to finally trigger the overhead sprinkler system. As water drenched them, Cole heard something approach at high speed and jerked his head hard to the left. A bullet whizzed past, cutting a swath through the shower and striking the wall beyond. Up ahead, a short figure wearing a red cloak held a gun up under the rain and fired again. All three men ducked down and charged for the turn in the hallway just a few short feet away while bullets flew past overhead.

"I'll hold them off," Cole said, giving Corhagen a shove. "Find us a way out of here."

Cole turned back as the red-hooded figure approached. At a

distance, and through the net of water still pouring down, Cole could have sworn it was a little girl. The figure took aim again, but he was ready. Calling power to his hand, he rolled toward her. The skeletons on the ground, all that remained of the scarecrow golems, twitched and came to life. The water might have grounded ordinary magic, but he was sidhe and as much a part of the natural order as anything could be. Flowing water would not stop his power.

The skeletons formed a line, blocking him from Red Riding Hood's view. With a wave of his hand, Cole sent them forward, and they formed a phalanx that swarmed the little figure. Cole had hoped the skeletons would be enough to deter her. Unfortunately, however, they didn't.

There were terrible crunching sounds over the roar of the water coming down. Cole's eyes widened as the figure kicked one skeleton hard enough that it was flung backward out of reach, its ribcage shattered. The others didn't hesitate, but that single opening was all the girl needed. Cole saw now that it was, in fact, a little girl barely older than thirteen. Rolling forward, she swept out with a leg in a fighter's kick, breaking the skeleton's legs out from under it. Another hand reached for a basket strapped to her thigh and pulled out a grenade. Expertly, she yanked the pin free and flung the grenade up in the air. Then, the pin still spinning around her finger, she ran past Cole wearing a childish smirk and waved goodbye.

Cole, however, was faster on his feet than Red Riding Hood gave him credit for, and he ducked for cover behind the corner before the grenade went off. The twinge in his left hand told him his resurrected foot soldiers had been destroyed. Making a fist, he released the power and returned them to their former state, choosing instead to go after the crazy girl with the basket of goodies. Whoever she was, it seemed no coincidence that she'd arrived while they were outnumbered.

"Get back here!" he called out, racing after her.

"Nah! Nah!" the girl teased, turning around to stick her tongue at him. "Can't catch me."

"I sincerely doubt that."

Cole put on the extra speed and caught up to her in seconds. Seeing this, the girl narrowed her eyes, and reached into her goody basket once more, pulling out a Smith & Wesson M&P pistol. It should've been too big for her fingers, yet she gave it a practiced spin once before taking aim. Cole tried to stop, but she had him in her sights too fast. It was a sad fact that even the sidhe were susceptible to the principles of physics, specifically those pertaining to wet floors and friction. Cole's feet fought for traction as the bullet left the chamber and flew toward him. With nowhere else to go but forward, he turned sideways just as the bullet would've pierced his flesh and it flew past. Still moving, he adjusted his balance and ducked as two more bullets were aimed at his head.

Just as she was about to fire again, Cole came in close. Red Riding Hood was backing away as she fired on him once more, but Cole was prepared this time. Bringing his leg up to avoid being shot, he swung his hips around and brought the foot down hard, knocking the gun right out of her hands.

"Ow!" Red Riding Hood cried out, clutching her fingers in pain. "That hurt! You're a meanie."

"I'm not the one shooting at people," he corrected, reaching for her.

"Uh-uh. You won't get me that easily," she taunted, slipping out of his grasp. "Don't take another step, sidhe, or I'll use this on you."

The girl flipped open her basket and reached inside it almost in the same movement. Up close, Cole could see she was dressed rather oddly, wearing, of all things, a camo uniform underneath the red hood. The upper half formed a tank top that exposed enough of her midriff that her bellybutton showed. She was dressed for war right down to the boots, as if the goblin hordes themselves had come and she were ready and willing to take them all on. It was such an odd ensemble that Cole had to blink to fully register what he was seeing.

That was probably why he didn't notice the bomb in her hand right away.

"You can't be serious," he scoffed, eyeing the napalm bomb. "Using that would hurt you just as much as it would me, if not more."

"Hmph," Red Riding Hood replied, sounding offended. "You don't use your nose very much, do you? Everyone said you were once one of Titania's wolves, but they must've been wrong if you're this close to me and can't smell it. And this is napalm, by the way. Running water won't put it out."

"I know what it is," Cole argued. "And it was the water that made it difficult for me to place your scent. You're half-gnome, aren't you?"

Her eyes widened. "Good one, but I'm not putting the bomb away."

As she said this, the sprinkler system shut itself off. Corhagen and Vallimun came running down the corridor from a side hallway and stopped short, eyeing the girl with the weapon in her hand with an understandable wariness.

"Guys," Cole said with a sigh, "meet Little Red Riding Hood. You might want to avoid her basket of goodies. It isn't filled with cookies, and I'm pretty sure she didn't get those to take to her grandmother's house."

"Don't call me that," she pouted, sticking her tongue out again. "I hate it when people call me that, and just so you know, my grandmother made these for me."

"Her grandmother makes her bombs," Vallimun muttered disbelievingly, gazing down at her. "Only in New York."

"I can't even make myself believe that a grandmother from New York would do that," Corhagen countered.

"Neither can I, really," Cole added.

Red Riding Hood, meanwhile, was busying herself by picking her gun up off the floor and giving it a good shake. "I'd love to just stand around in the puddles and chat with a bunch of old men and a loud-mouthed sidhe," Red Riding Hood broke in, suddenly very annoyed, "but the last time I checked, there were a bunch of creepy scarecrow men chasing me around. I'd like to get out of here before they come back."

Corhagen couldn't keep his mouth shut. "They were chasing after you too?"

"Of course." She shrugged, putting the napalm bomb away. "They chase after anybody not under that stupid glamour spell that put everybody to sleep. I just came here to find a renegade nightflyer and collect the bounty on his head, not get the runaround by a bunch of Wizard of Oz rejects. Speaking of which, I wonder what happened to all of them?"

The last part she said more to herself than anyone else, but Corhagen answered anyway. "We checked all of the stairwells. The scarecrows have blocked them off. We're basically trapped on this floor until you can pull off that thing with the cigarette lighter becoming a flamethrower."

"Wow, you can do that?" Red asked, looking impressed now. "Can I see?"

"You've got some questions to answer," Cole stated. "Who hired you to hunt down Mr. McKnight? Was it the same one who set these scarecrows on the hospital?"

"Sorry," she said, shaking her head firmly. "Customer confidentiality. See ya!"

Cole watched her reach for something in her basket again and moved to stop her, but she was faster. He'd figured she would reach for another weapon, but instead, out came something flat and metallic that reminded Cole of the old joy buzzers sold to children years ago. This one had some sort of adhesive on the underside, allowing it to stick to the glass window beside them. There was a high-pitched whine, like something being wound up. It reached a critical pitch, making all three men duck down and cover their ears. For Cole, however, it was the worst. The pain made him fall to his knees, unable to stand. Meanwhile, the glass beside him cracked, spreading out like the strands in a spider's web until it shattered. Red Riding Hood hadn't moved the entire time.

When the window broke, it shattered outward, flinging the glass through the air. With the glass gone, the high-pitched sound stopped. Riding Hood gave a wave to all of them, then leaped for the window. Corhagen attempted to stop her, whether to arrest her or to stop her from committing suicide, Cole didn't know. It was pointless, in either case. Before he'd stood up to check, Cole already knew she would be gone. She'd never have jumped in the first place unless there was some way for her to survive the fall, and her gnome heritage meant she might have.

"Where'd she go?" Vallimun wondered.

"It doesn't matter," Cole said. "We've still got problems of our own. It won't be long before the scarecrows come after us. They only sealed the floor off so they could corner us. Pretty soon, they'll be hounding our asses again."

"You lose some of your eloquence when you're under stress," Corhagen noted. "I've noticed that before."

"Not the time or place, James."

"Much as I hate to say this, I think we should split up." Vallimun spoke as though he were swallowing something foul. "Backup will be here soon. With the building on lockdown, someone is bound to notice something is wrong sooner or later. We just have to stay alive and keep our heads until then. Fighting those things is pointless, since there's only one of us that seems capable now, and he's a civilian. If everyone else in the hospital is still safe for the time being, we should avoid doing anything to endanger them. Corhagen, I want you to take Cole and find cover. Wait there while I go and see if there isn't some other way for me to contact the outside."

Corhagen turned toward Cole slowly, as though anticipating the look on his face. "I am not, as you say, a 'civilian'.'"

"You're a citizen of New York, buddy," Vallimun stated, jabbing a finger into his chest. Cole's eyes narrowed at that. "And I outrank both of you. Corhagen tells me you've lived here for decades, so that means you fall under the authority of the NYPD. This is my job, and I'll handle things how I see fit. Now both of you make your asses nice and scarce."

Vallimun walked off as though that were it. Cole watched him leave, not moving a muscle.

"He actually believes that would work on me."

"You don't get to be inspector without knowing how to give other people orders," Corhagen replied, looking as though he were about to undertake something highly unpleasant. "Vallimun might be something of an asshole, but he takes his duty to protect and serve very seriously. And for the record, you are a civilian. I don't care what you think you used to be on Avalon, or wherever the hell it was, but it doesn't make a bit of difference. Here, you're just another face in the crowd."

Corhagen paused as he took old of Cole's arm and pulled. "Granted, a pretty, pretty one."

That, and that alone, got Cole moving. "I never thought you'd live long enough to say that to me."

Despite the seriousness of the situation, Corhagen stiffened. "Don't take it personally. Remember, I'm married."

The simple stripe of gold on Corhagen's finger brushed against Cole's skin for a brief second. In that instant, he felt a flash of heat go through him. It struck against his power, his aura, as scalding hot water would against cold flesh. At the same time, a pair of brown eyes flickered in front of him, blocking his vision. They were narrowed and angry. Beyond the anger was the sort of loathing that seemed particular to humans.

"Believe me," he mumbled softly, "I remember."

Chapter
Five

THEIR hiding place ended up being another office in an area where the floors weren't wet. Apparently, the sprinklers hadn't gone off everywhere, just in the hallway with the flaming scarecrows. This one had an unconscious woman lying halfway outside the entrance. From the looks of things, she had been on her way out when the glamour took effect.

Lucky her.

Cole was careful as he propped her up against the wall as best he could. She looked dreadfully uncomfortable, but didn't rouse from the spell at all. He could feel the magic around her, the glamour forcing her consciousness down.

"Can you wake her up?" Corhagen asked, bending over close to his shoulder.

Cole inhaled, letting the smell of James's aftershave and the lingering scent of stale cigarettes that never seemed to wash away fill him. "Not likely," he admitted. "I could try, but if the spell is that powerful, whatever did this might fight back. If that happens, it would come down to who was better at glamour, with her serving as the battleground. Although she means nothing to me, I'd rather not bring an innocent bystander into this. Even if I were to win, her mind could be torn apart. It would be a Pyrrhic victory."

Corhagen sighed. "Just asking."

Cole watched as he stood up and glanced aimlessly around the room. "You're not at all happy with the inspector's orders, are you?"

James frowned. "Truthfully, no. He might not be vulnerable to iron the way you are, but that doesn't mean one of those things couldn't rip him to pieces with those claws. Or just run him through with the pitchforks coming out of their chests."

"The pitchforks are the core of the spell animating them," Cole explained, getting up from the floor. "Destroy them, and the scarecrows fall apart. If any of them find us, make sure you take that out first and foremost."

"When did you learn that?"

"I saw it happen when I used your cigarette lighter," Cole replied absentmindedly. Closing the window blinds, he turned around and looked at James for a moment. "Do you want it back?"

James didn't answer but silently extended his hand. As Cole passed it to him, James's fingers lightly brushed across the inside of his palm. Something inside of Cole quickened, like the string on a bow releasing an arrow. His abdomen clenched, and the sound of his heartbeat roared in his ears. James didn't close his hand over the lighter or draw it away as he had so many other times before. Instead, his eyes narrowed slightly as they stared across into Cole's. Cole swallowed and watched as the detective's irises shifted.

James's irises were usually a dull grey color. That did not mean they weren't captivating on their own, but as Cole watched, their dynamic changed. The color deepened, going from a plain grey to smoke blue, the color of stone mountains at sunset. The color rested closest to the pupil and took up the most space. Around the edges, however, were two more rings, one a slate-grey, the other a dark azure-blue. They were sidhe eyes.

Cole had known for a while and suspected as much even longer, since that first night when James had been drunk, intoxicated to the point where his inhibitions had been thrown to the wind. When he'd put his hand on Cole's stomach and playfully stroked the muscles there, Cole had looked up to see his eyes shift from ordinary human to the mark of high faerie. Somewhere along James Corhagen's bloodline, one of the high sidhe had conceived a child. Most likely, it had been abandoned. The sidhe did not tolerate mortality among them, seeing it as a kind of plague. Cole wondered briefly how far the sidhe blood went back, since the sidhe genetics almost never gave way to anything else. If something bred with the sidhe, the sidhe side was almost guaranteed to be the dominant force in their blood, until it was buried under many generations of human genetics.

Looking into those tri-colored smoky eyes, then and now, was like standing out over the sea and watching the waves wax and wane on the shores of his homeland. Before he realized it, Cole was tearing up. Among the fey, it was considered no great shame to cry. They were an emotional bunch, to put it mildly, and felt things with all the subtlety of a summer thunderstorm. But Cole had lived in the world of humans for a while, and he found himself wanting to turn away. It surprised him, but not as much as James dropping the lighter and linking their hands together did.

The shock must have shown on his face, because when he blinked, James's mouth curled up halfway in a smug sort of grin. Cole should've found it annoying, but for the moment, nothing could get past the drumming of his heartbeat. Cole gave James's hand a squeeze, which sent a spark between the two of them. It made things below his waistband tighten, and James's eyes fogged over with a darkness, the kind he'd only shown when one of them had been drunk. Now, there was only magic between them. It was older than a spell, older than time itself: the heat between two who were joined by blood, battle, and lust for each other.

The ring on James's other hand was a constant reminder, but Cole didn't care. He felt the desire for Corhagen rise up inside of him and spill out like a gale force wind. Pages scattered off the desk and picture frames on the walls rattled as his skin glowed. James's tri-colored eyes shone, reflecting off the gold, copper, and topaz of Cole's. Their breathing intensified like they were racing together, but Cole didn't move a muscle. Another glow filled the room, joining with Cole's the same way their hands intertwined, and Cole realized with a jolt what it was.

James was glowing alongside him.

A sidhe could grant power to a lesser fey, or a mortal, through sex. Cole had worried at first the morning after that something might have gone wrong, but when Corhagen hadn't demonstrated anything beyond his normal range of precognitive dreams, he'd relaxed. Now, it looked as though he should've worried more. There was wind in the office now, a true wind that held the same heat of their touching skin. Cole's skin glowed like the moon, whereas James shone like the dead of midnight. Most people didn't believe the night sky glowed, but it did. It was there, coming off the surface of the detective's flesh. They were still doing nothing but gripping one another's hands, and it was not enough. Cole reached for James first and threw his arms around him as their mouths pressed together.

The room swirled with wind and light. Cole could see it. Even behind his closed eyelids, he could see it all. He'd expected James to pull away, to push him back and tell him all the reasons why they couldn't do this. Reasons that Cole already knew and didn't care about. Instead, James opened his mouth to meet Cole's, letting him press his tongue inside. Their tongues danced together as their bodies met and ground against one another. Clothing was suddenly a hindrance, and Cole was first in opening the fly on James's pants. James let out a soft moan, barely audible over the wind in their ears, as Cole reached in between them and yanked back the waistband of his briefs to free his manhood. James was already hard and ready, leaking the first few drops of precum. Brushing his thumb across the slit, Cole sucked on James's lower lip for a moment while spreading the thick fluid back and forth over the shaft.

James moaned again, this time a high-pitched whine like he was in pain. His fingers curved like claws and raked across Cole's backside as Cole began moving the hand between them up and down.

Their kiss finally broke, leaving them breathless. Cole waited, unsure of what would happen next. The wind around them had died. Or rather, they were standing in the eye of the storm now. James's skin had turned an odd gray similar to one of the rings in his eyes. Those eyes seemed to be waiting for something now, unsure of what to do. Cole tightened his grip on James's shaft, then ran both hands up along the front of his shirt. When he reached the collar, Cole began working his way back down, freeing each button as though he'd done this numerous times before.

The skin underneath was the same as everywhere else. Cole yanked the shirt open, tearing it from James's pants in the process, and savored the feeling of having his fingers play through those chest hairs once more. Body hair was a rarity with the high sidhe. It was considered a mark of lesser fey, yet Cole had always been fascinated by it. James gasped and tensed slightly when Cole's fingernails scraped over his taut nipples, but he didn't pull away. Pulling him in for another kiss, Cole felt himself being pushed down to the carpet. He went willingly, drawing James down with him. Their groins pushed against each other, rubbing and thrusting in a rhythm that brought them closer and closer to the same goal.

Somewhere, at some point, his own cock had been let loose. The juices from both mixed together as they gave one last thrust. Cole's eyes flew open as he felt himself release in time with the creature above him now. James Corhagen had vanished, and in his place was a ferocious-looking beast of the high court. James didn't cry out; he roared. Cole let out a roar of his own, their cries mixing together along with the cum puddling on his abs. Cole's left hand flared to life, reaching down with power of its own accord, stretching to touch the earth. Instead of ground, it brushed against something else. Cole felt them moving now, stirring to life once more. He thought of the scarecrows guarding each and every way out, and that thought somehow traveled down to them along with his power.

James was still crying out, his voice deep like thunder now. It was a sound of the hunt, the cry of a predator in the wild ready to sink claw and fang into fresh, bloodied meat. Cole could sense the curtain around them now, the net of glamour used to subdue everyone else inside the building. At the sound of James's voice, it began to tear itself apart from the inside. The veil around the hospital gave one last feeble attempt at pushing James's will back, then disintegrated into nothingness. Only then did he grow quiet.

Cole pushed James away slightly to have a better look. There were horns—antlers, really—rising out from the bridge of his forehead to shape around his dark, spiky hair like a crown. Once, in the times long before Cole's birth, they would've been considered a mark of indisputable masculinity, signifying a direct link to the Consort himself. Cole couldn't help but feel a pang of wistful envy, even as his eyes drifted farther down. The full lips were James's, always had been. So were the tri-colored eyes that still shone brightly in the dark alongside his. The skin had a tint of purple mixed in with the graphite color, which complimented the black light hue mingling with Cole's winter-frost glow.

James's shirt and jacket were completely ruined. The underside of his forearms were marked with a kind of tribal web design that went all the way up to his elbows. On the other side were rows upon rows of what looked like dangerously sharp quills. Cole might have mistaken them for some sort of ornamental gauntlet if he were human. Even in the dark, his sidhe eyes could tell they were extensions of James's body.

And it was James. Cole breathed in his scent as the air around them at last fell silent. The scent was the same. No, it was more *him* now that he'd ever been before. Cole gazed up into the face of his old friend as he was always meant to be. Consort bless them all, but he had found flesh of his own flesh this night.

"What's wrong?" James wondered, sounding a little panicked. "You're grinning like... I don't know what, but it's really disturbing. And why do I feel so weird?"

Cole tried to fight back the smile on his face, but it was impossible. For the first time in a very long while, he was touching another sidhe, a real sidhe. Cole couldn't grasp how it had happened, how the miracle had come to be. In truth, he couldn't have cared less at that moment. James's eyes, meanwhile, drifted downward from Cole's face to his own arms, which were still propping him up slightly in a midway push-up.

"They're beautiful," Cole whispered, running a hand over his quills carefully, just on the off chance they were poisonous.

In a flash, James was up off the floor and standing as far away from Cole as he could possibly get. "What... what are these?" he shouted hysterically. "What's happened to me? What did you do to me?"

"Oh, that's encouraging," Cole said with a scowl as he got up off the floor. "Anytime something happens to you, it's automatically my fault. Just so you know, I wasn't the one who initiated it this time. For that matter, I don't believe I ever initiated anything between us, and I'd appreciate not being held solely responsible for what happened in the past from now on."

"I don't...." Corhagen swallowed and tried again. "I'm sorry. Now, would you mind explaining why this happened and what made you do this to me?"

"I couldn't even if I wanted to," Cole bit back, turning away as he zipped up his fly. "I don't know how it happened or why. Sex with a sidhe can grant a human immortal powers for a brief period of time, assuming the sidhe has the power to give in the first place, but I've definitely never heard of a mortal being made into one of the fey like this. I'm sure I would've heard something about a human becoming full sidhe."

"Sidhe?" Corhagen looked nauseous. "You turned me into one of you?"

"For the last time, no." Cole was dangerously close to shouting, but remembered in the nick of time that they weren't out of the woods yet. "Us having sex shouldn't have triggered something like this. I don't know how it happened, and I haven't the first idea as to why. All things considered, there are countless people, humans and lesser fey alike, who would see what you have at this very moment as a true and rare gift. Lucky for me, I've been exposed to your ingratitude for a while."

Corhagen took several long, deep breaths as Cole quietly fumed on the other side of the room. "Okay," he offered softly. "Let me try this again. I get that this wasn't your fault. I get that neither one of us understands why this happened. What I don't get is how. You said that humans get power by having sex with the fey sometimes, right?"

Cole nodded. He had the distinct feeling then that James was about to make things needlessly complicated. "How is that a hard concept to grasp?"

"Easy. What we... did... wasn't sex."

Cole blinked. And then laughed. "You're really fighting for a way out of this, aren't you?"

"We didn't," Corhagen insisted, sounding more and more like a petulant child. "I couldn't have, because...."

"You're married?" Cole offered.

"Yes," James stated, holding up his wedding band as if it could somehow drive Cole away. "And I distinctly recall you telling me that marriage vows are sacred for the sidhe. There's no way you and I could've had sex just now, because that would mean I had cheated on Sarah with you. So...."

"We didn't have intercourse," Cole admitted. "But the world of the fey is not so easily cut and dried as that."

James frowned, and it made his lips look positively kissable. Cole, however, pushed his own emotions aside for the time being and struggled to focus. "This is really not the time or the place. In case you'd forgotten, we still have a hospital full of people who've just had a major enchantment lifted off them. And there are scarecrows running lose."

"Oh, right."

Cole snickered. "Once again, I am in awe of your sense of timing. You probably could have chosen a better time and place to ascend to a higher state of being, but that's water under the bridge, I suppose. Let's try and focus on taking care of...."

Something hummed deep and low, cutting Cole off in mid-sentence. It took them each a moment to realize it was James's cell phone, set to vibrate. "Hello?" he answered, whipping it out. "Inspector?"

Cole listened carefully as Vallimun's voice came through from the other end, sounding especially unhappy. James's face grew more and more slack with each sentence, until finally, his eyes were as wide as dinner plates and his jaw hung nearly to his waist.

"He's right here," said James after a moment, passing the phone to Cole. "It's Inspector Vallimun. He needs to ask you about something."

"Inspector," Cole answered after taking the phone from James. "You're still alive. I'm impressed."

"What the hell did you do?!"

Cole remained silent for a moment. "I'm sorry. That wasn't quite vague enough. Perhaps if you left out a few more details, or maybe some vowels?"

"It's pandemonium down here," Vallimun shouted. Indeed, from the other end of the phone, it sounded as though a riot had broken out.

Women and children both were crying and screaming as though the world had come to an end. With a growing sense of dread, Cole began to think that shattering the veil of the glamour wasn't connected to it at all.

"What's happened?" Cole asked, serious now. "Have the scarecrows attacked anyone?"

"Fuck, no!" Vallimun swore. "The walking dead took care of that! How did you manage to pull that one off?"

Cole's eyes widened. "The walking dead?"

Slowly, as though recalling a dream, he remembered the power he and James had shared, remembered it building up in his left hand, his Hand of Power, which enabled him to raise and control any dead thing provided it was cold and lifeless. That power had spilled down through the floors into the earth. Or, from the sound of things, right into the basement of the hospital where the morgue was located. Cole had a sudden, sneaking suspicion as to why so many people in the hospital seemed to be having hysterics all at the same time.

"The whole hospital's been flooded with zombies," Vallimun went on, furious. "They just exploded out of the morgue and came charging through the hallways like the proverbial bats outta hell. I thought the world was coming to an end, but then they all swarmed over the scarecrows and tore them to shreds. People are shitting themselves crazy down here. A few of the families here had just seen their relatives pass away, only to have them rise up along with the rest of the horde and go on a rampage. One woman keeps jumping around like a lunatic, going on about how it's a miracle and her husband has come back to life. The trouble is, he doesn't look too thrilled about it."

Cole sighed, feeling a deep swell of pity. "None of it is real," he explained. "They're just empty shells, vessels for souls that aren't there anymore."

"You've got to put them back," Vallimun demanded. "I can only deal with so much shit at one time. Seeing it done once in the morgue for the purpose of interviewing a murder victim is one thing, but I watched *Night of the Living Dead* once as a kid, and it gave me nightmares all the way into my college years."

"Sorry about that. We had a situation of our own up here."

"Oh, Lord," Inspector Vallimun moaned. "What now?"

Cole wracked his brain for a delicate way of putting it, but one look over at Corhagen was enough to change his mind. "We're not entirely sure how, but James seems to have transcended his mortality and become one of the sidhe."

The silence on the other end was deafening. "Huh?"

Cole smiled slightly. "I mean he's no longer human. When a sidhe comes into their full powers, it usually generates a release of pure energy. In his case, it was a really big release."

Corhagen's eyes narrowed, but Cole ignored him. "He and I were touching when it happened, which is why the dead in the morgue came to life. The power had to go somewhere, so it picked the nearest available conduit, which was myself in this case. James's power was sufficient to break through the veil of glamour, but it just so happens that they woke up just as my Hand of Cold Death woke everything without a pulse or body temperature. I'm pretty sure I can put them all back, though. After we do that, however, I've got to figure out a way to get James out of here. A newly born sidhe with no control over their powers whatsoever can't be a good thing to have in a human hospital."

Vallimun didn't say anything for a moment. "How will you get him out of here?"

"Discreetly, I hope. Our best bet will be to throw a veil of glamour over him, then take him back to my loft."

"What's the address?"

Cole gave it and could hear the inspector scratching it down on something. "Get these people back down to the morgue where they belong before you do anything else. I've got a shitload of paperwork thanks to this fiasco, and a hell of a lot of explaining to do to my superiors. Right now, the only thing that's keeping me from arresting you is that it's less of a pain in my ass to blame all of this on a chemical spill or some other bullshit. That, and nobody wants to hear any more stories about the jaywalking dead from me." Vallimun took a deep breath. "They're not going to eat anyone, are they?"

"Not unless I command them to," Cole assured him. "They're going back just as soon as I hang up."

"I'm coming by your loft tomorrow morning," the inspector

warned. "By then, I expect some answers."

The click on the other end told Cole that the inspector had hung up.

"What did he want?" James asked, taking the phone back. "How bad is it?"

"We have to put the dead that rose when you came into your power back into the morgue," Cole explained, keeping his hand held out. "It seems they've taken care of the scarecrow problem for us, but because of the glamour being broken, everyone downstairs is getting ready to join them. I sometimes forget how mortals have such weak hearts."

Corhagen didn't take his hand. "What do you want me to do?"

"We're going to put them back together," Cole replied, motioning him forward. "Your power is what helped raise them. Therefore, it must be used to help put them back."

"I raised them?" James didn't look pleased at that thought. "I can raise the dead like you?"

"Not likely," Cole said. "Two sidhe having the same Hand of Power is very rare. It felt more like your power combining with mine, allowing me to do more with it. Now, would you please stop pussyfooting around so we can put everyone downstairs back before I get another angry phone call from the nice inspector? Or, worse yet, George A. Romero!"

At last, Cole was able to persuade James to take his hand. From that, it was child's play to thread the power through them into the Hand of Cold Death. James resisted at first, though Cole wasn't terribly surprised by this and simply kept prodding at him until the detective let go. Both let out a single breath at the same time, and the power came to life between them again. Cole felt the urge to touch James once more, flesh to flesh, until the need was overwhelming. The power seemed to want that more than it wanted anything to do with the dead below, which was unsettling. His power had never behaved this way on its own before. Concentrating, Cole shoved it into his left hand forcefully, making them both flinch from pain in the process. The Hand roared to life, and with a single command of thought, Cole sent the dead back to the morgue and their resting places.

"That's one problem taken care of." Cole nodded, satisfied for the time being. "Now to get you out of here."

"Is it supposed to hurt like that?"

"This won't," he assured him. "Take my hand again. I'm going to throw a curtain of glamour over you so you'll look like your human self to everybody else."

"I'll be able to walk down the street and no one will notice?"

"We're not going outside," Cole told him, taking his hand forcefully this time. "I've got a better idea. Just hold still."

In a moment, the other-worldliness of Corhagen's new sidhe form melted away. The glamour poured over him like melted glass into a mold. In a moment, the old Detective Corhagen was standing in front of him again, wearing the same clothes he had worn before, and in pristine condition, no less.

"You know," Cole remarked wistfully, "it's really a shame."

"Not to me," said James, looking over his faint reflection in the window. "I feel much better now."

Cole frowned, but said nothing for fear of rattling the man further. As he opened the door, the woman against the wall whose office they'd commandeered stirred, then came awake rather suddenly. "Relax, ma'am," Cole told her when she let out a sharp scream. "Believe it or not, we're the good guys."

"Don't bother getting up," James added. "We'll show ourselves out. We thank you for your time and the use of your office."

Cole made a beeline for the stairs with James close behind. The hospital was much noisier now, and the hallway was filled with people wandering around back and forth, clearly trying to find out what had happened. Some of them took one look at his bare chest and jumped back, as though the sight of him had scalded their eyes. Cole ignored them and kept going. Behind him, Corhagen kept running a hand over his head, as though checking for something. Once they were on the stairs, Cole paused long enough to turn around

"You might as well stop picking at them," he warned. "I understand that feeling them when no one else can see them is unsettling, but if you don't stop, the glamour will fade. And it won't just be your horns that are showing. People will get a full view of the whole show."

"Where are we going?" James asked, shoving both hands into his pockets.

"Back to the morgue. Or, to be precise, the storage closet that you summoned me into."

They kept to the stairs the whole time, which were considerably less crowded than the hallways or, Cole suspected, the elevators. Once at the bottom, it took James a minute to figure out which way to go. After getting turned around once and going the wrong way, he finally located the closet. Cole spotted the circle at the other end of the room at once and led James over to it.

"You won't need that," he said when James pulled out a small knife. "Come and stand in the circle with me."

For once, James didn't hesitate. "Now what?"

"I'll be directing power into the circle this time," Cole explained. "Your power will join with mine while you chant, 'From whence they came, return them now'. And you have to say it three times. Got it?"

"Okay," James said, looking confused. "Is this going to be like when I would send you back to wherever you came from?"

"A bit," Cole said, making sure their feet were safely tucked away behind the circle line. "Remember how I told you the circle acts as a portal to transport whatever you summon? The summoning spell is just a variation on teleportation. Whatever is inside the circle is brought to you. I can pour enough magic into it to get us back to my loft, but you were the one who cast the spell in the first place, so you have to perform the chant that will open the portal again and send us away. Understand?"

"I think so." James closed his eyes and repeated the words. "Just tell me when," he added, keeping his eyes shut.

Cole pressed his own magic into the circle, sealing it. Once it was closed, he took James by the hand and entwined their fingers together. James was being surprisingly cooperative at the moment, something Cole thought was nothing short of astonishing. For a moment, he considered commenting on it, but changed his mind at the last second. James had endured enough for one day. For that matter, so had he. Cole was looking forward to a hot shower and maybe something to eat, after the summoning circle returned them both to his loft. So long as James chanted properly, it would work just fine. Cole began visualizing his room exactly as he'd left it, and gave James's hand a light squeeze.

"From whence they came, return them now."

"From whence they came, return them now."

"From whence they came, return them now."

COLE opened his eyes as the sensation of being teleported across the city ceased. The first sight that greeted him was his bed, which looked as warm and inviting as ever. His guns and swallow were exactly as he'd left them, and though James was standing right next to him, that didn't stop him from marching over and picking them up. He would never again let his weapons out of sight or reach as long as anyone knew his name and could summon him to their presence.

Behind him, James gave a shudder. "Does it always feel like that?" he wondered. "It felt sort of like I was being stuffed through a wet rubber tube."

"I know," Cole said, walking past him to his walk-in closet. "Believe me, I know."

James stood there in silence for a moment while Cole dug through his closet. "I know they were here somewhere," he muttered, pushing some old boxes aside. "One of the downsides to being immortal is how much junk you can accumulate in a little under a century. I should really consider having a garage sale. Or maybe getting an eBay account. Some of this crap could be valuable...."

"How valuable?" James asked, sticking his head in. "Like, 'novelty Pez dispenser' valuable?"

"Found them," Cole exclaimed proudly, holding up what looked like a bunch of straps.

"Great," said James. "What are they? More importantly, are they worth anything?"

Cole ignored him and began attaching the straps to his legs. "Way back in the day when I worked for the Irish mafia, I had custom holsters crafted for my guns and swallow. They used genuine leather back then, and the stuff held up nicely through the years."

Cole smiled as his guns slid down into place in the hostlers that were wrapped around his leg. The swallow slid into a slot sideways on the belt, just above his ass.

James took in the sight of his guns and whistled. "I've never seen guns like those before," he noted. "You got a permit for those things?"

"Later," Cole dismissed. "Time to take the glamour off so I can have a look at you."

James frowned hard. "Do we have to?"

Cole held a hand up but didn't break the glamour yet. "If you want to know what happened, and why you've suddenly become one of the hidden people, yes."

James stiffened and shut his eyes tightly, as if anticipating something very unpleasant, but objected no further. Cole gathered his power to him once more and tried to ignore the slight pangs of fatigue. Living around so much metal and plastic, it was harder to do real glamour or break it apart. The sensation was more of a nuisance, like background noise playing while he was trying to sleep. If he ignored it, it didn't bother him so much. With a push, Cole felt the glamour fall, and he rose up to see James's sidhe glory unfold before him again.

James looked as human as ever.

More than that, he looked more confused than usual. "I thought I felt something for a second there, but I still look like myself."

"I'll try again," Cole said, frowning. "Maybe...."

Cole refused to finish that train of thought, and this time, he swung his hand out as far as the closet would allow, intending to sweep all traces of the spell away in a single gesture. Instead, James flinched as though he'd been struck, and staggered backward out of the closet.

"Ow!"

Cole blinked. "That shouldn't have happened."

"It felt like someone smacked me over the head," James whined.

"I've always thought you needed more of that," said Cole shutting the closet door behind him. "Why don't you try it, instead?"

"I'm not going to hit myself over the head. Whether I need it or not is no concern of yours."

"I meant the glamour." Cole did smack him over the head this time. "Try taking the glamour off yourself. Just picture yourself unzipping a full body suit and stepping out of it. Your own power will do the rest."

Rubbing his head, James glared for a moment, but consented to trying. After a moment, he opened his eyes once again and looked around. "Anything?"

"You still look like yourself." Cole couldn't hide the disappointment in his voice. "Which can only mean one thing."

"What?" James asked, very worried now.

"You've changed back. The glamour is gone, but you've gone back to being human. Or, at least, looking like one."

"Really?" James looked positively ecstatic, which annoyed Cole to no end. "How d'you think that happened?"

"I couldn't begin telling you how you changed into sidhe in the first place," Cole replied. "Don't even ask me to explain how you were able to change back on your own. All I know is, it is very late and I have had an exhausting day. There will be plenty of time to work all this out in the morning, assuming we wake up before the inspector gets here. Either way, I'm going to sleep."

"Oh," said James. "Well, good night. I can let myself out."

"Were you planning on going home?"

James stopped at the door, frowning as though the question were rude. "Yeah."

"I wouldn't, if I were you," Cole warned, dead serious. "You've undergone some serious ascended transmogrification."

"Well, I'll deal with it." James didn't sound happy, but neither did he move any farther out the door. His hand gripped the door frame as though steeling himself for something. Cole couldn't figure out what, though. Or if James was holding onto it to keep from leaving, or trying to drag himself away.

"What happens if you go home, and the change is somehow triggered again?"

James's grip on the door frame tightened.

"Stay for the night," Cole suggested. "You can call and say you're working late on a case and won't be home. It's not lying and will be much safer for everybody on the off chance that something else just as decidedly dramatic happens tonight."

James wouldn't look at him. "Fine," he said quietly. "I'd better go ahead and call so they don't get worried. Where am I going to sleep, incidentally?"

"Here?" Cole offered.

James left the room at once, muttering, "I hope the couch is comfortable."

Chapter *Six*

INSPECTOR VALLIMUN arrived at Cole's loft bright and early the next morning with three freshly baked bagels and packets of cream cheese for all of them. Cole graciously accepted one, having just gotten dressed to face the day ahead, wearing his guns and double-bladed sword over a fresh pair of leather pants and knee-high boots. He'd foregone a shirt and instead draped an old black jacket over his shoulders, one that contrasted nicely with his skin. Vallimun had taken a good look at him as he passed the cream cheese and smirked. Behind them, James was holding his cell phone against his ear as if it had taken root there. His voice was low, but each word was punctuated to the point that none of them had trouble overhearing.

"I know," James hissed, sounding more and more urgent. "This is important, though. And you know I can't discuss police business over the phone."

Cole chuckled, and even Vallimun smiled as he bit into his bagel. "Look, I can't talk about this right now. The inspector just showed up, and he's ready to leave right now."

"It's amazing how pistol-whipped he acts when he's talking to her," Cole remarked, upon swallowing.

"Her?"

"I... don't... care!" James snapped, loudly.

"His wife," Cole explained, trying not to laugh too loudly. "Sarah. Corhagen got engaged to her when she told him she was pregnant with his kid. Three months before the wedding, they had a *huge* fight over something stupid, and she told him the baby wasn't his. Since they were living together by that point, it made things somewhat inconvenient. He was in a really bad place for a while, and wound up staying here with Katalina and myself. One night, after we'd gone out for drinks to cheer each other up, Sarah showed up at my door wanting to talk to him. To this day, I can't imagine what she could have said that would get James to agree to take her back. Somehow, though, she did it, and they were married a few weeks later in a short ceremony. The kid was born a month later, and to this day, Corhagen will tell anybody who'll listen that the kid looks just like he did when he was a baby."

Vallimun took another bite of his bagel and chewed. "Hmm. Does it?"

"I promise I'll call you later, but right now, I really do need to go...."

Cole shrugged. "No idea, really. James was very careful not to show me any baby pictures of himself as a child, and to be honest, most human babies look alike to me."

Vallimun finished off the last of his breakfast and tossed the napkin he'd been holding it with over toward a nearby trash bin. The paper nearly missed, but Cole waved his finger, causing a light gust of air to land it right on the top.

"Impressive." Vallimun nodded. "Corhagen and I hadn't spoken much until several months ago, but I'd heard rumors before then."

Cole watched as James hung his phone up and sighed, slumping his shoulders in defeat. "I don't doubt it," he whispered softly before raising his voice. "Trouble in paradise, Detective?"

"No," said James unconvincingly. "Are we ready to go?"

"Almost," Cole assured him. "I just need to check on one thing first."

Katalina hadn't emerged from her room yet, which meant she was most likely still asleep. Cole raised a hand to knock but was stopped short as his ears picked up what sounded like chanting. Chanting, and rhythmic drum beats coming from a stereo system. There was a male's voice as well, speaking along with the foreign language of the chanting, but the voice had to have been coming from another set of speakers. There was a faint distortion that Cole only heard when sound equipment played. Katalina began speaking, using the same odd language. Hesitating for a moment, he rapped his knuckles on the door and stood back.

Behind it, Katalina let out a very exasperated sigh. "Just a minute!"

Cole wasn't sure what to expect when the door finally cracked a minute later. "Cole!" Katalina exclaimed, as if she'd been expecting someone different. "Umm, could you maybe come back later?"

"I was just about to leave," he said, getting a whiff of incense. "Were you in the middle of something?"

Katalina looked behind her, careful not to open the door any farther. Cole thought he caught a glimpse of a magic circle in the background, but she quickly put herself between him and it, blocking his view. "Kind of," she said hurriedly. "Was there something you wanted?"

Cole had a number of questions, suddenly, but he stuck to the one that'd brought him to her door. "The hair sample I gave to you yesterday. Did you ever get a chance to look at it?"

"No," she said, almost spitting it out. "No, sorry. Um, but a friend of mine took a look at it, and said that it came off of an infant that was part brownie. It had to have been the baby's hair, because there wasn't enough mystical weight to it. You know, that whole thing with experience and auras. But the child definitely had brownie blood in it. He was sure about that."

"Got it." Cole nodded, stepping away. "That fits in with my theory."

"Listen, I've got to get back to something," said Katalina, bringing the door almost to a close. "Can we maybe finish this later?"

"Sure." Cole nodded, but the door had already slammed shut.

Vallimun and James were waiting for him when he came back across the room, but neither of them looked ready to leave just yet. Cole glanced back and forth from one to the other for a second, wondering what he could have missed. Deciding it didn't matter, he looked into the inspector's face.

"The children being taken are part fey. Whoever is behind this has been using their magic to murder the parents in the most spectacularly gruesome way possible so that when the police arrive, they're too distracted by a crime that shouldn't, by their standards, be possible. Nobody gives much thought to the missing kids because the murders are just so horrible."

Neither James nor Vallimun said a word at first. "And when did you come to this conclusion?" the inspector finally asked.

"I began suspecting it when we found the nightflyer in the coroner's lab," he explained. James gave an involuntary shudder, but Cole ignored him. "The nightflyer said that something came for his son the minute the curse had taken effect on both of them. Susan Brown, the other victim, had a daughter. I just learned she was part brownie. Since the forensics teams haven't found anything at any of the crime scenes, it was probably those scarecrows that grabbed the kids."

"What's a brownie?" Vallimun interrupted.

"It's a lesser fey that will sometimes do things like cleaning or repair work," James broke in. "But since Susan Brown was just under five feet tall, I'm guessing it must've been the father who passed the brownie to the kid, since they're said to be really small."

Cole looked at him.

"What?" James said defensively. "I read too. Or," he went on, "the mother was part brownie, and the father a full-blooded fey. Either way, that doesn't really matter."

"So why go through the trouble of killing the parents?" Vallimun wondered, studying Cole carefully. "Why not just snatch the kids?"

"Missing children reports," Cole answered immediately. "People would look for them, at least for a little while. With the parents dead, the city is more likely to write the missing children off as a lost cause. Kids go missing from the streets every day, so it would be no sweat off anyone's back if they never turned up again. Humans breed ridiculously fast, so if one or two that aren't the offspring of somebody important happen to vanish, it'd just be more paperwork to waste time tracking them down. If the parents were murdered first, however, the police need to find out who could murder grown adults without coming anywhere near them, because that puts their own lives in danger."

James looked offended, but Vallimun simply nodded and began

jotting some things down in his notebook. Cole had to respect him for not denying the obvious facts. "It sounds like some psychologist's game of hide and seek," he mumbled, writing very fast.

Cole nodded again. "We're dealing with something old, older than either of you, and probably older than all of us put together. They understand how humans think, and how the police would react to a situation exactly like the one we're facing. They've had the time and energy to plan ahead, and they've got the power to back up everything they do."

"In other words, they're not human."

Vallimun spoke with little emotion in his voice, but Cole heard the fear and anger buried deep underneath. "I can't imagine a human doing this," Cole admitted. "So it has to be an older fey, maybe even an older sidhe who was exiled."

"Why the kids, though?" James cut in. "What sort of fey would go to all this trouble just to kidnap a bunch of kids with mixed genetics?"

"That," Cole said with a sigh, "is what I haven't the slightest clue about. Human children were always regarded as something of a commodity among the different courts. Some would send the lesser fey out to bring human children in and then barter with more powerful fey in exchange. The sidhe were prone to keeping humans as pets or raising their children as their own if they couldn't have kids."

James didn't look happy now at all. "That's really sick."

Cole's eyes narrowed at once. "And what of all the human children in this city right now?" he challenged. "Humans breed like crazy, then toss their unwanted out like trash when it becomes too much of a hassle for them. Mothers dump their infants into the arms of strangers because raising them interferes with their jobs and careers. Women complain nonstop of all the sacrifices they make. Men leave their wives and newborns without looking back. The sidhe are far from perfect, but children among the fey are considered the rarest and most precious of gifts. The children we took throughout the eons were barely thought of by their sires, yet were treated among the courts as something beautiful and to be envious of. How many human parents have done the same for their kids outside of a poorly scripted sitcom?"

Cole couldn't keep the rage in his voice out, and frankly, he didn't want to. James's eyes had widened to the point that they might have passed for silver dollars. Vallimun had backed away, keeping himself out of the sharp glow that had begun emitting from Cole's snow-colored skin. When nothing else happened, though, he leaned forward again and stood between them.

"Calm down," he said, meeting Cole's eyes for the first time. "Not that I entirely disagree with you, but this discussion gets us nowhere, so let's try and stay focused."

It wasn't a demand but a request. That alone gave Cole the clarity to bring his emotions under control. "Okay," he said, letting out a long, deep breath. "Fine. Getting back to the task at hand, we're looking for a fey that is either older than dirt or higher up on the food chain, and understands how New Yorkers think. There aren't many who fit that bill, so it narrows down the list of suspects considerably."

"You just wanted to use the word 'suspects' in a sentence," James taunted.

"Quiet," Cole glowered. "Or I won't rest until I've located the cemetery where your Great-Aunt Miriam was buried and brought her back. She was the one who loved pinching your cheeks anytime you got within an arm's length of her, wasn't she?"

Vallimun didn't reprimand Cole this time, but instead turned to face Corhagen. "Something I've been meaning to bring up since I got here," he said, giving James a very penetrating stare. "This fucker here said something last night about you...."

"He became sidhe," Cole finished, arms crossed. "I'm still not sure how, but the process reversed itself. I don't understand how that could have happened, either, but he seems perfectly human today."

"This sort of thing happen a lot?"

"To my knowledge, it's never happened at all," Cole replied. "At least until last night, that is."

"Well, if you're feeling normal, we've got a job to do." Satisfied, Vallimun then turned back to face Cole. "I don't normally condone bringing civilians into police investigations, but the truth is a bitch and, honestly, I can't picture us solving this one without some sort of guide into the world of the freaky and hairy."

"The sidhe don't have much in the way of body hair," Cole retorted. "And very few things are regarded as 'freaky' by us. We appreciate the beauty in all things."

"Whatever," James grumbled. "Are you going to help or not?"

Cole took his time thinking. "I'm still getting paid, right?"

"We'll work something out," Vallimun muttered. "Time to get our asses in gear before the trail gets cold. Forensics was able to snag a hair sample and some fibers off the glass from that window the adrenaline junky grade-schooler jumped out of at the hospital yesterday. She's probably long gone, so I wouldn't worry about tracking her down."

"Actually—" James began.

"Actually, we can track her down with that no problem," Cole finished, grinning ear to ear. "Things are starting to look up."

Vallimun followed him and James out the door and down the steps, but not quietly. The entire time, he pressed them about what they had in mind, but Cole maintained a tight grip on his mouth, though that didn't get rid of the smug smile plastered all over his face. Once they were out the front door, he pointed toward an alley down the sidewalk a little way.

"In there," he said. "We don't want anyone watching us for this."

"For more than one reason," James moaned.

"What's he going to do?" Vallimun worried. "It's not going to get us decommissioned, is it?"

"The last time I did this, some of the lower-ranking officers threw dollar bills," Cole explained with a wink once they were out of sight. "One woman wanted me to be the guest of honor at her younger cousin's bachelorette party, but that was before she caught the whole show. I guess the NYPD doesn't accept enlistees with a furry fetish."

Vallimun opened his mouth to speak again but was stopped short as Cole began stripping out of his jacket. "Must you do this every time?" James flinched, hiding both eyes with one hand. "Some of us just ate."

Cole's eyes narrowed to thin slits, but he didn't stop. Corhagen was putting on a show for the sake of the inspector, who hadn't turned away just yet. Rather than get offended, he opted to have a little fun instead. Taking his time, Cole let the jacket slide off his skin, the interior caressing his arms as it fell to the ground. From there, he took off the belt first, making sure to remove his swallow so that the strap would slide through the notches in his pants smoothly. Vallimun had cocked an eyebrow in response, but otherwise, he was showing very little actual interest. It was Corhagen whom Cole wanted to tease, anyway, and regardless of what the detective did, the outline in his pants made it clear he was enjoying this. Even if he didn't want to.

Cole could feel James's eyes on him. James still had half his face covered up with his hand, but there was a small slit between the fingers, barely visible to the human eye from this distance. And Cole could feel the heat of James's gaze burning through to rake across his back. It was more than the January winter air that sent chills down his body. His cock stirred in response, and Cole was careful to turn just enough so that it would show a little as he opened his fly. James looked away again, giving his status as a peeper away, but Cole slid the leather pants down slowly anyway.

"Enough with the cocktease," Vallimun grumbled. "Did we walk all the way out here just so you could give us a free strip show?"

"I always strip before I do this," he explained, stopping. "The detective can vouch as to why."

"He doesn't want his clothes to get torn," James admitted, risking a glance. "If he shape-changes while still in his clothes, they'll be ripped to pieces. I've seen it happen a couple of times, once while he was wearing my favorite Tornado Blue Jays T-shirt. Speaking of which, you never paid me back for that, either."

"He expects us to spend the rest of the day wandering around New York City streets carrying another man's clothes in our arms?" Vallimun raged. "Not on your life."

"Even the underwear." James nodded seriously. "The last time he did this, they got left in the backseat of my car and Sarah found them. I don't think she ever believed me when I told her how they'd gotten there."

"You don't have to worry," Cole replied, sliding the pants down so they could see. "I'm not wearing underwear today."

"How thoughtful of you," the inspector grumbled, rolling his eyes. "Can we get on with this, please?"

Cole relented and finished stripping quickly, folding his clothes into a neat pile and handing them over to Corhagen, who didn't look pleased with the task he was being saddled with. Cole savored the discontent for a moment, then extended a hand out to the inspector.

"The fiber and hair samples, if you please," he asked. "Don't worry. This won't take long."

"You're going to do some kind of tracking spell?" the inspector wondered, his eyes drifting downward. "Naked?"

"Not exactly," Cole replied, taking the bag from him. "Just watch me work, Inspector. This is something you won't want to miss."

"Most men would've said that before taking their clothes off for us," Vallimun muttered to Corhagen as Cole took several long sniffs from the bag. "Oh, and by the way, you can go ahead and look now."

James brought his hand away and immediately jumped at the sight of Cole standing in the raw, calmly passing the bag back to the inspector. "I thought you said it was safe to look," he accused.

"I never said it was safe," Vallimun reminded. "I just said you could look. If I gotta stand here and take getting an eyeful of his wiener, you're going to suffer through it with me."

"James has already seen the show," said Cole, getting on his hands and knees in front of them. "More than once."

Vallimun looked like he wanted to ask what that meant, but in the next instant, Cole had shapeshifted to his wolf form, leaving the inspector completely speechless. Vallimun dropped the evidence bag and jumped back out of the way, his jaw hanging wide open. Corhagen, on the other hand, doubled over laughing and managed to pick the bag up off the ground before the wind took it away.

"Thank you for that," he told Cole. "I admit, I owe you one now."

The inspector looked pale. "He just...."

Corhagen held the still-open bag up for Cole so he could sniff its contents once more for good measure. Once Cole had the scent imprinted to memory, he held his nose up high in the air and took several breaths. Something on the wind caught his attention and whispered for him to get up higher. Heeding its wisdom, Cole turned around and ran for the far wall of the alley, leaping with paws out just before he would have smashed headlong into it. His claws screamed for purchase and found it, pulling him up the layers of brick. Cole ran vertically, racing up the wall a few feet, then pushed off and jumped higher, landing on the wall adjacent to it. Up higher and higher he climbed, until finally, he was over the side of the building and out of sight.

Vallimun watched him go, and remained in that position until his neck finally developed a crick. He looked like he had about a million questions, but finally settled on, "How will he get down?"

James looked at him. "I don't know."

As if to answer, Cole landed catlike on his feet a short distance away, and shook himself off. "Oh," James replied, gesturing. "That's how."

Cole rose up, shifting back to his original form in the process and shook himself. "I have her scent, but she's a good distance from here. We're going to have to hurry if we want any chance of catching up to her."

"My car's parked not far from here," Vallimun said at once, already moving. "We can drive. Can you still keep hold of her scent in a moving vehicle?"

"I should be able to," replied Cole, taking his clothes from Corhagen, who had his eyes closed at the moment. "If not, I can take to the rooftops and lead you there."

"Let's go."

"Sure," he said, struggling with a pants leg. "Just as soon as I'm dressed for the humans' comfort level. And James's."

"Gotcha," the inspector called out, laughing. "Since I've already seen the show, why don't I go bring the car around for us?"

Corhagen waited until the inspector was out of sight before he turned around and shoved Cole against the wall. It was only because he was off-balance with one leg stuck halfway through his pants that Cole staggered backward and was left with James fuming in front of him. Cole was several inches taller than James, average height for one of the sidhe, but James himself was a little over six feet. Cole had relatives who'd towered over him at seven feet tall or more. As it was, at that moment, he could see that the little human detective meant business.

"What the hell are you playing at?" James demanded, pushing against Cole's bare chest with one hand. "Do you think this shit is funny?"

Cole looked down at the hand spread over his torso, then met James's eyes, tri-colored and three-ringed once again. "Your eyes," he whispered, looking into them.

James shut them at once and seemed to wrestle with something internally. When he finally opened them again, they seemed to be human again, but one look from Cole caused the pupils to dilate, and the irises shifted back once more.

"I know you see us all as one huge joke," James tried, his voice sounding thick and hoarse. "But people are dying, and someone is taking their kids. Meanwhile, you won't stop with the innuendo, and that man that just left is an inspector of the NYPD. One word from him could have me out of a job and never working behind a badge for as long as I live. Do you understand what that would mean for me?"

"I understand," Cole said with a nod, slipping his shirt back on. James didn't move his hand at first, but as the fabric slid over it, he tried to pull away. Cole was too quick, however, and seized him by the wrist, reminding the detective of his strength.

"The question is, do you really care so much?" he finished, leaning in for a kiss.

"No," James said flatly, backing away as far as he could get. Cole let him go, and watched him move to the middle of the alley. "No," James repeated, as if it were a prayer. "We are not doing this again."

"Is it because of what happened last night?" Cole pressed. "Because touching me made you remember what it was like before? Or because what we did may have been what made you into something more than human for a few minutes? Or is it just because it's me, and I'm not a woman?"

James didn't answer. "Or," Cole pressed, emphasizing each word, "is it just because you liked it too much?"

A sour expression fell over James's face. "I didn't like it," he muttered angrily.

"Bullshit."

James stared up at him, and Cole wondered for a second if he'd ever seen the detective look more hurt and angry than he did now. Not even a year ago, when Cole had tried to convince him that Sarah was just using him and that the child he had married her over wasn't his, had Corhagen looked so hurt. It actually made Cole regret his words a little.

"I'm married," James spat out. "Married, do you get that? No matter how much you may want this, no matter how much we both might, nothing can ever come between me and my family. I have kids now and a responsibility to them. And before you say another word, they are *my* damn kids. Nothing is ever going to change that. I don't want to have anything more to do with this... whatever it is between us. I love my wife, and she's the one I chose. I don't need this magic or glamour or whatever you're using messing my life up."

Cole remained still, as cold and as distant as the icy north wind. "Like I would use glamour to seduce you."

James didn't reply.

"You're worried over the inspector for nothing," Cole went on, his voice empty of everything but his cold, fiery rage. "Unlike you, he's capable of taking a joke. And even if he were to go to your superiors, it wouldn't make any difference, because I know you. You'd just deny any accusations they brought against you. Because that's what you do, isn't it, Detective? If there's something you don't like or would rather not deal with, you just cover it up with denial and your own feigned ignorance. You're the one who's been hiding under a blanket of glamour all this time."

James stared down at the concrete, refusing to meet his gaze.

"What you just accused me of is tantamount to rape, since it'd be so much easier for you if anything that happened between us was just the result of alcohol or fey magic, instead of what's really in your heart. That way, it's my fault in the end, because you're just an innocent victim of circumstance." Cole turned away and walked off, leaving James to stand by himself in the alley. Just as he reached the sidewalk, Inspector Vallimun pulled up alongside it with his car and blew the horn. Without turning around, Cole knew James was coming up behind him slowly. Cole climbed into the front seat and fastened his seatbelt. The silence in the car was thick enough that it seemed to block out the noise of morning traffic. Vallimun seemed to notice it, but he didn't comment as James walked around to the other side of the car and climbed in the backseat behind him. There were bad guys to defeat and monstrous fey to stop, so Cole was willing to set aside his personal feelings for the moment. Once this was all over, however, he had plans to pound James's face into the ground with his bare hands.

The thought of doing so put a smile on his face as the inspector slapped a cherry light on top of his vehicle and began ducking through traffic.

COLE was furious during the whole drive. Constantly having to strip and climb out of the car in wolf form in order to retrace the scent didn't help things. Each time he leaped back onto the front seat and shifted back, Corhagen would cover his eyes a little too conspicuously. It stoked the cold embers in his chest, but Cole took great care to not rise to the occasion. Calmly, he put his clothes back on and pointed the inspector toward their moving target. The scent had changed directions twice now, which meant their target was on the move. Cole had a hunch they were being led somewhere, but at the moment, he was too furious with the detective sitting behind him to care much.

That thought made him reconsider his actions. It was getting to the point where his skin was glowing lightly in the car. Vallimun had already put on shades to keep the glare from affecting his driving. He hadn't asked what the change in moods was about, but Cole suspected the inspector had wagered a guess. It was no sweat off his back what the human thought of him. Cole had given up trying to explain sidhe sexuality to anyone years ago. Having the humans brand him as some sort of deviant was annoying, but it was a problem he'd grown somewhat accustomed to. Human ignorance was something he wasn't obligated to cure or drive away, and it wouldn't have been worth the effort. At this point, all Cole wanted to do was finish the task at hand so he could go home and crawl back into bed.

Detective Corhagen hadn't spoken a word the entire time. The car was thick with the lack of conversation, the sort that only came from people not knowing what to say. It wasn't a comfortable silence, to put it mildly, and Cole was pleased when the quiet began to make the detective antsy. Vallimun was doing a fair job of keeping his emotions in check, but Cole saw him glance back in the rear-view mirror more than once to stare at Corhagen for a moment before looking discreetly his way. Thankfully, they pulled up alongside the building where the trail ended a few minutes later.

Vallimun placed a hand lightly on Cole's arm as he moved to climb out of the vehicle. "You have to leave the guns here," he said, drawing away. "Unless you've got a permit for them."

Cole shut the door without getting out. "I'll wait in the car, then," he said. "After what happened yesterday, I'd rather not go anywhere unarmed."

Vallimun didn't argue, but he wasn't happy. "I probably shouldn't have let you come along with them in the first place," he said tensely. "Unless you can show me some sort of permit."

"It was years ago when they were first crafted," Cole replied. "Back then, having a permit for weapons was the least of my concerns."

Corhagen went ahead and climbed out of the car, leaving them alone. "How long ago?" the inspector asked, curious.

Cole thought. "The early 1920s. It was not long after I'd been banished, and I wound up on the shores near here. I needed better weapons than what they had at the time, and a man from the Old Country had been trained as a blacksmith before coming over on a boat. He was helpful, even reverent, to me. Apparently, his family had educated him somewhat on the customs of the fey, so being asked for help was something of an honor. I showed him the magics of fey metalworking, something that should've been a crime punishable by death, and he made these for me."

Vallimun looked at him over the sunglasses. "You've been in New York since the Roaring Twenties?"

"On and off," Cole answered, shrugging. "Why?"

"It's just...." The inspector looked flabbergasted now. "I can't quite wrap my head around it. You'd have to be ninety years old, then."

Cole laughed, then. It felt good and actually pushed some of his anger back. "I'm a little bit farther along than that," he revealed, wondering what had made him so chatty. "Although, time in the faerie realms isn't the same as it is here. Still, I assure you that I'm well over a century."

"Must be hard buying candles for birthday cakes," Vallimun muttered. "So, what did you do in the twenties?"

Cole cocked an eyebrow. "I was an enforcer."

"What?" Vallimun took a moment to absorb that bit of information. "You were a gang member?"

"Brian Fitzgerald's right hand, actually."

Inspector Vallimun paled. He was familiar with the name, it seemed. "The Fitzgeralds were some of the biggest in organized crime for years. You worked for the boss of the Irish Mafia?"

"I was banished," Cole said, and even to him, it sounded defensive. "Among the sidhe, there is no higher punishment than to be cast out to live amongst mortals. At the time, I'd simply wandered into a local fight club, hoping to get my bearings. There were people, and one of them had something to say about my pale face and snowy hair. He thought I was in the wrong sort of club, if you catch my drift. I was alone and terrified, but more than that, I wanted someone to take my frustrations out on. We climbed into the ring together and the bets went rolling. I walked out of the den that night with quite a bit of cash, a job offer to come work as one of Fitzgerald's bodyguards, and one of the serving wenches on my arm."

"And the other guy?"

Cole grinned. "Let's just say no one ever made fun of how I looked to my face ever again."

Vallimun turned to face the dashboard. "No, I just bet they didn't."

"Fitzgerald liked me," Cole went on after a moment. "He was a hard mob boss, but fair. He tried to treat everyone under him as though they were extended family. In those times, I wasn't the only one who took some comfort in that. After a while, he confronted me about what I was, and I admitted the truth. He thought that my coming to him was a sign of good fortune and began moving me up in his organization.

Gradually, the inner circle became aware that I wasn't human. Many were unnerved by it, but they all feared what I could do to them. The other mob bosses learned that to insult Fitzgerald or raise a hand against him was to invite my wrath. As time wore on, we became more than simply friends."

Cole waited for Vallimun to say something, but the car was silent. "His wife became entranced by me. It wasn't something I'd done on purpose, but rather than being upset, Fitzgerald brought me to their bed. The three of us were a true threesome up until the day Fitzgerald was shot and killed."

Vallimun spoke quietly now, recognizing that Cole was deep in his thoughts. "What happened?"

"An ambush," Cole whispered, his voice carefully neutral. "I should have seen it coming. After he died, the rest of his organization took to fighting amongst themselves. The only thing any of them seemed to agree on was that it was my fault and that I was to never set foot in their territory again. I left New York and Branwen behind along with her unborn child, thinking I'd never see either of them again."

"Whose was it?"

"We're not sure," Cole confessed. "Or, to be more exact, I think the child was both mine and Brian's. We were together on the holy night of Samhain, and the veil between worlds is always thinnest then. The power to bend the rules of what is and isn't possible is at its peak during that time. Branwen wrote to me after she gave birth to her daughter and told me the child had her eyes and Brian's mouth, but the baby's hair was the same color as mine. No ordinary human could have been born with hair that particular shade of white."

Neither of them said anymore. It was odd telling the inspector about his life, a life that had been so very different than his life was now. He rarely spoke of it, and having a bonding moment with the human left the car feeling very stuffy and awkward. Vallimun picked up on it and moved to get out. When he had one leg on the asphalt, he looked back around curiously.

"What did you do to get banished?"

Cole rose up, eyes narrowed. "Sorry," he said, keeping his face partially concealed behind his curtain of hair. "Privileged information."

Chapter *Seven*

IT WAS warm in the car, much warmer than it should have been. Cole sat for what felt like an hour as the heat built up steadily until it could have been a hot, muggy afternoon in July. Only then did it occur to him what was happening. Cole checked his hands, and his skin wasn't glowing the way it had before, yet a twinge of light hovered just above his flesh against the sun shining through the windows. It could almost have been mistaken for a trick of the light. There were enough pedestrians outside at the moment for Cole to guess the halo around him hadn't caught anyone's eye. Nobody had stopped to stare through the glass. Many times, Cole was thankful humans in this city were so horribly cynical.

The halo of sunlight could mean but one thing, of course. Cole had presumed for years that his powers came primarily from his father, the Lord of Hoarfrost. They had many things in common, at least outwardly, but now the magic he'd inherited from his mother, the Summer Duchess, was growing inside him. The cold from outside should have seeped through the openings in the car, yet it was as warm as if Vallimun had left the heater running at full blast. The air held a trace of moisture to it, like a hot night in the countryside.

Cole wasn't sure what to make of it. More unsettling was the fact that these outbursts of power he kept having were so random. It was common amongst sidhe who were new to their powers to have difficulty controlling them. It was why the education in sidhe magic and how it worked was so important, and why it began at such a young age. Children were expected to understand the basics before they'd gone on their first hunt. Cole was over two hundred sixty years old according to human measures of time. His power shouldn't have been acting so unpredictably.

His thoughts were interrupted when the front and rear driver's side doors swung open at the same time. "It's about time," he grumbled, looking up. "I was wondering when…."

Bugaboo was already in the backseat with his enormous tongue dangling out of his mouth, leaking drool on the seat, when his older brother climbed in and settled down behind the wheel. He looked like a small, hairy child trying to pretend he was driving, but the look on Bugbear's face was anything but friendly.

"Finally found ya," Bugbear growled, snatching his hat off. "Couldn't stand ta turn the blasted air on for us, eh? Feels like a freakin' sauna up in here."

Cole glanced back to Bugbear's younger brother. "No drooling on the seat," he warned. "Or you clean it off."

Bugaboo just grinned and flopped his tongue around, causing saliva to splatter on the passenger window. "Never mind, then," Cole muttered. "Something tells me neither one of you traveled this far just for a ride in a police car. I hope this means you've got information for me."

"Maybe," Bugbear said, stripping out of his coat. Most of his body was covered in layers of clothing, which explained how they'd been able to wander through the city unnoticed. Then again, the residents of New York might have noticed, and simply not cared. "First," Bugbear went on, "we want our payment."

"I haven't got any donuts on me," he said, making an effort to lower the temperature slightly. "Tell me what you know, and I'll make a quick run for them before the police get back. And does your brother normally slobber this much?"

"It's hot," Bugbear grumbled, shifting uncomfortably. "Let's just leave now. I'd rather not be in front of this place when I tell you what I know."

Something in the way Bugbear spoke made Cole take notice. The fey, as a rule, didn't lie to each other, but painting the black-and-white truth every color of the rainbow was a spectator sport of theirs. Bugbear and his brother had been away from fey culture long enough that it looked like they were out of practice.

"This isn't my vehicle," Cole explained. "I don't have the keys for it, and the nearest donut place is too far to walk to. Give me the information you have, and I'll give you cash so that you can buy your own donuts. That way, you can pick and choose whichever cream filling you like."

Bugaboo seemed to like that idea, if the amount of saliva was any indication. Bugbear didn't seem pleased, though. "And what're we supposed to do wit cash?" he grumbled. "Just waltz in like we are and ask for a box of crispy creams with sprinkles?"

"This is New York," he reminded them. "You both walked all the way here from Central Pak, unless you're trying to tell me you took the subway. In any case, no one's going to care. So long as you're paying and refrain from biting anyone's fingers off, the people behind the counter won't think much of it. As far as they're concerned, you two would just be two very hairy circus midgets with a serious sweet tooth."

Bugaboo climbed up the back of the driver's seat very quickly, letting his tongue hang down just to the side of his brother's head. Not a sound came from him aside from the doglike panting, but Cole watched closely as some silent communication passed between them. After a moment, Bugbear sighed in defeat and slumped his shoulders, while Bugaboo slid back onto his seat behind him.

"People ain't been talkin' much lately," Bugbear began. "And it ain't just a case ah 'em not likin' me, neither. Folks around here lately, they be scared of sumthin', and I don't know what it is. Whispers are spreadin' all over the streets about some strange power on the move again. Whatever'n Consort's balls is goin' on, most are ready to piss themselves."

"Again," Cole repeated. "This sort of thing has happened before?"

"Shhh!" Bugbear hissed, putting a claw in front of his non-existent lips. Bugaboo mimicked the expression, which caused both of them to be soaked in spittle. "Right," Bugbear snarled. "Ya don't wanna go around just mentionin' shit like this, ya know? Never can tell who's listenin' and who's ready ta tear yer bloody throat out. That's anuther thing, though. People're actin' as though this is some sort of bad storm terrible to be around for when it hits ya, but it'll pass over soon enough. Get it?"

"I've got it," Cole said with a nod.

Bugbear stuck his claw out and waved. "Fork it over, sidhe. I didn' risk my ass and me brother here just to have you welsh on us."

Cole paid him and watched as they slipped out of the car more quietly this time, all wrapped up once more in their disguises. "Not that this is my problem," Bugbear stated, pausing to shut the door, "but by any chance, did the lunkhead ya rode here with happen to go into da building right behind ya?"

Cole turned around to look. "Yes. It's where the scent I was tracking lead us. Why?"

Bugbear chuckled, and it wasn't a pleasant sound. Bugaboo was standing next to his brother the whole time, keeping his dark little eyes focused on the very same building, as if he were watching some vicious, rabid dog. "Didya not know why Wood Goblin're considered advantageous even by humans? We're not the most likeable bunch around, but one thing dats always been goin' fer us is that we always know when evil's afoot. What's inside a dat place right there, I wouldna sent nobody inside to look in on. Not even a human!"

Realization settled in like a punch to the gut. Cole tore out of the car and ran up toward the building as Bugbear and his kin took off down the street, laughing their asses off. He could have kicked himself for being so stupid. It had been over an hour by this point, and the inspector hadn't had a warrant. Cole knew enough about police procedure to know the most they could've done was have a glance around and maybe knock on the door. Without a warrant to properly search the place, they had no official authority.

It was his own anger that had led to this. Cole hated to believe it, but being furious with James had distracted him. Now, something had clearly happened to the both of them, and in a place he should've been able to sense before the goblin did. He was sidhe, for crying out loud.

And his rage at Corhagen had done him in.

There was nothing impressive about the building, just a few steps up to the front door. Something about the place gave Cole the feeling that no one had set foot in it for years, but once he was close enough to get a good long sniff, he knew. It was the same glamour as before, the one woven around the hospital to keep all the humans tucked away in a deep slumber while murderous scarecrows went on a rampage. Funny that he would find it here now. The door was chained up. It was the only thing about the whole place that looked new, and Cole somehow sensed the chain hadn't been in place when Corhagen and the inspector had gone up those same steps earlier. Cole couldn't remember seeing them go inside now. It was as though they'd walked toward the building and vanished. And he'd been so caught up in his own drama that it'd slipped by him unnoticed.

He hoped Corhagen never found out what really happened. The bastard would never let him forget it.

There was no other way in, except maybe the roof. Cole wasn't about to risk shapeshifting on a street in the Bronx in broad daylight. The turning-into-a-wolf part might slip by unnoticed, but he'd lay dollars to donuts someone would make a complaint about indecent exposure in a heartbeat. Humans were just that weird in this city. Taking aim with Bandersnatch, Cole cleared his head of his worry and gathered up all the anger he had. Emotions could be simplified, distilled into power, and then put to better use with practice. He'd had lots of that through the years. The gun made too much noise on its own to pass for something small, but with a little twist of glamour, anyone within earshot would most likely pass it off as a taxi cab backfiring. One lone shot wasn't enough to alert people in this type of neighborhood.

Once the spell was in place, he fired. The bullet cleaved the chain in half, and it fell in two pieces on the ground without him laying a finger on it. No one moved; nothing on the street suggested anyone was disturbed or alerted by the noise. The glamour had done its job.

Cole sheathed Bandersnatch and checked the doorknob for spells. The glamour that kept this building unobtrusive was there, and so was a curse. It was small, almost miniscule, but all the more dangerous as a result. A major spell to cause him physical pain or damage would be far too easy to detect. A human might find it unsettling and feel an inexplicable hesitancy toward grabbing the knob, but a subtle spell was much harder to catch. Had Cole not checked first, he could have been bewitched by it and never noticed.

The curse was designed to open one's mind and make him or her more susceptible to persuasion and glamour. If Corhagen and the inspector had both touched the knob before entering, it might explain why they'd never come back out. The spell had been expertly crafted. Whoever designed it knew the intricacies of the mind, and how to nudge one toward the caster's intent. Cole waved his hand over the doorknob, freezing the spell at once. His action left a layer of frost over the metal, easily brushed aside. Cole tried the door then, but it was locked. Smirking, he leaned back slightly and kicked out with his right foot. Being an enforcer for the Irish mafia meant he had done this sort of thing a lot. Brian Fitzgerald had seen to it Cole got in lots of practice. To this day, he would never have to fear locking himself out of his loft, only the rising cost of replacing the door each time.

The door swung in, and Cole dove forward with Bandersnatch and Jabberwock in each hand before it had time to rebound off the wall and snap shut. Before he'd finished the roll and risen up, his sidhe eyes got a good look around. The place was decorated like some swank hotel downtown. The carpet felt brand-spanking-new and freshly cleaned. The walls might have been painted white only last week. A fresh vase of flowers rested on a wide, varnished table at the end of the long foyer.

One quick sniff confirmed it was all a lie. The glamour that blanketed this place felt older, woven into the walls and floors of the building like a handmade quilt. This was a place of power, where the owner in question gathered on a regular basis. It might have been their home. Cole strode confidently down the foyer with both guns at the ready, giving them a quick twirl every so often. The place felt deserted, but he knew better than to go on what his eyes and ears told him, especially in a place where his enemy had the home field advantage.

He was near the vase full of flowers at the end of the foyer when the door slammed shut behind him. The sound made Cole turn around, but it wasn't the closed door that bothered him. Just before the carved wooden panel swung back, he had smelled something. Something decidedly not human, and looking down the corridor, Cole saw what it was. She was young by human standards, young enough to still be in school, but her height made her seem older somehow. Almost everything about her was dainty and youthful except her eyes. One look at them, no matter how innocent she tried to make her face, told him this girl was not to be trusted.

Keeping his guns up, he walked casually back the way he'd come. The girl smiled at his approach. "Welcome," she said, in a voice much deeper than he'd expected. "Nanny Goodwynch has been waiting for you, Tuulois MacColewyn. Tea is nearly ready in the drawing room."

She'd even pronounced it right. "I apologize for keeping your lady waiting, then," Cole said, looking down on her. "And sorry about the door."

The girl giggled. "My name is Spinner. I was instructed to lead you to her. She's been wanting to speak with you for a while now."

Nodding, Cole stepped back to let her walk past him. "Lead the way."

It was dangerous to enter the home of another fey uninvited or unannounced. Cole had been expecting a couple of things, but not an invitation to have tea, and not with someone who knew his real name. That made him nervous, since knowing a sidhe's full name allowed certain types of creatures power over them. Even still, there were loopholes to slide through. Cole occupied himself by keeping an eye on where the almond-skinned Spinner was leading him, and watching for any signs of Corhagen or Vallimun.

When they reached the drawing room, Spinner stepped to the side, allowing Cole to pass through first. He did, keeping both guns at the ready in case anything happened.

There were only two women waiting for him at the table. One was an elderly lady, looking for all the world like she could have been someone's grandmother. The other stood not far away with an empty cookie sheet in hand as though she'd just finished delivering some baked goods. She glanced up as Cole approached and visibly stiffened. His presence had alarmed her somehow, though he wasn't sure why. Cole was used to people on the street doing double takes whenever he walked past, but somehow, that didn't seem right this time. She outright refused to meet his gaze as he walked up to the table.

The old lady smiled at him, showing two rows of perfect human teeth. "Tuulois MacColewyn," she gasped, as if greeting a long-lost child. "The Fallen Sidhe and former wolf of Titania's. Welcome, dear child. Welcome to teatime. Please, have a seat."

Cole put his guns away but didn't sit down. "Am I to assume I'm a guest here?"

The crone, whom he assumed was Nanny Goodwynch, smiled. "Of course, dear. We don't serve tea and cookies to intruders."

He knew she was referring to the door he'd kicked in. Cole nodded in response and took the seat across from her. "Very well, then," he said. "And who is this lovely young creature here?"

The young woman flinched at the word "creature" but otherwise didn't look up. "Here, we call her Raywing."

"It's a pleasure to meet you," Cole said, lowering his head ever so slightly. "Raywing. And behind me is Spinner, correct? You have very exquisite taste in names."

"I name all of my children," Nanny Goodwynch said, as though it were something to be proud of. "They all know how a name from me means they're special."

"Of course."

Nanny Goodwynch spent a moment pouring tea into a cup for him, then pushed the tray of cookies toward him. Cole picked up his tea cup and breathed in the vapors, pretending all the while that he was savoring the aroma when, in actuality, he was checking for poison. It was against their laws to harm a guest in any way. Nanny Goodwynch, no matter how much glamour she wore, was certainly old enough to know this. Still, it never hurt to be cautious, and Cole had learned all about paranoia when he'd first arrived in the city years ago. The tea smelled delicious, and clean of any toxins. More to the point, however, it both smelled and tasted familiar. Picking up a cookie, he studied it for a moment.

"Something wrong?" Nanny Goodwynch asked, watching him closely.

"Forgive me," said Cole, taking a small bite out of one. "I was just wondering what sort of cookies these were."

"Homemade gingersnaps," she answered at once. "I made them myself."

He nodded. "And the tea?"

"Cran-apple with a touch of honey."

Cole smiled and took another sip. "You know what I like. I'm impressed."

"I try," she said, looking pleased. "I confess, I was expecting you to show up sooner."

Cole paused in mid-bite, then recovered and hurriedly finished off the rest of his cookie. Nanny Goodwynch saw the hesitation, however, and her eyes seemed to sparkle in the room's dim light. "You must have been awfully uncomfortable sitting in that policeman's car for so long. I thought perhaps you would simply walk up the steps and knock on the door as they'd done. Why wait for so long?"

"It was warm," Cole answered, shrugging. "And I had company show up unexpectedly. Plus, to be honest, I wasn't especially happy with the detective at that moment."

Nanny Goodwynch blinked. His blunt honesty had caught her off-guard. Cole picked up another cookie and smiled at her. "May I?"

Nanny Goodwynch motioned with a wave of her hand, recovering herself quickly. "Go right ahead. Help yourself."

"Do you want one?" he offered, holding the plate up to Raywing. The woman looked positively shocked, as though no one in her entire life had ever offered her a cookie before. She stared at the silvery platter as though it contained nothing less than death itself and shook her head frantically.

"It's alright, Raywing," Nanny Goodwynch cooed, stroking her arm gently. "The nice young gentleman sidhe was just being polite. That was very sweet of you, Master Cole, but Raywing doesn't particularly care for the sidhe much. She's had some bad experiences."

"Haven't we all?" he asked, taking the opportunity while she was distracted to reach out with his power.

The room was absolutely soaked with her glamour. It clung to every aspect of the room, right down to the floor. Cole couldn't be sure anything he was seeing was real; most fey couldn't work real glamour on a sidhe, but he wasn't willing to put anything past her. True glamour could bewitch all the senses, not just sight. For all he knew, he'd been biting into the backsides of beetle shells the whole time while sipping sewer water. It wouldn't kill him, but the thought was disgusting enough to make him put the cookie back down. He had to break her hold over this place, but for the life of him, he was having trouble thinking.

Which made no sense whatsoever. He was certain nothing he'd had contained poison of any sort, nor did it have any spells put on it. Looking down at the table for a moment, Cole thought he saw a flicker of someone in the warped reflection of the cookie tray. He fought not to turn around but instead focused on it. The distorted image seemed to steady itself after a second, like water smoothing out after the wind stirred it, and a face looked back at him. The person staring back at him was much younger. Cole hadn't seen that youthful face in years, except perhaps in photographs taken when David was still a child. Cole licked his lips, and the taste of Cran-apple tea clung there like a faded memory bursting out onto the surface of his mind.

The spell hadn't been in the tea or the cookies. It was on the bottom of the cookie tray. His skin had absorbed it when he picked the blasted thing up to offer Raywing a cookie.

"Damn," Cole swore, looking up slowly. "So what was the spell? Something to make me more susceptible to your glamour?"

"Just a little tweak to make you more open-minded," Nanny Goodwynch replied, picking up a cookie for herself. "Would you like some more tea?"

It wasn't so much that the room was spinning for him. The spell wasn't designed to make Cole nauseous, just eat away at the mystical barriers of his mind and spirit until he was wide open for attack. He could sense it now, like ants stripping flesh away from a carcass on the side of the road. His aura weakened with each second that ticked past. Any time he fortified one area, the spell would simply shift its attention and move to another space and start again. He had to keep her distracted long enough to deal with the problem. Trouble was, Nanny seemed adept at multitasking.

"Is this the part where you tell me your evil plan, giving me enough time to escape?"

Nanny Goodwynch laughed. "Oh, you're a clever one, aren't you?" Nanny gave Cole a smile as she stroked Raywing's side absentmindedly. "I thought perhaps you might have some difficulty seeing things my way. The spell won't take away your free will. If you are truly sidhe, removing it shouldn't be a problem."

"Ah." Cole nodded feebly. "So we've reached the villainous taunting segment of the tea party. And here I was worried you might not monologue for me."

"What a wicked tongue you have," she noted. "If you were human, I might have had it cut out before we sat down."

She was still stroking Raywing as though the woman were a cat. "You murdered those children's parents," he breathed, forcing each word out. "You wanted them to die in the most gruesome way possible, so the police would be too focused on their deaths to worry much about the vanished children. With them distracted, no one would bother to go looking after a while. They'd just write it off as an unexplained event. Then I got involved, and it all went to hell. McKnight survived the curse because he wasn't human, just using a husk to move around in daylight hours, so you glamoured everyone in the hospital to fall asleep while those scarecrows went hunting for the both of us."

Nanny Goodwynch shook her head. "You won't get me started on some rant about my means or motives that way, young Master Cole. I'm not so dense as to spill my secrets to whomever worms their way up to my doorstep. Speaking of which, I would be interested in learning how you found me so fast. No one has ever gotten this close before. Are all of the Lady's wolves this resourceful, or is it one of your specific talents?"

What the hell? "I followed your flunky," he whispered, the spell rolling down over him completely now. "She left a trail. Some fiber and hair samples from a window she'd crashed through at the hospital."

Nanny Goodwynch stiffened, then forced her body to relax. The movement was a dead giveaway, however, even in his bespelled state. She didn't know who the girl in the red hood was. Cole steeled himself as the devouring spell pushed deeper against the weaknesses in his shields. It was getting close to time.

"Raywing," Nanny Goodwynch called out, "Spinner, it's time. Why don't the two of you show the exiled sidhe what he's really been dealing with all this time?"

Cole waited as Spinner joined Raywing in standing beside their mistress. The air around both women warped and bubbled for a split second, and that was all Cole needed. It seemed like the bitch would keep talking forever, but she'd finally dropped one of her disguises, and that was all he needed. Instead of fighting the curse on him, he'd held it in check, hoping for her to undo something within his line of sight. As the glamour around both women melted away, revealing their true forms, Cole sprung his trap.

The spell seized up suddenly, thrashing and twisting over the surface of his aura like a caught mouse. Concentrating, he flung a rope of energy out from his body at the two, keeping the curse from following the trail until it hit both targets. Once he felt his energy anchor against theirs, Cole let it go and watched as the spell shot out toward them and slammed against both auras. The women gasped, even as the glamour continued to melt off them. Nanny Goodwynch leaped up out of her chair and held a hand out to stop it, but it was too late. Cole felt the spell move downward to the floor and keep going. When it touched the carpet, the curse spread like wildfire, devouring all of the glamour it could touch.

Spells such as this had a side effect when lowering someone's defenses. They also caused glamour to fade, leaving the person under it exposed. Cole hadn't been holding any glamour over himself, but the entire building had been saturated by Nanny Goodwynch's. The glamour itself was like a barrier, and the spell had been going for the weak points in his. Now that it had a choice, the curse moved toward the biggest barrier of them all: the one wrapped around the entire room.

There was maybe a split second where none of them moved. Then, Raywing let out a scream and took off into the air. Cole was too distracted by the spell leaving him completely to notice more than a flurry of dark wings and an odd sort of shape shooting up to the ceiling. Spinner staggered as her body stretched slightly, showing just how tall she really was. Her arms and legs were pulled thin, far too thin for any human. The ends of each contorted like claws, the sort of claws one would find on a praying mantis except that two more appendages burst forth from her sides at the same time. Her mouth stretched wide, too wide, and was filled with fangs. Her lower abdomen was split wide open straight down to her groin, and lined with a row of what looked like teeth.

Cole's eyes drifted toward the plate of cookies, the only thing that hadn't changed. Lucky for him, they hadn't been beetles after all.

And the tea really was just tea. Hooray.

Nanny Goodwynch herself wasn't so lucky. She kept trying to draw her glamour back around herself. Each time she managed to pull one part of herself back together, though, another would get eaten away. The spell was turning ravenous and wouldn't let her go. She kept ranting incoherently as her body appeared to fall apart in front of him and then draw itself back together. The spell, however, was having none of it. While she wrestled to placate her own vanity, everything else came apart at the seams. Cole took one last sip of his tea as the whole building shook. It might have been an explosion, except nothing came apart. The glamour had given way with one last tear, ripping the very fabric around the building in half. All that remained was Goodwynch herself, and with one final cry, the curse tore her real form free from the illusion at last.

Her skin was pale and wrinkled, yet it somehow defied its age by remaining glossy and smooth. Her face showed the least amount of damage done by the passage of time, yet there were age spots dotted across her forehead and down one side, almost artfully so. Her hands extended outward into claws, straight and razor-sharp, meant for tearing muscle from bone. The hair was as dark as a starless sky, and ran down her back in curls that could've been knots, yet it shone in what little light there was. In all, she was a study in contrasts, age and youth woven together into some sort of perverse creature of dark fetishes.

But it was Nanny Goodwynch's eyes, burning like tri-colored emeralds, that gave it away. "You're... sidhe," he whispered, lowering his cup. "And...."

"Naryssa," she spoke, her voice carrying with it a light hiss.

"Naryssa Goodwynch, to you. Never forget that name, fallen child, because I will never allow myself to forget what you've done to me this day."

Despair filled the room, and it wasn't his own. Up above, Raywing hovered over the table near the ceiling like some giant, pesky moth. Her wings were like a bat's, and she bore the unmistakable mark of being the child of a nightflyer. Yet her body was too long for it. Instead of arms, she had her wings. There were no tentacles, but what had once been her legs fused together about halfway down to form her tail. Her head was a little too wide now to ever be mistaken for human. Whether it was her mother or father, she'd been the bastard offspring of a union between a human and a nightflyer.

And she carried all the bitterness of one. "Wicked sidhe," she spat. "Wicked, wicked sidhe."

"May we eat him now, Nanny?" came Spinner's voice from the side of the wall. Cole spared one glance away from Naryssa to get a good look at her. In her half-spider goblin form, she clung to the wall amidst a quick net of webbing she'd spun for herself. All of her eyes focused on him as her tongue ran itself hungrily over row upon row of fangs. Both her and Raywing's bodies shuddered as the despair touched them, caressing their forms the way a tender lover might after years of being together. The power from Naryssa Goodwynch flared for a moment, and she drew herself up to stare him down.

"Night hag," he stated, understanding. "You're half sidhe and half night hag. You feed off negative emotions like hate, fear, and despair."

Naryssa snarled.

"That's why you need the children," he went on as Raywing hovered down closer. "You feed off their misery to stay powerful."

"Never!" she screamed, even as their despair soaked into her aura. "You couldn't possibly understand what they mean to me. They are my children!"

Cole drew his guns and aimed for her head. "Lady," he said with a grimace, "you are one lousy parent."

"Attack!" Naryssa screamed. "Tear the asshole apart, my children."

Spinner threw a loogie of webbing right at his face. Cole threw himself backward in his chair, letting the webs pass overhead, then went with the momentum to roll back up in a fighting stance. One hand held Jabberwock, but the other was drawing out Aed Deigh. The trio in front of him hissed and snarled as the red-hot blade snapped to life out of the hilt. All around them, the room had fallen apart into dilapidation with the sweeping away of Naryssa's glamour. Great gaping holes in the floor stretched out around them. The curtains by the enormous window framing Goodwynch and her two daughters were in tatters. Cobwebs and dust covered everything save the table separating them. Nanny Goodwynch, it seemed, was meticulously polite.

The lack of a mess at the scene of Susan Brown's murder now made sense.

Raywing dove at him, lashing out with her tail as she swooped past. Cole swung upward with his Aed Deigh, missing as she looped around the room to make another pass. Spinner managed to pin his feet to the ground with more gobs of her sticky fluid, but Cole freed himself by swiping at the webbing with his blade. It caught fire as he backflipped, then hand-sprung off the floor and landed feet-first into Raywing's stomach. Cole could hear the air rush right out of her lungs as she rolled to the floor in a heap. Spinner gave a startled growl at the sight of her injured sister, then leaped right at him.

Cole had his gun ready and fired before she reached him. Naryssa screamed, causing dust to rain down on them as Spinner's wounded body landed with a satisfying crunch at his feet.

"Sister!" Raywing gasped, reaching for her with one injured wing. "What have you done to her?"

"I shot her," Cole replied, taking aim for Naryssa next. "Like this."

Cole's shots missed and broke through the window as Naryssa took to the air. The white gown she wore fanned out around her, making her seem almost ghostly as she spun herself down in a spiral, swiping at his throat. As he dodged, the claws brushed against the tender flesh above his pulse, spilling the hot blood underneath. Cole staggered, falling to the side, and clutched at the place on his neck where blood flowed down onto the floor. Naryssa had claimed the advantage with her hag blood, willing herself to fly without aid. Cole had never flown on his own before. It was not one of his powers.

Raywing, though still hurt, struggled up to her feet, then flapped both wings and took to the air again alongside her mother. Spinner was still bleeding on the floor. Thinking to himself, Cole rose up and retracted the flame blade back into the hilt. With a thrust downward, he shoved the ice blade into the floor and held both hands away from the hilt as though praying.

"Ice," he commanded, letting his voice fill with magic, "freeze!"

Spinner was struggling to get to her feet when the spell hit. Cold filled the room like the biting chill of a giant freezer. Ice from the sword spread out over the floor; creeping frost covered the dust and cobwebs, until they glistened like Christmas tinsel. Icicles hung from the beams criss-crossing above. It was snowing now, and the frozen cold covered Raywing's bat-like arms, causing her to plummet out of the air. The floor shook with a noisy thud as she landed a few feet away.

"That's one," he noted, aiming Bandersnatch. "And here's number two."

Spinner took two more bullets to the chest and stumbled back, hissing in pain the whole time but she was at least one-half spider goblin. Cole had no delusions that she would die so easily. Nevertheless, her appendages were far too close to him for his comfort, and he kept on firing.

"Stop this!" Naryssa screeched. "You're hurting her!"

Cole snatched up Aed Deigh before she could make another pass and leaped on top of Raywing's body. The nightflyer spawn went rolling out of control across the icy floor of the room, screaming and cursing him all the while. Cole endured the flapping of her wings trying to knock him off and kicked out with his foot, propelling them forward as Naryssa came after them in a gale of fury. Cole fired a few warning shots and steered clear of her claws as she attempted to take his head off. Raywing, meanwhile, did not appreciate being used as a skateboard, and she snatched up a chair in one of her hands as they passed it by. The wood shattered against Cole's back, forcing him off of her, and only his fingernails digging into the frost prevented him from sliding all the way down a hole in the floor at the far end near the window.

Raywing was helped to her feet by Naryssa, who landed next to her. "Are you alright?" she whispered, her voice thick with concern. "Did he hurt you?"

"He...." Raywing was gasping for air as Cole slipped on the icy surface. "He touched me, Nanna!"

"It's not like I tried to cop a feel," Cole grumbled. "Never mind the fact that you're all trying to either kill me or bespell me. Quite a way you have of treating guests, Naryssa. Maybe that's why your kids don't bring their friends over more often."

"I swore sidhe flesh would never again touch Raywing's," Naryssa spat, glaring daggers at him. "You will pay for this, sidhe spawn, Son of the Glittering Courts."

Cole rolled his eyes. "Must you be so dramatic about everything?"

The skin on the back of his neck crawled. At the same time, the doors on the other side of the room behind Naryssa burst open. In rushed a mismatched cluster of some of the most oddball mixing of fey blood Cole had ever seen before. His eyes flickered over one who might have been part human, snake goblin, and brownie; and another who might have been a very small ice mountain troll, were it not for the face being so round.

"Get him, my children!"

Cole ducked, not in an effort to hide, but because something chose that moment to come flying through the window. What little glass there was left rained down, leaving shallow cuts all over his back and arms as he shielded his face as best he could. The figure rolled across the floor and stopped at Naryssa's feet as the hail of shards stopped pelting him, and Cole had enough time to rise up and see the pepper bomb before it went off. A pair of small feet thudded against the broken window-pane, and a second later, they crunched across the floor to stop beside him.

"You okay?" a familiar voice asked. "Wow, that's a lot of blood. I didn't know it would cut you up that badly. Sorry!"

Cole stared up at Little Red Riding Hood. "I'll heal," he groaned as the glass was forced painfully out of his skin. "What are you doing here?"

"Saving your lazy butt," she replied, pointing toward Naryssa's gasping horde. "What else?"

"You're helping me? Why?"

Red Riding Hood scoffed. "You want answers, or help kicking someone's ass?"

Cole sighed as the cuts on his arm began closing. "How about ass-kicking first, followed by answers later?"

Riding Hood grinned and pulled out two homemade Molotov cocktails from her goodie basket. "We'll see."

Chapter Eight

COLE slammed the door shut behind them and broke into a straight run, catching up to Red Riding Hood quickly. "How long until it—" he began, but then there was a rather loud explosion from the room they'd just left, which shook the whole floor. "Never mind," he finished.

"That won't stop them," she warned. "Nothing that small could. We'll have to bring the whole building down around their heads."

"Can't," Cole replied. "Some people I know are in this building, and it's sort of my fault they're in this mess to begin with. I've got to find them first before we do anything more to make this place more structurally impaired than it already is."

Red Riding Hood stuck her lip out as they dashed around a corner. "You're no fun!"

The fight hadn't gone as well as Cole had hoped. Even with her on his side now, the odds were stacked against them. Cole hated to leave the battle without a clear victory, but the thought of Vallimun and Corhagen trapped in this place somewhere was enough to make him grab her by the hood and split.

"I don't suppose you have another one of those," he pressed as they reached a set of stairs. "Or, a dozen?"

"Does this thing look like Aladdin's lamp to you?" Riding Hood grumbled, sliding past him on the railing. "I have my limits, you know."

"It's a bottomless purse," he countered, foregoing the steps entirely. Cole jumped, and the floor shook as he landed next to her. "I haven't seen one of those in a while, but they should still work the same way they always have. Incidentally, where'd you get that thing?"

"Grandma," she replied. "And my name is Robyn, incidentally. Just so you don't start calling me 'Red Riding Hood'."

"Too late," Cole said, grinning. "How about Robyn Hood instead?"

She scowled. "Not another word. Let's find these friends of yours and get out of this madhouse."

Cole was all for that idea. The problem was, without Spinner there to guide him, he had no idea where to go. The glamour Naryssa had thrown over the place had faded completely, devoured by the curse she'd attempted to inflict on him. Without it, everything looked completely different now. Moreover, it was far more dangerous than before.

"For someone who loves her kids so much, she doesn't seem to mind them running around a place that's loaded with booby traps," Cole muttered as yet another axe swung down from the ceiling, narrowly missing bisecting him. "She's really campaigning for mother of the year."

"They live here," Robyn stated as if it were obvious. "All of her kids know where the traps are. The only way they'd get hurt is if they're dumb enough to fall into them."

With a pang, Cole realized she was right. It was just like he'd been taught growing up amongst the other sidhe: if you knew where the dangerous places were and still strayed into them, you deserved whatever fate befell you. He'd lived among humans for far too long if he'd forgotten something like that. Naryssa, apparently, had not.

"This way," he said suddenly, turning a hard right. "I hear something."

"Is it dangerous?" she asked, and for once, she didn't sound hopeful. "It could be dangerous."

"It sounds like... moaning." He paused, standing outside a door. "Lots of moaning."

"It could still be dangerous," she pressed.

"Or it might be them," Cole countered. "In which case, we grab them and get the hell out of here."

From her goody bag, Robyn pulled out a small rocket launcher. Cole watched as she loaded it, then took aim at the door. "Okay," she said, looking through the scope. "Open the door. I'm ready."

Cole blinked once. "I see that."

Reaching for the doorknob, he pressed an ear as close as he dared to without touching the wood and listened hard. The sounds were still coming from inside, along with what might have been snickering. Deciding to risk it, he flung the door open and stepped out of the line of fire as Robyn's finger twitched over the trigger but didn't pull. Confused, Cole peeked around from behind the door and looked inside the room. A soft, crimson glow had spilled out into the hallway, and he immediately saw why.

Not far into the room, two soft figures hung lightly in mid-air, their arms wound tightly around each other. Both women were naked, and touching one another in a way that many humans would've found objectionable. Cole, however, just leaned against the frame and watched as one ran her fingers lightly over the other's breasts, drawing out a soft moan that reverberated off the walls. Their light cast shadows all over the room as their tongues wrestled with one another. Cole felt himself harden instantly, and he groaned painfully as the one on the right began to reach down between the other's legs and slowly stroke the soft flesh there.

"Okay," Robyn said loudly, stepping into the room a little. "Admittedly, that isn't dangerous. That's just… two lesbians making out with each other while levitating off the floor."

"Yes," he said. "It is."

Robyn was silent for a moment as the two women gasped and licked nonexistent sweat from each other. "We should be looking for the others, remember?"

"We should," Cole agreed. "But they've waited this long. A few more minutes won't kill them."

"I'm pretty sure it could."

"Or," came a different voice in the shadows, one high-pitched and squealing, "it could get the both of you killed along with them!"

Both forms collapsed to the floor in a heap, one on top of the other. The strings holding them up were black and almost invisible in the darkness of the room. A little glamour had helped, no doubt, but Cole was ready for them, anyway. When the strings came for him, he'd already unsheathed Aed Deigh and was swinging it around in an arc in front of him. The strings were cut to pieces, left smoldering on the floor at his feet. More had gone for Robyn, or rather, the rocket launcher in her hands. Grinning, she deftly pressed down on the button and fired.

"No!" Cole cried out, but it was too late.

The rocket at the tip roared to life. At the same time, a strange, eerily thin creature whisked past them out the door, dragging his strings along with him. The strings yanked the launcher off its target at the last second, causing the miniature missile to go flying out the door and blast through a wall on the opposite side. Cole snatched Robyn up and dove farther into the room, choosing it over the possibility of being impaled by flying debris. Sure enough, a second later, the hallway exploded and sent bits of plaster, wood, and extremely tacky wallpaper through the door where they'd been standing.

Cole gazed down at Robyn, who looked strangely intrigued by the sound of the explosion. "Let's put the rocket launcher away for now, shall we?"

A pair of feet landed on the floor just above their heads. "Let her keep it," the jack-in-irons grunted, grinning around his tusks. "She's a lot of fun. Not that it will help either of you."

Cole rose up off her and stood up, sniffing. "You're not part-human," he said, surprised. "You're full-blooded jack-in-irons. What are you doing here?"

"He's... ow!" said the high-pitched voice behind him. Cole turned to see a staggering marionette the size of a human, impossibly thin and covered in dirt. "That really smarts. He was the runt of the litter in his clan. They chucked him out for being weak, and Nanny found him."

"That's none of his business!" the jack said, roaring. "Shut your gaping hole, Pine Nut."

Pine Nut, the marionette, turned to the jack and stuck his tongue out, which was shaped like a party favor used for human children's birthdays. Cole helped Robyn to her feet while looking back and forth between them. "You're a fetch," Cole said, pointing. "You were left in place of a human child when it was taken away. And you," he added, pointing at the jack-in-irons, "were thrown out by your clan."

The jack-in-irons cracked his knuckles menacingly.

"What of it?" the marionette glowered.

"This isn't a prison," Cole said as it all came together. "She found the both of you after you'd lost your homes. She's been taking in faerie refugees all this time, giving them a place to stay when they have nowhere else to go."

"What's it to you?" Pine Nut snarled, and several knives sprouted from his fingers. In response, Robyn pulled out another rocket from her goody bag and loaded it. Cole quickly stepped in front of her, however, and shook his head.

"You were, what?" Cole pressed. "Some kid's toy? They brought you to life and covered you in glamour so you'd look just like him. But the spell must've worked a little too well, because you kept growing. You grew like a normal kid would grow, but underneath it all, you were still nothing more than a puppet."

"He talks too much," the jack-in-irons snarled, raising his fist.

"Hold it," Robyn warned him, aiming her launcher. "You wouldn't want me to fire at this close range. He would survive it, but can you promise me the same thing?"

"I am a jack-in-irons," he declared angrily. "I can survive anything."

Without looking around, Cole pulled Bandersnatch free from its holster and fired. The jack-in-irons staggered backward clumsily as blood leaked from the bullet hole in his forehead. "Oh, shut up," Cole retorted sharply, as Pine Nut came toward him with both hands raised. "The bullet won't kill him. I just wanted to talk for a second without his bad breath going down the back of my neck. He'll be fine, eventually."

"Murderer," the fetch bit back, stopping in his tracks.

"He's right," came Naryssa's voice from what remained of the doorway. "A bullet won't stop our dear Tobolt. Once he wakes up, though, he will be in a terrible mood."

Cole put his gun away again. "I can handle it."

Naryssa came forward and stood next to Pine Nut. She appeared as she had before when Cole first arrived, looking for all the world like somebody's grandmother. He wondered for a brief second if Robyn didn't see her grandma in that face, but then Naryssa began to speak again. "Pine Nut has no sense of smell," she explained, touching him gently. "He has spent his whole life without that pleasure, watching others take their senses for granted. The faerie who brought him to life many years ago didn't want to waste magic, I imagine. The spell lasted longer than they expected, for some reason, but the glamour was the first to fade. It was supposed to go when he died, but it didn't somehow. His parents accused him of being a monster and chased him from their home. He was on the verge of death when I found him hiding in a toy warehouse. The power keeping him alive had nearly run out."

"You saved him," Cole finished, looking at Pine Nut differently now. "He's alive now because of you."

"I would have asked you to join us," Naryssa went on, nodding. "Something tells me you don't approve of my methods, though."

"Parricide, magical poisoning, and trying to kill me," Cole named, ticking each one off on a finger. "Yeah, those rub me the wrong way."

Naryssa sighed and moved away from the entrance, taking Pine Nut along with her. "Then go."

Cole hesitated, sure he had heard wrong. "Leave now, unless you plan on staying forever," she warned, her voice taking on some of the aspect of the night hag in her blood. "Make no mistake, sidhe. I haven't forgotten what you did to me, or to Raywing and Spinner. But revenge will have to wait. There are more children I have to help, and their lives take precedence. We will just have to cross swords once my business is finished."

"You already have a family here," Cole said, gesturing. "Why kill more people? Why take other children from their homes and loved ones when the people here adore you?"

Naryssa laughed. "You are too naive to be a sidhe. Do you honestly believe that any of those people will love their children? Will they care for them in spite of the hardship that raising a child in a land that fears, hates, or doesn't believe in them brings? Their parents will abandon them eventually. Sooner or later, the hardship will be too much, and they'll toss their kids out on the street to be devoured by whatever predators happen to come by first. I've seen it happen far too many times to believe otherwise. Better that they lose their families before time has given them the chance to develop feelings of love. I can save them from the abuse, but love is incurable."

"You can't save everybody," Cole tried. "No one is immune to suffering."

"And yet more suffer needlessly," she countered. "The ones who still remember their old lives are forever tainted. They can never completely let go of what they were, what they had before it all fell apart. The blood of the night hag that flows in my veins may force me to feed from the children's painful pasts, but I can see to it that no other harm comes to them. That's why I must do this. It is a necessary evil, whether you agree with me or not."

Cole drew himself up and met her gaze. "Where are the others?"

"Alive," she answered at once. "For the time being. I have ordered my children not to harm them in any way. They are to be left alone until my business is finished. Once I have the last one, the cycle will be completed. Then you can have them back, provided you stay out of my affairs."

"And if I don't?"

Naryssa leveled her eyes at him. "Then it will be as if they'd never existed. Go, fallen one. Leave us and never come back. This building is no longer a haven for us, so it will be destroyed. You will find nothing here of further use to you."

It was a mistake to trust her, even if a small part of Cole found the offer tempting. "I have your word that they'll be safe? You don't have to promise my well-being. I know you plan on killing me sooner or later, but the detective and inspector will be kept alive and well, yes?"

Naryssa nodded. "I give my word that no harm will come to either of them while they are my captives, provided you stay out of my affairs until I release them."

Cole said nothing. With her word given, Naryssa could not harm either of them so long as he did nothing to stop her. Yet she'd called him a guest before and then tried to magically entrance him. Under the laws of the courts, that was grounds for a trial by combat. Cole could challenge her here and now on those laws, but they weren't at court anymore. There was no one here among the humans that would call her forsworn, and she was already living in exile. An exiled fey had nothing left to lose, which meant Naryssa had nothing to lose by lying.

Still, that wasn't why Cole looked up at her again with Bandersnatch and Jabberwock pointed at her chest. "Give me back my friends," he commanded. "Now."

If Naryssa was surprised by this turn of events, she didn't show it. "Why risk your life to save humans?" she insisted. "What has either of them done for you?"

Cole didn't answer. "You have until the count of three," he warned, both fingers itching to shoot. "One... two...."

"Tobolt, take him!" she ordered.

"Three!" Cole spun around and crouched low to the ground, firing into Tobolt's chest as he leaped up off the floor toward him. Blood poured down from the empty hole in his forehead to mix with the streams coming out of his chest now. Cole holstered Jabberwock and drew forth Aed Deigh even as the jack-in-irons staggered toward him. Robyn kicked out with her foot as Tobolt came in close and caught him at the knee. Strong as she was, the kick didn't do more than make him stumble, but it was enough. Cole thrust with the frost blade into his chest, and the flesh hissed as arctic cold met with the heat of his blood. Tobolt was a pure-blooded fey, regardless of his being exiled. Aed Deigh wouldn't freeze him solid or incinerate him.

It would, however, stop his heart cold for a few minutes. Not enough to kill a jack-in-irons, but most anything would find that a deterrent.

"Tobolt!" Pine Nut screamed.

"Eat this, Pinocchio!" Robyn yelled triumphantly. "You jackass!"

"Don't!" Cole cried out, trying to turn. Aed Deigh, however, was still stuck in Tobolt's chest. Cole swore and retracted the blade, but the movement cost him. The rocket was already in motion as Naryssa forced Pine Nut out of the way and stood there to take the blast meant for him. At the last second, however, she reached up and snatched it out of the air in one hand and crushed the still-flaming end with her bare hands.

Something rolled over into the darkened corner to the right of them. Cole's eyes landed on it as Naryssa glared over at Robyn. "You've been a very bad girl," she hissed between her teeth. "And bad girls get punished for doing bad things."

Cole ducked down and grabbed the unconscious lesbians, who were still lying in a heap, as the floor on the far end of the room exploded. "Hurry," Robyn said, racing past him for the opening she'd made. "We don't have much time left."

Hefting both women up at the same time, Cole was startled by the amount of weight to their thin-looking frames, but he didn't stop. Pine Nut came after him as he dove down the opening into the second floor, but the marionette didn't come after him. A second explosion, one far more powerful, came from somewhere in Naryssa's vicinity. The roof above them shook and came apart as Pine Nut was thrown through a wall by the force added to his own momentum. Naryssa let out a wail of pain that rattled through the building.

"That's likely to bring help for her," Cole noted. "We'd better get out of here."

"What about your friends?" she wondered. "And why'd you save those two?"

Cole noted the suspicion in her voice and extended the red-hot end of Aed Deigh down toward their bodies. As the heat drew close, the glamour surrounding them melted away to reveal the unconscious forms of Corhagen and Vallimun, deep in a magical sleep.

"I can smell the glamour that was hiding them," he explained to a surprised-looking Robyn. "It seemed like the sort of stunt she would pull, hiding them right in front of me."

"Clever," she said. "Now can we go?"

Cole lifted both men up over his shoulders. "If you know a way out of here. Nice job with the delayed charge on that rocket of yours."

"Thanks," Robyn replied, reaching into her bag. "But wait till you see this one."

"I NEVER want to see that again," Cole muttered once they were outside. "If I live until the sun explodes, I never want to see anything close to that again."

"I thought napalm would melt through the floor faster," she quipped, opening the car door for him. "Anyway, they're less likely to come after us now, what with the building burning down around their ears. Assuming all of them have ears."

"You do realize," Cole groaned as he hefted Corhagen into the backseat next to Vallimun, "that you've done their work for them. Naryssa was going to destroy the building, but you've made that completely unnecessary. She's probably already escaped through the basement and is long gone. The fire will destroy any evidence of them being there, and tracking their scent now is going to be even harder. Not that I have the time to do that, since these two won't wake up."

"You're being grouchy," Robyn derided. "I just saved you from a potentially dangerous situation and helped you locate your missing friends. The very least you could do is show your appreciation. I mean, is a 'thank-you' really that much to ask for?"

"The older sidhe don't like being thanked," Cole replied, satisfied that both men were secure now. "It's considered insulting."

Robyn snorted. "You aren't that old."

"No, I'm not," Cole admitted, holding the keys he'd palmed from Inspector Vallimun's pocket. "But I am an asshole, and it's time you answered some questions."

"Can't," she replied, backing away. "I hear the sweet sound of police sirens and fire trucks in the distance. Something tells me neither of them will be pleased to see me. You might want to think about getting out of here yourself. Being found at the scene of an arson with an inspector and a detective unconscious in the back of a car you're holding the keys to probably wouldn't look good."

Cole turned around to look back at the two sleeping officers, and in that moment, he knew she was gone. He didn't bother turning back around, but instead, he walked around the car and climbed in. He was a police consultant, and while that didn't carry much clout, there were people at Corhagen's precinct who *might* back him up. Assuming they were in a good mood, that is, or could be bribed with Starbucks coffee. Since neither man was conscious at the moment, however, that could make things more difficult. It wouldn't surprise Cole if the arriving officers decided to forgo asking questions and arrested him on sight. That might sound a bit paranoid, but years of being on the wrong side of the law when he'd first come to New York had left him jaded about due process.

So, with that in mind, Cole started the car and drove off as inconspicuously as possible. The glamour he'd thrown over them when they'd first crawled out of the flaming basement into the street collapsed as soon as he'd started the vehicle. Too much metal combined with motion made glamour tricky. Cole couldn't keep the whole car concealed, but he managed to disguise himself enough that when the first wave of cop cars came through, no one would identify him as being at the crime scene. Anything beyond that was out of his reach. He was simply too nervous now.

Cole hated to drive. It was why his bike was so precious to him. Anytime he'd driven a vehicle before, something bad eventually happened. He'd been shot at more times than he could count back when he was a gangster and had been in numerous car accidents. The subway was tolerable, but just barely. If given the option, Cole would have walked, but both men in the backseat were too heavy for even him to carry all the way back. So he gritted his teeth and plunged into the maze of havoc that was New York traffic and tried desperately not to lose hold of his glamour too soon. By the time they made it back to the loft, his teeth were sore from clenching them for so long and his knuckles had cramped from gripping the steering wheel too hard. The glamour had faded away from him too.

Finding a place to park was maddening. Cole gave up hoping for somewhere close to his loft and drove several blocks down to an area he felt was reasonably well-lit. Getting both men out of the car proved to be a chore, and much harder than getting them inside. Cole considered for a moment just taking them one at a time, but that would mean coming all the way back and forth again. With this a deciding factor, Cole steadied both grown men on his shoulders and wandered back up the street, sighing.

Several women stopped in their tracks to stare at him, wide-eyed. "It was this or let them sleep it off in the car," he explained without looking toward them. "And it isn't my car."

His shoulders were sore by the time he reached his building. No one bothered to help him open the door, of course, but it was really annoying when the receptionist just stood there and watched as he struggled to press the button for the elevator. Needless to say, he was in a bad mood by the time they reached the stairs. At the top, Cole struggled to keep both men supported as he fished his keys out. The ones to the inspector's car fell out of his hands a second before Corhagen began to slip. It was only after Cole got them both balanced against the wall and the door opened that he realized he hadn't locked the inspector's car.

Fuck it.

Katalina had come out of her room when she heard the door open, and she watched, wearing an amused expression, as he dragged both men over to the couch and set them down. "Long day?" she asked as he straightened the pillows so they'd be more comfortable.

"You know that bottle of solid black liquor in the very back of the refrigerator?" he breathed, leaning his weight into the couch. "The one you took a single sip of last Summer Solstice before making out with Ann Ritchkins and passing out face-first into the punch bowl?"

"If I don't remember it, it didn't happen," she insisted, turning away.

"Bring it to me, please. I need it after everything I've been through so far."

Katalina returned a moment later with the bottle in hand, holding it out in front of her as though the licorice-colored fluid might leap out of its container and bite her hand. "You look terrible," she noted, handing the bottle over. "And why do you smell like ash, gunpowder, and...." Katalina paused to sniff him. "Napalm?"

"I'd love to know how you know what napalm smells like," he replied before taking a long, deep draft. "Ah, that's much better. Honestly, this could be the worst day that I've had in almost sixty years, unless you count the weekend I was at Woodstock. What's really weird is that driving through New York traffic remains the most abhorrent experience so far. I've had to deal with murderous fey chasing me everywhere I go, a flaming building that almost fell on top of me and buried us all alive, a crazed gun nut, and a delusional half-sidhe who has power over glamour that I haven't seen since I left Faerie. And yet, in spite of all that, the drive back remains the worst part. I think there may be something seriously wrong with me."

"You're just now starting to think that?"

Cole glared before turning to point at the two on the couch. "Oh, and these two won't wake up. The best I can figure is they were put under some sort of magical enchantment. They slept through the building catching fire and everything. I was hoping you might know of some way to wake them up. My brain's too fried from everything to think straight right now."

"I don't," Katalina admitted nervously, watching both men sleep on the couch. "But I might know of someone who can."

Cole stopped in mid-sip of his drink and stared hard at her. "Why are you looking as though I might shapeshift at any moment and tear your throat out?"

"I haven't been totally honest with you," Katalina said softly, looking away. "For a while now. There's someone I've been wanting to introduce you to, but I was worried how you might react."

Cole wasn't sure what to say. "Alright," he began. "Wait, does this have anything to do with your mystery boyfriend?"

"He's not my boyfriend," she countered, then turned away again. "Not officially, at least. He's... well, come to my room, and you can see for yourself."

Cole followed after her, bringing his drink and leaving the two on the sofa to sleep it off. Something made him turn back just as he reached Katalina's bedroom door. Cole looked around to find that Corhagen's head had slipped down somehow and was now buried in Vallimun's crotch.

"If only my camera weren't broken," he said with a sigh, before walking away.

"What was that?" Katalina asked.

"Nothing," said Cole, shutting the door behind him. "I'll explain later. So, where's the mystery man you wanted me to meet?"

Katalina glanced sheepishly over at her computer. "He's right over there," she pointed, blushing red. "Just sit down and type something."

"You're having an online relationship? That's your big secret?" Cole sat down anyway as Katalina walked over to stand behind him. "No offense, but I was expecting something a little more ominous with the way you were acting. Where's he from?"

"Presently, inside the computer," she said, taking the mouse away from him. "Before that, he lived inside a book that was shipped here from either Germany or Scandinavia. I forget which."

Cole waited for her to tell him she was joking. "You're not going to tell me you're joking," he said flatly after several minutes of total silence. "Are you?"

"I'm afraid not," she admitted, pulling the screen up. "For the past two months or so, I've been having a relationship with the ghost of a sorcerer whose soul was imprisoned inside of his spell book. Remember that vintage book fair Rainette wanted me to go to, and I dragged you along for company?"

"I remember she spent the day insulting me," he replied.

"I found the spell book there," she went on. "I was afraid to handle it much since it looked so old, so I scanned the pages and converted them into JPEG files. Somehow, it scanned Mal into my computer. He was watching me for a long time afterward and finally worked up the nerve to say hello. We've been talking ever since."

"He can hear us right now?"

"Not unless I turn the microphone on," she explained, pointing. "You also have to use the speakers to be able to hear him."

Cole stared at the computer a moment, saying nothing to Katalina. When he opened his eyes again, she was looking down on him with a frown that stretched across both cheeks. "Here's what I want you to do," said Cole, getting up from his seat. "If you would, go online, or whatever it is you do, and speak with Mal. See if he knows of a way to wake Corhagen and the inspector up. I'm going to leave you two alone so you can speak with each other in private. Come and get me when you're done."

Katalina looked at him, worried. "Why can't you just ask him yourself?"

"Because this really isn't the time or the place for me to have a relevant conversation with your new beau. Plus, I'm old enough that asking others for favors is a very difficult thing. To the sidhe, it's a sign of weakness, and Mal may or may not have been a human at some point, but he's probably old enough to understand. I'd rather our first official introduction not involve my pleading for help."

It pained him to see the look on her face. This was obviously not going how she'd planned. Cole privately thought she should be grateful he wasn't being totally honest with her at the moment. As cruel as he could be sometimes, though, he wasn't about to break her heart so easily. Once again, he'd failed a human under his protection by not paying close enough attention.

"You're worried about making a bad first impression?" she wondered, looking surprised at him.

"Something like that, yes," Cole admitted. "Among us Old World types, that's very important. Besides, Mal knows you best. He won't mind it if you ask him, and he'd probably be more forthcoming."

"Mal's not a bad guy," she countered, still smiling uncertainly. "But if it's important that you look good in front of my potential boyfriend, I'll do it."

"Thank you," Cole said, reaching for the door. "I appreciate it."

It wasn't until he was outside that Cole pressed his head into the wall, hoping he could force the anger at his own stupidity out of him as discreetly as possible. She had been acting strangely for a while now, especially recently, and he hadn't bothered to notice. She showed all the classic signs of a human who'd come into contact with some questionable power or entity. Whatever the thing was, she had been communicating with it for weeks.

Of course, it was entirely possible that nothing bad would happen. Not everything in the realm of fey and otherwise was a high-octane nightmare factory waiting to happen. Cole had heard enough stories about humans dabbling with seemingly innocent forces, however, only for it to end badly. Katalina had made a new friend, and a seemingly innocent one, but that didn't mean the relationship would stay innocent. Mal could have devious intentions or be planning something horrible for her.

"Or," Cole whispered softly to himself, as realization settled in slowly, "maybe she's just happy."

He couldn't play the big brother card now and go rough up the guy just because he'd gotten to her first without Cole noticing. The fault of that lay squarely on his own shoulders. What was more, he couldn't be certain his reaction was entirely altruistic. Cole would never admit it, but a part of him loved the little girl in the room next door. He had been the shield that guarded her when the world of the fey had come crashing through her window in the night.

There was nothing romantic in his heart. Cole couldn't picture a happily-ever-after between the two of them. They were far too different as a couple for anything more than friendship to occur, and for a long time, he'd been happy with that. Yet his heart couldn't help but ache a little at the thought of someone else sweeping through the front door one day and taking her off to sail into the sunset. It hurt even worse knowing he had so little time with her, regardless. Cole had been too busy lusting after Corhagen the past few years to realize she'd grown up.

Looking around the loft, Cole imagined for a moment the different times he'd had with Katalina, all the laughs and tearjerker moments they'd shared together. At this point, the loft was practically bursting at the seams with them. He couldn't remember a time when she hadn't touched the place somehow.

"Is it just that I want Mal to be a bad guy?" he asked to no one in particular. "Or am I paranoid for a reason?"

There was no reply. Cole couldn't remember the last time he'd prayed to Goddess and Consort without receiving a reply. Then again, it almost seemed as though the silence itself was his answer. Cole turned around until he was looking at Katalina's bedroom door, which was still closed. He could have listened in on their conversation, but that would be a violation of her privacy. Cole appreciated the freedom having her around allowed him. As the door opened, he forced himself to smile.

"Before you say anything," he said, stopping her, "I want to apologize for how I reacted."

The look on her face said she'd known he was upset from the start.

"When you told me about Mal," he quickly continued, "I started thinking about all the horrible things I knew of that had either been destroyed or sealed away, only to be brought back by a human's carelessness. I'm not accusing you of anything, but it made me wonder about him. I wondered if anything he'd told you could be trusted. And then, I started realizing that I was more worried about you, and what being here without you might mean."

Katalina's eyes clouded over as he spoke.

"I wouldn't blame you for being mad at me," he added, looking down. "I don't know Mal, but you do. I'm going to trust your judgment on this one, even though I don't like him."

"Why?" she asked, looking dangerously close to crying now.

"Because," he said softly. "I think he might be planning on taking you away from me."

Katalina frowned then and glared up into Cole's face. A moment later, she was in his arms and laughing softly into his chest as tears rolled down her face. "You dumbass," she mumbled through his shirt. "Nothing's ever going to take me away from you. Promise."

For a while, even though there was still an unbelievable amount of work for him to do, Cole set it aside in favor of holding Katalina in his arms. As he breathed in her scent, he pictured for a moment what his life, what their relationship, would be like had things turned out differently. He could see them now in the kitchen, still laughing and joking with one another like they'd always done, but with a lingering heat to their eyes as they held each other's hands. He saw them snuggled on the couch where Corhagen and Vallimun sat lumped together, watching TV and sharing a bowl of popcorn. Dancing through the empty space to music only they could hear.

He saw Corhagen coming through their front door laughing, carrying a spark in his eyes that he hadn't had in a long, long time. His wife was with him, a woman Cole had never seen before, but recognized at once as the one James had chosen to live a happy, fulfilled life with instead of the shamble of lies he was trapped inside of. There was no awkwardness between them, no hesitancy or regret on his face as he pulled Cole in for a warm hug. Katalina and the other woman entertained themselves for a moment by catching up in the kitchen while he and James lounged on the couch, watching TV, until both women pulled them away to help. The loft was brighter and warmer in his vision than it had been in years, thanks to the friendship and love they all shared.

Cole pulled away from her gently, and as he did so, the vision was ripped in two. In Katalina's eyes, he saw the love for a man she had never held in her arms like she'd held onto him, but one whom she was enamored with nonetheless. The friendship she felt for him seemed overshadowed somehow. Cole savored the waking dream he'd seen for a little longer before letting her go. He let it go, as well: let go of his wishes for a past that would never change and a future that would never happen. Today, he had to free the inspector and Corhagen from the enchanted sleep that a sidhe hag had put them under. Then, they would have to do something about stopping her and figure out how not to get killed in the process. There would be no reward for his effort, no chance to make things more like the place he'd seen in his mind.

Even for an immortal, living could really suck sometimes.

Chapter *Nine*

ONCE upon a time, Cole had purchased a complete set of camping equipment, the theory being that he and Corhagen would make a trip into the woodland areas of upstate New York. Cole was familiar with the territory, and Corhagen had expressed a desire to see some of it. It had looked like an enjoyable prospect, except for the fact that Corhagen had just begun dating Sarah at the time. Now, Cole couldn't recall what she had said to make Corhagen change his mind, but they hadn't gone. Cole had put the camping gear away and deliberately forgotten about it. It had gone into the area of his loft reserved for their other impromptu canceled plans, next to the hockey gear and two surfboards they would have used at the end of their canned road trip to Florida.

Cole had dug through the small but bitterly cluttered area of the walk-in closet until he located the roll-out sleeping bags. Katalina, meanwhile, had already begun making the salt circle on the hardwood floor. Cole was careful not to disturb her as she inscribed the necessary runes while he unrolled the three pallets. Katalina nodded when he was done and began adjusting the circle to where it would trace around the sleeping area without being disturbed. It might have been better if she'd waited, but she'd wanted to get started right away. Cole brought the inspector and Corhagen over, still unconscious, as she wrapped things up.

"I'm about to close the circle," she warned, as he settled down between the two. "According to Mal, the spell should put you to sleep within a few seconds. All you have to do, then, is find both of them in the shared dream and bring them out of it."

"Right." Cole nodded, shifting slightly to where he was facing Corhagen. "How long do you think this will take?"

"No idea," she replied. "And I can't bring you out of it once you're unconscious. You'll just have to hurry and figure out a way to wake both of them up. Just remember that dream time isn't the same as real time. You could spend what seems like a few minutes inside their dream while the day passes by."

"I know," Cole said. "Close the circle for me. None of us have much time left."

Cole watched Katalina closely as she sealed the circle, allowing the magic to fill it and cut them off from the rest of the world. For Cole, this wasn't such a jarring experience as it might have been for some. He had been inside magick circles before, and the sensation of isolation was muted compared to the first time he'd endured it. A sense of peace and contentment settled over his body like a blanket. The longer he lay there, the more he felt like dozing off. Cole waited for sleep to fully claim him, but it never did.

Finally, he risked opening his eyes. James was still stretched out in front of him, his eyes fluttering open slightly with each breath he drew in. The room had grown dark, and he had a surprisingly tranquil expression. Cole could feel the inspector turn slightly to spoon against his front. The movement caught him off-guard, but Cole did nothing to discourage it. When Vallimun's arm snaked around his waist, he allowed himself to be drawn up against the man completely. Heat passed back and forth from their bodies as he reached for James, drawing him in closer. The circle around him flared to life as their skin touched, eliciting a soft cry of protest from Corhagen, yet he shifted into Cole's arms willingly.

Rather than putting Cole to sleep, the flare of magick sent shock waves down his skin. The movement caused Vallimun to jerk awake behind him, while Corhagen's eyes opened more slowly.

Corhagen stretched, inadvertently pushing his body farther into Cole's, and Cole seized the opportunity to wrap his arms around the stocky man. It had been ages since he'd felt like this. The years apart from Faerie had left Cole starved for contact with sidhe flesh. They still had no idea how he'd been able to change James from human to sidhe temporarily. Now the scent was unmistakably human, but it didn't matter. For the first time in a long while, Cole felt at peace with himself. The gnawing hunger for more of his own kind had diminished to a tiny speck. Somehow, he understood that it was but a temporary reprieve. Nevertheless, he was thankful.

"Where are we?" Vallimun's voice reverberated through him like a cat's purring. "And why are we all naked?"

"We're not," Cole began, only to look down at himself. "Oh, wait. How did that happen?"

"Here's another question," stated Corhagen, rising up slightly. "Where the hell are we, and how'd we get here?"

Cole thought hard for a moment. His brain felt muddled, clouded by fog. "My loft," he said slowly. "I think, but then we all came here somehow. I think there was something I was supposed to do, or warn you about, but I don't remember what."

"We were together earlier," said Vallimun, looking up over Cole's shoulder. "How did we get separated?"

"I don't know," Cole answered, truthfully. "Do any of you recognize where we are?"

"No," answered Vallimun.

"Me either," said Corhagen. "It looks familiar, though."

At last, Cole released James to stand up and have a look around. The ground beneath them was grass, which seemed a little odd to him. Behind him was a circular pond surrounded by concrete and park benches. Walkways leading up to the water cut through the grass, carving it into sectioned areas. Lampposts provided enough muted light for him to take in the flower beds and shrubbery that went all the way to the iron fence that surrounded the area. Beyond that, however, everything was pitch black.

"Bowling Green," he whispered.

"Where?" Corhagen asked, getting to his feet beside him.

"Bowling Green Park," Cole explained, looking around. "This looks like Bowling Green Park."

Both men turned around in a circle, taking the place in. "I've never been here before," Vallimun admitted.

"I've walked past it," Corhagen replied, scratching himself idly. "Several times, really, but I never bothered going in. Should we be standing out here with our cocks flapping in the breeze, though?"

"It's fine," Cole nodded, sure of this, at least. "No one will find us. This isn't the real thing."

"How do you know?" Vallimun wondered, turning around.

Cole's eyes nearly wandered down south a little, but he made himself stop and pay attention to the task at hand. "I used to come here all the time, back when I was first exiled. It looked a lot different then, but no matter how much things changed, I felt safe when I stepped inside the circle. There was something comfortable about it, something I couldn't put my finger on. I think...."

Cole hesitated before continuing. "I don't think this is the actual park. We're in some kind of illusion or dream world."

"It is the park," came a voice from behind them. "And, isn't."

Vallimun and James turned toward the voice, but at its first utterance, Cole's entire body went rigid. Shaking, he drew in a rattling breath and steeled himself for what would come. The sound of her footsteps came closer, and Cole forced himself not to run. Corhagen and Vallimun hadn't moved; they were struck dumb by the site of her. Queen Titania gave a half-smile as Cole made himself turn around and look at her.

"My Queen." He bowed humbly. "Have you come on your Lord's orders to slay me now?"

The half-smile turned into a full-blown one. "Lord Oberon does not rule everywhere," she replied assuredly. "Despite what he himself may think. What lies within the world of humans is beyond his authority to command. As I am here now, what I choose to do is of my own volition. To answer your question, child, I bring you neither harm nor ill will. You may rise and greet your queen as you would another, for here there are no courts to speak of."

"Why are you here, then, my Queen, if I may be so bold?"

"Boldness was a trait I admired in you," she said. "I come because it is time for you to begin what you were secretly sent here to do."

"I was never sent anywhere," Cole reminded her, harsher than he'd intended. "I was banished, and for what amounted to Lord Oberon's petty jealousy."

"Perhaps," she replied, and there was something in the queen's voice that suggested she knew better. "You have encountered the night hag Naryssa's dreamscape. As it was a willing decision that you made to save the two mortals next to you, I cannot interfere directly. The decision to come here was yours, so you must break free yourself. However, there is a gift I bring so that you may finally come into your true self. Use it on yourself and the others, so that they may aid you in the ensuing struggle for dominion over this place."

Titania reached into the folds of her cloak and drew out a small vial. "You remember on the day we stood at the shores of Avalon, during your official exile from the realm of Faerie, I told you there were but three ways I could help you. You'd begged me to allow you to stay, but I could not overturn a direct order from my liege. Instead, I gave you your family heirlooms to take, one of the Chalices of Dagda and Aed Deigh. Now, I present the final favor from me to bring you out of the nightmare in which she holds you."

Cole accepted the vial. Under the light of the lamppost, he could see it contained an amber-colored liquid. "What is it?"

"Touch them with it," she explained, nodding to both men. "Let it breathe along their skin so that you all may awake. Once you return to the waking world, time will be short for you to do what must be done. I will not interfere any more from this point afterwards until the title that is rightfully yours has been claimed. For now, I bid you farewell."

Cole looked down at the vial in his hand. When he glanced up, Titania had vanished. Corhagen and Vallimun were looking around now, as though they'd just woken from a daze. "What happened?" James wondered. "Who was that woman?"

"The Queen of All Faerie," Cole answered, tossing the vial up. "She gave this to me so that we could wake up."

"From what?"

"From the dream Naryssa put you in," he replied. "I remember now. We're supposed to use this on ourselves so we can escape the dream world and then... do something."

"That's informative," James quipped.

"This is all a dream?" Vallimun looked around. "All of it? Why did we come here, though?"

Cole stared at the spot where Titania had been standing. A part of him believed it was because he'd entered the dreamscape last, and this place had been important to him at some point, regardless of how long it'd been since he forgot. The better part of him knew otherwise, though. Titania had snatched them out of the normal dreamscape and brought them here. Cole couldn't complain too much, even though the Queen of all Faerie rarely performed good deeds for others out of the kindness of her heart. She ruled over all fey and was as wily and cunning as the best of them. Most likely, they'd been shown this place for a reason, though Cole was less interested in why at the moment. Whatever Naryssa had intended for them to see in their dream was no doubt far worse than this, but Cole didn't entirely trust his former queen anymore. Odds were none of them would enjoy the trip.

Still, it wasn't as though Cole had any other options at the moment.

The stopper for the vial came off with very little resistance. The liquid inside smelled sweet and syrupy and reminded him of some type of cologne without all the added chemicals that irritated his nose. There was a hint of roses as well. The scent trailed out of the bottle and up into the air between them.

"What is that?" Vallimun asked, his voice thicker than usual. "It's smells...."

Corhagen summed it up best. "Wow."

Cole tried to dab the liquid out, but most of it came loose in a thick puddle in the palm of his hand. The substance was somehow thick yet runny all at the same time. The moment it touched his skin, Cole felt a jolt run through him. Immediately, snow began falling in the air around him. Within seconds, a light cover of it had blanketed the grass surrounding them. Only the space they stood on remained clear and green. It should have been cold, but the air felt warmer. Cole reached out with his hand that had the sticky fluid and smeared a light trail of it over Corhagen's chest, letting it bead in his nest of chest hairs. He'd expected the man to jump away, but instead, James threw his head back and sighed. When Cole withdrew, he began rubbing the stuff deeper into himself, making the carpet hair stick flat against his skin.

Cole turned to Vallimun to do the same thing, but the inspector stopped him. "There's been way too many questions so far," he warned. "And nowhere near enough answers. How do we even know this stuff is safe? Do you honestly trust that broad who gave it to you?"

"No," he admitted softly. "But what other choice do we have, unless you'd rather stay here? We still have to find Naryssa and stop her before she finishes her big killing spree."

Vallimun said nothing more, but consented to let the sticky fluid be rubbed up and down both arms. His breathing grew deeper the longer it stayed on him, until he was running it down his own hairy chest and onto his groin. Cole finally spared a glance and saw that the inspector was fully erect. More to the point, he was impressive. The shaft was thick, like his, and very long. The mortal actually had him beat by an inch or so in length, but otherwise, they were nearly matched in size. It made Cole's mouth water.

Before he realized it, Cole had reached out with his sticky hand and was stroking the inspector. The mortal threw his head back and sighed, clearly enjoying the attention. James, meanwhile, was rubbing his cock and balls as his own shaft grew in length. Cole had a moment's hesitation as the last twenty-four hours or so came rushing back to him. He nearly stopped what he was doing, stopped completely and walked away from the men. There was something about this that seemed a little too convenient. Neither man should've been okay with him touching them, especially James. When Vallimun reached over and placed a long kiss on James's mouth, Cole felt a pang of unnatural jealousy. Reaching down, Cole gently brushed against James's shaft, earning him a soft moan. Satisfied, he threw his doubts away and got down on his knees, closing his mouth around the man's hard dick in one gulp.

James was neither as long nor as thick as he was. This wasn't a problem for Cole, who had always enjoyed being able to take most of it on the first try. He'd suspected after their first tryst together that James had been intimidated by his size, but those doubts appeared to have melted away. Seizing both of James's hips, Cole rammed the cock down his throat as far as it would go, taking a deep breath each time his nose was buried in the mat of groin hair. James smelled rich and manly, just as Cole remembered. As he teased the mortal with his tongue, running it over the helmet of foreskin at the tip, his hands played lightly with the low-hanging balls underneath. Titania's elixir slicked both bull-sized orbs up, and the heat from them increased as he forced himself back down on the shaft. Whatever substance she'd bewitched them with, it did its job well.

Vallimun's thick, callused fingers were running traces through his hair. As they dug in, Cole pulled away from James to take on the more monstrous cock hanging down between the inspector's legs. It took considerably more effort on his part to encompass the thick club, but Cole was nothing if not determined. Once he managed to push the head down his throat, the rest was easy. Vallimun was much more vicious and force-fed his meat to Cole with painfully hard thrusts. It made his head spin, but Cole never let up.

Vallimun let his head go after a while, and Cole took the opportunity to catch his breath. The other men were still kissing each other passionately, their tongues dancing together in the summer night air. The park looked like a winter wonderland around them save for the undisturbed circle of grass beneath their feet. Cole brushed the blades stuck to his legs away as he stood up, moving in between James and Vallimun to break up their kiss. Cole had tasted Corhagen's mouth already. He remembered its taste, the way the hairs around his mouth tickled and bit lightly into his skin. The inspector was an enigma so far. He was anxious to see what the seasoned policeman had to offer.

Some part of him was still waiting for the realization to slam into them, but Vallimun grabbed him by the jaw at once and captured his mouth roughly. Cole seized the back of the other man's head in response and jerked him in closer, responding in kind with the strength that was his blood right. The promise of violence excited Vallimun, and a droplet of precum splashed against the top of Cole's foot as the inspector ate at his mouth like some hungry beast of the woods. James, meanwhile, had wound his arms around Cole's chest while lightly tracing a row of kisses down his shoulder from his collarbone to his armpit. When he got there, Cole dimly felt his arm being raised as Vallimun stroked his cock in time to the thrusting of his own tongue, fucking it into the sidhe with a vengeance. James shoved his nose into Cole's pit and breathed deeply, savoring the scent there. The detective licked a row up along the hairless patch of skin again and again like a cat drinking cream.

All of James's fears and insecurities had melted away the instant Titania's elixir touched him. Cole broke his kiss with the inspector to push James down to his knees. Then, bracing himself against Vallimun's sturdy frame, he threw one leg over James's shoulder and forced his cock down the detective's throat. James gagged, turning red in the face as he struggled to remember how he had handled the cudgel over a year ago when they'd first spent the night together. Cole didn't give him a chance to recover and bucked his hips forward as he reached around to bring the inspector forward so that they could resume kissing. The inspector's hands ran the length of Cole's body, stopping where he was joined with Corhagen to force more cock down James's throat. With the senior ranking officer guiding him, James's muscles took over, remembering how to take the thing all the way. Before long, he was taking Cole's length of him all the way to its root without choking.

Cole, meanwhile, was feeling the length of Vallimun's own impressive tool with his hand. Vallimun rocked his hips back and forth more slowly, letting Cole glide his palm across the thick, veiny length of him. What remained of the oil there mixed with the inspector's precum, causing the two scents to mingle and fill the air around them. The air grew heavier, pushing all three of them down to the ground. Cole withdrew his leg from James's shoulder, and James collapsed on top of his legs a minute later, still sucking away as though his life depended on it. Cole seized the inspector by the legs as his knees came to rest on either side of Cole's head. The man's cock dangled low, and without prompting, Cole sucked it down his gullet.

Their eyes met as Vallimun pushed his cock deeper. "You're glowing," he whispered. "It looks like your skin is glowing."

Cole had to draw the cock out of his throat before he could speak. "I am," he said softly, not blinking. "And so are you."

Vallimun looked down at himself. His whole body glistened as though kissed by a hundred sunrises. He was shining brighter than a summer day, a perfect contrast to the winter moon of Cole's own pale glow. At the other end, Corhagen radiated the purple licorice of dusk. The three colors combined together as Cole lapped contently at the juices dripping down from the inspector's wondrous cock.

"Why is it not snowing here?" the inspector wondered.

Cole knew, could feel it in the ground. "It's more than just lights," he said between gulps. "Our power keeps winter at bay."

Vallimun looked confused. "What does it all mean?"

"Nothing," he replied. "It can mean anything you want it to mean, or nothing at all. The whole point here is for you to be true to your feelings, and let them guide you."

Vallimun thought on that for a moment, then lightly brushed a stray hair away from Cole's vivid tri-colored eyes. Leaning forward, he bent down near where Corhagen was still happily drunk on Cole's dick and placed a kiss near his bellybutton. Vallimun worked his way back up, licking his tongue into the crevices that formed between Cole's abs, giving special attention to both perfectly erect nipples, before pulling Cole up to meet his deep, passionate kiss.

"I haven't done anything like this in years," he whispered, cradling Cole in his arms. "Not since I was a kid. I hadn't realized how much it meant to me or how much I missed doing it."

"What do you want?" Cole pressed, lightly scratching the back of Vallimun's neck.

"I want to fuck you," he hissed fiercely. "And I want to watch as you fuck him. I want for you to be on top of me, taking all of me inside of you, as you force your way into his ass. I want the three of us to make the most of what we have here, since we'll never do it again. I want to slam into your ass over and over again. I want to fuck you silly, until you can't think of anything but my cock tearing its way up your chute, and I want you doing the same thing to him the whole time."

James had stopped sucking, finally, and was lightly rubbing his thumb over Cole's piss slit. "Sounds good to me."

VALLIMUN lay stretched out with the warm grass under his back, his shaft standing proudly up in the winter night as the snow at the edge of the circle tickled his feet. Cole admired the sight for a moment, balancing himself with his feet planted firmly on either side of the man's hips. Then, taking a few deep breaths, he lowered himself down.

Cole's eyes widened as the thick cockhead touched his sphincter, causing the inspector to grin. Undeterred, Cole breathed in deeply and forced himself down. This was all a dream, he had to keep reminding himself. There was nothing here that could hurt him if his will was strong enough to combat it. He just had to will his ass to open and accept the baton-sized intruder. Something gave way at that thought, and Cole felt his body slide down an inch or two. It still hurt, but he knew he had to accept the pain, that it was necessary. The pain was as much a part of this as anything else. Being familiar with Titania's magics had helped him to understand that. Gasping, he continued down, crying soft moans like a she-wolf in heat. Vallimun seized his hips and helped with the last bit, until Cole's ass sat all the way down on his tube steak.

"Give me just a second," Cole gasped, enjoying the feel of being so full. "I need to adjust. It's been a few years."

The grin never left Vallimun's face. As Cole leaned back a little, the inspector dug his fingers into the flesh of Cole's glutes and thrust upward. Cole's cry wasn't so much a scream of pain as the howl of a hunting wolf. His feet slipped, causing him to fall backward, and it was only the inspector bringing his knees up that supported him. Cole threw caution to the wind as pain, pleasure, and desire overrode his thoughts. Bucking like a bitch in heat, he dug his fingers down into the inspector's carpet of chest hair, groaning and growling right along with the mortal as his cudgel slammed up into his guts.

Cole wasn't sure how long they fucked together, but Corhagen was suddenly in front of him with his own cock out. Cole reached out to bring it closer to his mouth, but the detective had other ideas. Turning around, James pointed his ass at Cole's face, then slid down to sit down just above Vallimun's face. Cole's own dick had been slobbering and drooling precum for a good while now, enough that it had left a puddle on the treasure trail leading to the cock buried in his ass. James reached back around with his fingers to scoop some of it up, then proceeded to finger-fuck his own asshole, lubing his hole in preparation. Cole got the message and coated his own thumb with the stuff, then brushed James's hand aside so he could take over.

The detective grunted when the appendage first pushed past his ring muscle, but he quickly adjusted and began asking for more. Cole obliged by withdrawing and replacing the thumb with two fingers, then three. Corhagen's ass was surprisingly receptive for once, to the point that Cole soon had him humping back and forth on all three fingers, and begging for more.

"Just do it," he grunted when Cole pulled back slightly. "If you're going to do it, go ahead, before I change my mind."

It was hard to think, what with Vallimun's big cock still in his ass. His ears worked fine, however, and it was as open an invitation as he would ever get. Yet enough of his head cleared for him to realize it wasn't enough. James had just offered to take one up the ass, to take his dick up into his ass, but Cole wanted more.

"Say it," he barked, pulling his fingers out.

"What?" asked James, turning around slightly.

"Say it," he repeated. "I want to hear you say it. Tell me what you want."

James grew quiet, his body not moving. Even Vallimun slowed his pace a little to watch the parade of emotions cross the detective's face. Though Cole couldn't see his face, he knew from the way the inspector reacted what James was thinking. It almost made him change his mind. Almost.

But Corhagen had earned this. At least, Cole thought so.

"Fuck me," whispered James softly.

"What?" Cole pressed, shoving his finger back in. "I couldn't hear you."

"Fuck me!" he cried out, more loudly. "I want you to fuck me. Now!"

Cole grinned. "Say it again."

Corhagen gasped as Cole's finger struck his prostate. "Fuck me," he tried again, gasping. "Fuck me, please."

"Again."

"Fuck me," whispered James, getting into a rhythm. "Please, fuck me. Fuck me, man."

Cole removed his finger and pointed the head of his pale cock toward James's hole. "I am not a man," he hissed back angrily. "I am sidhe. And you are mine."

One good thrust, and it was all in. James jumped forward with a yelp, trying to get away, but both Cole and the inspector grabbed hold of him to keep his body firmly in place. Cole waited a moment, allowing for time to let James's asshole get used to the invader planted squarely away there. He couldn't wait long, however. Corhagen's sphincter had more give to it than he'd expected, but it was still tight. Tight and warm. Plus, the added comfort of his own pre-cum made it a tad slippery. As Vallimun eased James back, the detective's ass clamped down over the cock lodged there, and he sighed. Cole felt years of frustration give way with that sound. As Vallimun bucked his hips up hard into his ass once more, Cole drove forward to plow James like a madman, using the inspector's own momentum to add to the weight of his own thrusts.

"Uhh!" James cried out, wincing. "Oh, God. Yes. Fuck me!"

"Again," Cole grunted, feeling Vallimun's cock deep inside him.

"Fuck me," he squealed. "Fuck me. Just fucking fuck me."

Cole roped his arms under James's armpits, forming a link with his fingers behind the big mortal's neck. Holding him in place, he braced the soles of both feet into the grass, lifted himself a little up off Vallimun's cock, and pistoned forward. James grunted and gasped, feeling the strength behind Cole's thrusts as Cole shoved more cock into him, only to get a dosage of his own medicine when he came back down. On each return, Cole howled his pleasure to the sky above, to the snow still landing around them, forming hills in the park. Then, he thrust up again, taking claim inside Corhagen, filling the man up with the length of himself. On and on they rode one another, with Vallimun helping to keep Corhagen in place. Corhagen didn't seem keen on leaving anymore, however, and when one especially hard thrust pushed him too far up, he seized the opportunity to kiss the inspector full on the mouth.

The unexpected shift in movement made Cole lift too far off Vallimun's cock, and it sprung free from his ass at the same time his own was dislodged from James. James went right on kissing the inspector as Cole lowered him back down. Vallimun, however, pushed up a little with his legs, until his own cock was pointed at James's worn out entrance. Cole got the idea and lowered the detective back down onto the rod that had just plowed him senseless moments ago. James rose up in shock and made a noise halfway between a moan and a shout, but he didn't stop. Cole watched as he took control for himself and sank all the way down, driving Vallimun's big dick home.

The two rode together for a little bit, with Cole providing help by lifting Corhagen up higher so he could feel the full thrust of it on the way back down. James was flogging his own cock madly as he rode Vallimun, painting the inspector's chest with cum as volley after volley shot. Still, he pushed back down on the cock embedded in him, feeling it load him up for another round. Corhagen's balls seemed bottomless. Cole amused himself by watching as he licked and kissed up and down Corhagen's spine. When Vallimun motioned to him, however, he rose up and left James to stand beside the inspector's head.

Vallimun stroked one leg and gestured for him to come close. Cole knelt down until his balls rested just above Vallimun's chin at which point, the inspector took over by dropping them straight down into his mouth. The hard-worn policeman licked and sucked both orbs as his thrusts grew faster and more determined. Corhagen had gone soft, though he still stroked himself as Cole felt his own cock twitch in preparation to shoot at last. Vallimun's mouth was doing the trick, adding the last little bit of stimulation to bring the sidhe over the edge. Cole's dick exploded, spraying all over Vallimun's chest and stomach, adding to the mix Corhagen had already left there. A second later, Vallimun himself unloaded in Corhagen's ass. The three of them collapsed at the same time in a heap, as the snowy world around them faded to black.

Into nothingness.

When his eyes fluttered open finally, the first thing Cole became aware of was how heavy his body felt. For a moment, he couldn't stand, until he looked down and realized his legs were tangled up with Corhagen and Vallimun's. At some point, they'd moved a whole lot closer together. Probably a little too close for either man's comfort, regardless of what might have transpired while in the dreamscape. Sensing movement behind him, he looked up to find Katalina leaning over him with a frantic expression.

"Finally, you're awake!" she gasped.

"What's wrong?" he wondered.

"Don't you realize? Cole, you've been asleep for *three days*!"

Chapter *Ten*

COLE shifted uncomfortably on his stool as he fought not to grip his hot chocolate mug too hard and break it. Every few minutes, his body would stiffen up as Katalina fell victim to another bout of snickering. At last, he set his mug down, spilling some of the brown, steamy liquid in the process, and whirled around.

"It's *not* funny."

Katalina merely laughed. She'd been doing that all last night and throughout the morning. "You should've seen the look on your face," she giggled. "How could anyone believe they'd slept for three days straight?"

"It was magic," he spouted out, and even to Cole, it sounded pathetic. "Magic makes things strange sometimes. Frequently, according to some people I know."

"Oh, quit pouting and finish your hot chocolate so you can get going," she reprimanded. "You're going to be late, and the inspector sounded pretty insistent last night. Besides, you've been cranky about this for way too long. Get over it, already."

"I'm immortal," he reminded her briskly before finishing off his drink. "Holding a grudge is a pastime of ours. And why is it I keep having to remind people of this?"

"Well, hold it against me on your way out the door," she replied, taking his cup. "I've got work to do today and need the loft to myself for a couple of hours. You might want to consider getting a few drinks with your new inspector friend and the asshole once you're all done battling the forces of darkness together."

Cole sighed, knowing that as irritated as he was with her at the moment, there was little point in putting this off any longer. If he were human, it might have been nervousness coursing through his veins at the moment. Neither James nor Vallimun had mentioned anything last night that suggested they were aware of what had transpired in the dreamscape. The inspector, honestly, he was less concerned about. James, on the other hand, had proven time and again he could make things very difficult following the afterglow.

That pretty much *was* his afterglow.

Cole needed them both to be alert. He'd filled them in on what had happened after they'd vanished yesterday, as well as shared the information Bugbear had brought him. Needless to say, their stay had run a little late, and the first thing James had done once the official meeting had ended was call his wife. That had gone over about as well as anyone could expect.

Cole reasoned it was just another hazard of living around humans for too long. The less he concerned himself with what either man thought, the better. As soon as this whole mess was over with, he could go back to his normal life, and James could resume pretending they'd never shared an affiliation with one another. At least until he'd dug himself a new hole and needed rescuing again. Cole thought, as he left the loft with his bike, that it would take Corhagen about two weeks.

Probably less.

THE subway ride to Brooklyn was crowded, as he'd expected. It had been years since he had strolled down a Brooklyn street. Some of the buildings looked as though they'd survived the march of progress that'd steadily taken over New York for decades, but for the most part, he was a stranger in a strange place once again. It might have been nice to have a look around, but Cole was already late, and the others were waiting. On top of that, he had one other thing to take care of afterward. He should have gone there first, of course, but curiosity had gotten the better of him. Going by what the inspector had hinted at last night, he would have regretted not showing up.

Once the subway ride was over, Cole happily mounted his bike and took off down the sidewalk, sending a couple of aimless pedestrians scattering. The ride took longer than he'd expected, but after making a wrong turn once, Cole managed to locate the warehouse owned by the NYPD's Central Records Division. There was little to be impressed about, save for the blond man standing next to Corhagen at the front door munching on what looked like a hot bagel. Cole waved, and the unfamiliar guy rose up from his breakfast to stare harshly at him. With a jolt, Cole realized he was looking at the inspector, whose head was now covered in long, silky, ice-blond locks.

"Um," he began, totally off-guard for once. "I like the wig. Never figured you for a Fabio fan, yet it works in a strange sort of way."

Neither man said a word. Corhagen seemed more than happy to keep his distance from Vallimun at the moment, and it wasn't difficult to guess why. Vallimun was glaring bullets at him now and looked ready to explode. The bagel held between his hands was falling apart from his grip, and cream cheese oozed out in dribbles onto his shoes.

"Explain," Vallimun demanded. "Now."

Cole shook his head. "I have no idea what you're talking about. Is that not a wig?"

"It's not a wig," the inspector clarified, still glaring. "I woke up this morning with it growing out of my head. It was down to my shoulders by the time I got out of the shower. Before I'd gotten off the subway here, it was down past my shoulder blades. Would you mind explaining to me why I seem to be turning into the surfer version of Cousin Itt?"

"Actually, I think it's stopped growing, finally," Corhagen said quickly, looking nervous.

"Thank God," said Vallimun, slumping a little. "I thought I'd never be able to show my face in front of the chief of police again. My barber bill would've gone through the roof."

"Okay," Cole said, holding a hand up. "Obviously, this is somehow a result of the time we spent in dreamscape together. I can't think of anything off hand that would've caused it, unless you were in contact with some other fey before then."

"No," Vallimun assured him. "This," he said, and he gestured toward his hair, "I suspect came from… what happened yesterday."

"Right," Cole said, noting the inspector's reluctance. "Fey magick is generally wild magic, unpredictable and untamed at most times. Strictly speaking, this could have been a lot worse than growing a full mane of hair. I know of some humans that walked away from an encounter with faerie and were never the same again."

"Tell me about it," muttered Corhagen, sounding very put out all of a sudden. "I guess I should be grateful I didn't wake up with horns this morning."

Cole ignored him. "Let's try and be practical. It isn't a bad look for you, and most men who were bald would give a lot more to trade places with you. Think of it as a gift, and be thankful nothing bad happened. You've managed to encounter raw magical power and come away more or less unscathed."

Corhagen snorted.

"So," Cole finished determinedly. "What made you bring us all down here?"

"Come with me," the inspector said, after swallowing what remained of his bagel. "This is one of the places where the NYPD stores its evidence from old crimes."

"I thought evidence was disposed of after two years," said Cole, following.

"Unless it's a homicide," Corhagen reminded him curtly. "There's no statute of limitations on murder."

"So we're going to have a look at the evidence from the other murder cases?" Cole followed them in. The interior was vast by human measurements, nothing but row after row of barrels with numbers marked on them stacked on top of metal girders. "I thought they'd be back at the precinct."

"We're not here to look at murder evidence," said Vallimun, leading them along the wall toward a man sitting on a stool behind a glass window. "There's something else in here I wanted to show you both."

The man behind the window did a double take as Vallimun approached. Vallimun reached into his coat pocket and removed a small piece of paper that resembled a voucher. The man took it as Vallimun slid it under the crack below the glass pane and held it a moment, his eyes drifting back and forth from it to Vallimun's head. Cole realized then that together, they must have made quite a sight. His hair was approximately the same length as the inspector's was now, and silvery white like snow. The inspector's hair was almost like lemonade in color. Together, they looked like part of an eighties hair band instead of a police investigation. For once, out of the group, Corhagen appeared to be the most normal. Rather than being thrilled about it, however, he looked sourer than ever.

The man behind the desk finally gave up looking for some reason to bar them entry and stood up without a word. A moment later, he returned and passed the voucher back to the inspector. "Row 13-S," he said in a surprisingly high-pitched voice. "All the way in the back. Please be careful not to disturb anything while you're there."

Vallimun took the voucher back without replying and walked away. Cole and James followed after, with James careful to keep several feet of space between them. "Back in the sixties," Vallimun explained, not bothering to lower his voice, "this sort of place was a nightmare. Cops who were injured or on disciplinary probation were sent here. It was what they called a 'no-show' job; cops were on the payroll here, but many of them never bothered showing up. It was a dumping ground for pricks with bad attitudes, so a lot of crap got lost or thrown out just because they needed the space. It was like that for years until the board cracked down on the place because some DNA evidence that would've cleared a convicted man got tossed out. The property clerk's office finally had to step in and modify the place. Hopefully, what we're looking for is still around, though it's probably just a wild goose chase."

"What are we looking for?" Corhagen wondered, eyeing some of the barrels higher up.

"Classified files," said Vallimun, leading them around a corner. "As far back as the 1950s, I hope."

"What could possibly have happened in the 1950s that would help solve this case now?" Cole asked, though he knew perfectly well what the answer was.

"Back in the mid-to-late fifties, there was a secret squad of police officers formed following an incident where several prominent citizens of New York went on a killing spree, murdering most of their spouses and loved ones in a freak panic. All these incidences occurred after they'd been visited by a famous psychic. Rumor had it he had done something to their minds to get revenge on them, since everyone involved had been a member of the board of directors on the company his father owned before it went bankrupt. The detective who solved the case was labeled a crackpot, but the city still saw fit to put him in charge of what they called Section Thirteen."

Cole stopped dead in his tracks. "*The* Section Thirteen?" he pressed. "It really existed?"

Both Corhagen and Vallimun stopped and looked around. "You've heard of it?" Corhagen asked, looking surprised.

"The fey in New York used to talk about Section Thirteen," he explained, moving in closer to them. "Not loudly, but there were rumors. Section Thirteen was like a cross between the Gestapo and the secret saviors of New York, depending on who you asked. I never paid much attention to them, to be honest. It all sounded like the sort of tales adults will whisper to their children before they go to sleep, warning them about how monsters will take them away if they aren't good. Hard to believe they were real."

"Very much real," Vallimun affirmed. "Up until the seventies, when the state board decided it didn't need to keep writing checks out to a bunch of kooks on acid, Section Thirteen handled cases dealing with the occult and supernatural. Most of the reports they turned in read like a really bad drug trip."

"But if any of their case files still exist," Cole said, putting it together, "it might help us figure out what to do next. You're thinking Section Thirteen might have tangled with her before."

"If she's been operating in New York for as long as you suggested, I don't see how they couldn't have."

"Then it also means they couldn't stop her," Corhagen added

gravely.

"Or they never found her," Cole pointed out. "Naryssa was hoping I might sympathize with her yesterday. I don't think I would've located her as easily as I did otherwise. She seems like a slippery customer."

Vallimun went on ahead and turned at the corner to their right, checking the serial numbers on the barrels. "Do you?" Corhagen asked quietly.

"Do I what?"

"Feel bad for her?" Corhagen looked at Cole, and there was a maze of emotions etched across his face. "Do you think reasoning with her is the way to go?"

Cole debated being careful with his words for a second, then threw caution to the wind. "I suppose I can't help but feel a little empathetic toward her plight," he admitted. "She's half sidhe and half night hag. I can't imagine anything remotely good happening to her, living in Faerie like that. Whether she was exiled or just fled for her own safety, it couldn't have been easy living among humans. I don't have any plans to join up with her, though, if that was what you really wanted to know. I would have told you, if you'd asked."

James looked away, careful not to meet Cole's eyes. "Found it," Vallimun called out. "Over this way. Give me a hand with these fuckers!"

Cole left James standing there and moved to help Vallimun with what looked like a rather hefty barrel. It was nearly as tall as his waist, and it rattled from within like something loose was shifting around. This turned out to be boxes filled with case files. There were three barrels of the stuff, one for each of them. Cole had been expecting a lot more, but Vallimun seemed pleased.

"Guess this was all they bothered to hold onto," he said, once they'd wrangled all of them open. "An old friend of mine who used to be a city official was the one who pointed me toward these things. He said that there was a UF49 sent down with instructions that these case files not be disposed of. Damn rubber gun squad never listens, but it's better than nothing. Each of you take a barrel and start going through this shit. If you come across something that looks relevant, throw the whole box to the side so we can look through it later."

"Shouldn't we take the stuff down to the station and look through it there?" Corhagen suggested, wrestling his barrel off to the side a little.

"Can't," Vallimun said, lifting one of the boxes out. "There's not enough room in my car to take all of this, and I'd have to get permission for the city to haul it downtown." Vallimun shook his head as his hair fell down in front of his eyes. "Dammit! Why can't this shit stay outta my face?"

"It takes practice," Cole replied, not looking up from the file in his hands. "It's all a matter of keeping your head tilted right and precise body movement."

"We should get you some ponytail holders," suggested Corhagen. "Or maybe just a pair of clippers to shave it all off."

"You could try," Cole admitted. "But then, it could grow back even longer than it is now."

Silence fell over the three of them following that, with Vallimun wearing a very irate look on his face at the thought. Cole put the file he'd been reading back into the box and moved onto the next. It was a tedious, dragging task, but some of the tales that'd been left by the members of Section Thirteen were interesting, to say the least. He wasn't sure whether the box he was searching through housed files from their early years or not, but the stories they held played the Section out to be a fairly competent bunch.

For humans, anyway.

When he was done with the first box, Cole pushed it a few inches out of the way with his foot and moved on to the next. The reports grew tiresome after a while, and the only place to sit was on the floor. "I'm beginning to see why the board thought these Section Thirteen boys were high as a kite," Corhagen said, breaking the silence. "Most of these reports sound like they were written by a Jim Morrison fan."

"I never liked his poetry," Cole answered, absentmindedly. "But a lot of people give him flak for things that weren't his fault."

Both men looked down at Cole. "He was talking about the lead singer from The Doors," Vallimun corrected.

"I know," replied Cole, looking up. "*I* was talking about the lead singer from The Doors. He may not have been much of a poet, but his concerts were something to see. Especially that one down in Florida."

Corhagen frowned. "The one where...."

Cole smiled. "I thought a live anaconda had gotten loose on the stage. Never saw anything like it in my whole life, and that's saying something!"

Cole went back to his file as the two men looked at one another, but then he immediately stood up. "I've got something," he said, pointing. "Look here. It talks about a disfigured couple in Queens. The initial report says their arms and legs were torn off, but there was no forced entry. Someone left an obituary clipping in here, as well. It says that Davis and Marigold Fine were survived by their twin daughters. Neither one was ever found."

"Any more like that in there?" Vallimun asked, interested.

"Yes," said Cole, after checking. "Hold on, though. Let me look through the rest of the box."

Cole dug out some more files and began checking. "This one has a lot of murder files in it," he added. "Let me see if...."

"I've got one," Corhagen called out. "Found a box with a bunch of deaths in it. A few sound a lot like our case, but there are others in it that are more or less normal, if you don't count the perps having multiple arms and acid breath attacks. It seems like Section Thirteen got handed a lot of weird murder cases."

"That's what they were there for," Vallimun replied, looking over. "How many look like they were the same as our case?"

"I'm checking," Corhagen said, flipping through the different file folders.

"As am I," Cole added. "And I believe I have all the ones from this box. Guess what, though? All the murders took place within the same month or so of each other, roughly the beginning of each year. These are from 1972."

"Mine are even older," Corhagen bragged. "Nineteen fifty-nine, and there were thirteen cases where the parents died suspiciously and left behind children that were never found. Some of these reports even go into details about how the parents didn't look entirely human. There's stuff in here about claws that had specially made gloves over them."

"Nothing like that here," Cole replied. "But here's something you might find interesting. I have almost the same number of cases. What month did yours take place in?"

"At the beginning of the year," Vallimun answered for him. "All these murders were around the same time of the year as yours were. Let's keep looking."

"Wait," Cole said, getting up again. "What year did you say those murders took place again?"

"'Fifty-nine," said Corhagen, looking again. "Between the months of January and March."

"Mine stopped before March," Cole said, thinking. "But the times... I need to look through these again."

Vallimun watched as Cole rifled through the boxes once more. "Some of them may have been thrown together with the wrong year," Cole surmised. "Or maybe I just overlooked them. Something she said to me yesterday has been getting under my skin, though."

"And here I thought you'd told us everything," Corhagen quipped. "What was it?"

"She offered to let me go and said she would release the both of you unharmed once she was finished if I agreed to stay out of her business," he responded coolly. "I told her she could go to hell. She also said something about a 'last one' and the cycle being completed. I think our killer has a schedule to keep and was afraid I was going to put her behind schedule."

Corhagen made a low noise that sounded almost like a growl. "What schedule?" Vallimun asked, ignoring the detective now.

"Thirteen children," Cole answered, holding up more than a dozen case files. "She takes thirteen children total, killing their parents and swiping them away while no one bothers to look for them, saving them from a life of torment for being different in a world that has historically never accepted such things. Naryssa sees herself as these children's rescuer, shielding them from any abuse they might receive. If you add up the times, there are thirteen years between 1959 and 1972."

"Section Thirteen was disposed of following that," Vallimun added thoughtfully. "If there were any more killings, we won't find them here."

"But it fits, doesn't it?" Cole pressed. "If you do the math, then the next batch of murders would've occurred in '85, then again in '98."

"And finally, this year." Vallimun nodded. "It's a long shot, but it fits. Why the bad luck number, though?"

Cole shook his head, putting the other files back. "I have no idea," he confessed. "Maybe it's a personal thing, or she's following some ritual I'm not familiar with. Either way, we've got until she locates her thirteenth child and kills its parents."

"What happens then?"

"Naryssa hasn't been caught in all this time," Cole explained. "Most people nowadays aren't willing to believe in fairies. My guess is she takes the children somewhere they won't be found. The building she was in yesterday was probably a temporary base of operations. Her real home is most likely somewhere humans can't penetrate. If that's the case, finding her after she obtains that last child is going to be difficult, to put it mildly."

Vallimun thought on this for a moment, then looked toward Corhagen, who was wearing an especially stiff-looking blank face. "You got anything you wanna add?" the inspector offered. "You've been awfully quiet about this. I thought you'd have more to bring to the table."

"I'm sorry, sir," Corhagen said, looking properly ashamed. "I guess I'm just preoccupied. I keep thinking there's something important I've forgotten about."

Neither Vallimun nor Cole responded at first. "Get it together," Vallimun said finally, looking away. "I need everyone who's on board with this to keep a clear head. Right now, we don't have nearly enough proof to get the sort of manpower it would take to bring that bitch down. I'm not sure the chief would approve the muscle we'd need to take down an immensely powerful hag woman who thinks she's Mary Poppins, anyway."

"Yes, sir," said Corhagen politely, suddenly glaring at Cole as if this were his fault. "Right away, sir. I do have one thing to add, actually."

"Spill," the inspector ordered.

"She was staying at a building in the Bronx." Corhagen paused and drew a sheet of paper out of his pocket. "I spent most of last night and early this morning tracing the name on the property. Turns out, the building was owned by a dummy corporation set up in the nineties, right before the killings would've occurred in '98."

"And?"

Corhagen looked past him to Cole. "It looks like whoever owned the building didn't want anyone knowing their fingerprints were on it. I'll need more time to work through the paper trail, since it's pretty thorough, but whoever's name is on it has enough clout and money to keep the trail cold."

Cole bit his lower lip, willing James to say nothing more. Corhagen met his eyes, and there was a flicker of something like sorrow there underneath his anger and resentment. Corhagen obviously remembered everything from last night, and blamed him for it. No matter that it'd been necessary, he still held Cole responsible for what he believed was a wrong committed against him. For the crime of making him feel, Cole was sure James intended to get his revenge. For now, however, he merely folded the paper up and tucked it away.

"That's all I have to add, sir," Corhagen finished, and he wouldn't meet Cole's eyes again.

Vallimun left the two of them to gather together any boxes full of case files that might be relevant while he signed the forms needed to check them out and bring his car around. Cole hefted the barrels back into place by himself while Corhagen watched. He could feel the man's eyes drilling into him. It made the muscles in his neck and shoulders stiffen painfully.

When Cole turned around, Corhagen had moved closer. There

was a heat to him, a quiet, boiling rage threatening to spill over at any second. For the time being, James was keeping it in check. His eyes held the knowledge that it wouldn't stay that way forever. What he'd learned had shaken him, shaken his faith in Cole. There were times when Cole regretted having shared so much about himself with the mortal.

It made what he needed to do next all the more difficult.

"I don't suppose you'd be willing to share with me what you found out," he tried, struggling to be optimistic in the face of the cold, stony look on James's face.

"Do I really need to?" Corhagen challenged. "Don't you already know?"

Cole sighed. "I guessed," he admitted. "I didn't have any proof until now, but I was going to talk to him about it. I just wanted a chance to hear his side of the story first."

"And impede a police investigation."

"Because it was personal," Cole snapped, his voice echoing. "Because it was family. My only family, in case you'd forgotten."

"So I'm supposed to give a crap about your family while you don't seem to care what happens to mime?" Corhagen challenged. "I put my life on the line every day, wondering each time I walk out the front door of my house if this will be the last time I see any of them. I have a home and people to care for now. That was what I'd always wanted; you knew that! And now I may have ruined it forever. You just couldn't leave me the fuck alone, could you?"

"*You* summoned *me*," Cole reminded him. "I gave *you* the power to do that, and no one else. You're the one who brought me into this."

"Like that excuses what you did to me last night?" James spat. "What I did? What we did to....?"

Cole shrugged. "He didn't complain."

"Life's just one big smartass joke to you, isn't it?" Corhagen snarled. "How long do you think I'm going to be able to keep something like what happened a secret? What if the inspector decides to spill his guts one night at the bar and people trace it back to me? I can't lose my wife and kids, Cole. I worked too hard to have them in the first place."

Cole cocked an eyebrow at him. "She got herself knocked up and told you the baby was yours so she could have someone to pay the bills and keep her from waking up at five in the morning. The only reason it's worked so far is because you refuse to look at the obvious. Your marriage is a sham, and that first kid isn't yours. Honestly, I wonder about the second one."

"She was under a lot of stress when she said that," James insisted, though even he didn't sound convinced. "She didn't mean any of it."

Cole sighed, then reached down and lifted a box under each arm. "Believe whatever you want to," he said, walking off. "I've got someone else I need to talk to."

COLE parted ways with the inspector with his word that he would meet back up with them at the precinct later. Neither man looked happy about it, for completely different reasons, but Cole wasn't worried. He hoped that there was a simple explanation, or at the very least, a forgivable one. If he were honest with himself, both were likely to make him feel worse.

It was another crowded subway ride back to central Manhattan, though not as bad as before. Cole tried to concentrate on what he planned to say, but nothing came to mind. Adding to his distraction was the fact that more than one mortal he shared the train car with hadn't bothered to bathe. The smell made the trip seem even longer. When the subway train finally came to a stop, he was one of the first ones off. No one else wanted to halt a man who was so obviously armed and dressed to kill. Cole had no intentions of killing anyone just yet, but if it got him off the subway faster, no one else needed to know that.

The stairs put him back on the street just a few miles down from where he was headed. There was no limousine waiting for him this time. As such, he mounted his bike and took off as quickly as he could without snapping the bike chain or knocking pedestrians out of the way. At the building, no one tried to stop him from going inside. The people there looked up, but upon seeing it was him, they went back to whatever it was they were doing. Cole brought his bike inside, not wishing to leave it alone, though he doubted seriously anyone would dare to take it. His godson would probably turn over the thief's hide as a show of what happened to anyone who dared mess with family.

Cole had always appreciated that.

When he reached the roof, Cole didn't stare out across the expanse of greenery like last time. His eyes were for the front door to the castle and nothing else. Cole rang the bell and waited impatiently, feeling his nerves tense and taut at the thought of seeing David now and what he would say to the man. When the door finally did open, it was to a young woman whose eyes widened to triple their size at first glance of him. Cole, however, had neither the time nor the inclination to deal with her.

"I'm here to see David Bryne," Cole stated flatly. "He has an appointment with his godfather."

The woman didn't move, didn't even blink. "Ma'am," Cole said, feeling his anger rise.

"Master Colewyn," came Hagan's voice as he appeared around the corner. "How wonderful to see you again. To what do we owe the pleasure?"

"I need to speak with David. Is he here?"

"In the back," Hagan said, gesturing and moving out of the way. "Come."

The last part was spoken not to him but to the woman still looking up at Cole like she was a bird caught in a snake's gaze. When she didn't move at first, Hagen took her by the arm and pulled slightly. The unexpected contact caused her to jump, and she looked at the old man like she hadn't realized he was there.

During the exchange, Cole walked on past them, happy to leave the woman behind. He'd forgotten how his appearance could rattle people. People reacted differently to seeing a sidhe for the first time. Many of them were struck by the beauty that was natural to their race and fell instantly into lust. Others went mad or were terrified beyond words. Cole hadn't had anyone strip naked and offer themselves to him for a while, though he could still part a crowd fairly easy. In the city, away from Faerie, the effects had withered a bit. He knew this was a good thing, for it would be difficult going from place to place when people kept screaming or humping his leg, but it was just one more reminder of what he'd lost.

Today, though, he didn't want to think about that.

David was waiting for him in the drawing room, his back to Cole as he looked out the window at the expanse of city all around them. Cole knew he could feel his presence, even if he hadn't reacted to it yet. "I thought you'd get here sooner," David said suddenly, not turning around. "Was traffic that bad?"

Cole felt his anger spill over into his words. "You knew."

David turned around slightly, his eyes concealed by the same sunglasses he'd worn before. "Beg pardon?"

"When I found her, she offered me tea and cookies. It was cran-apple and gingersnaps, the same cran-apple tea and gingersnaps I used to eat here. Don't try and tell me they weren't, because I remember exactly how those used to taste. We would sit by the fire for hours and drink gallons of the stuff while we ate cookies together. You almost wet yourself from it more than once because you didn't want to leave the room. It was nearly impossible to get you to go while I was there."

"I remember," David said, a smile on his face. "I was terrified that if I left for even a few minutes, you'd be gone when I got back."

Cole hesitated briefly. "I never abandoned you, David. Not really."

"No," he admitted, facing him at last. "No, you never abandoned me, but you couldn't stay."

Cole wanted to turn away, but he kept his eyes forward. His eyes stung slightly at the edges, but he made himself stay strong. "If you think bringing up past regrets will get me to leave, then you never knew me at all. I came to find out from you why you were helping Naryssa, before I go to the police."

David said nothing for a moment. "Is that the name she gave you?" he asked, when he spoke. "She's had others, but the only thing I ever knew her as was Nanny."

Cole's hands drifted away from his guns slightly. He hadn't been aware of where they were until he moved. David watched, pain drifting across his face like fog. "Did you come here to avenge their deaths?" he asked, looking up again. "For all the people she killed?"

"She was...."

"Nanny was here for me when you couldn't be," David said quickly, frowning now. "I was raised by her while you were away. My grandmother arranged it, though I never learned how they came to know one another. I thought perhaps you might have helped set it up, but it seems I was wrong. Mother and Grandmother both feared what the rest of the family would do to me, considering how hard of a time my mother had. The family was in shambles, fighting over every scrap they could sink their teeth into, tearing each other apart. They knew better than to murder me while you were around, but the problem there was that many didn't accept that Grandmother had repealed her banishment. Most still blamed you for what happened to Grandfather, and the younger ones were raised with the hate. They needed someone powerful around who would scare everyone off."

"Naryssa?" Cole shook his head. "I would've...."

"Smelled her?" David offered. "Sensed her? We thought so, too, but Naryssa survived outside of Faerie for as long as she did because she can hide herself better than anyone else. At least, that's her version of things, but I'm guessing you know better than me, if the two of you were fighting yesterday. Nice job with burning the whole building down to escape. At least I was insured."

"I didn't burn it down," Cole retorted. "Some gun-crazy girl in a red cloak named Robyn did it."

"I know," he replied. "Who do you think hired her?"

"What?"

David gestured toward the chairs. "Have a seat," he said. "This is a conversation best had with a brandy."

Cole almost argued, but he sat down in the end as David pulled out what looked like a finely aged bottle. "On the rocks," he said with a weak sigh. "If you wouldn't mind."

"Not at all," David replied, slipping ice into twin glasses. "So, are you still planning on going to the police?"

"They already know," Cole told him regretfully. "One does, anyway. He tracked the paper trail you left and found out the building was leased in your name."

"Is that what he told you?" David passed Cole his drink, then sat down. "I find that hard to believe."

"He insinuated."

"Then he has nothing on me. The building was leased to one of my companies, not specifically to me. And even if the place was in my name, that doesn't mean whoever lived there had my permission to stay there. Squatters take up residence inside old abandoned buildings all the time."

Cole held his drink but didn't bring it to his lips. "Was Naryssa staying there with your blessing?"

David looked across at Cole and quietly set his glass down. "Yes," he answered. "Happy now?"

"Not remotely," said Cole, doing the same. "Why was she there? Why would you help her in the first place?"

"Because I had no choice."

"There's always a choice!" Cole shouted, getting up. "You could've told her to burn in hell."

David got up and looked Cole in the face. "Then I would have lost you, as well."

Cole froze. "How?"

David sighed. "Sit down," he said, taking his own advice. "I'll explain everything, I promise. And would it kill you not to waste good brandy? If you don't want any or are afraid I might have poisoned you, at least pass it over here to me."

Cole frowned as he lowered himself back into his chair and picked up the glass in salute. "It's good," he admitted after trying some. "You've always had damn good taste in liquor, though."

"Thank you," David said, rolling his eyes. "I'm humbled by your praise, considering you were the one who gave me my first scotch. Now, do you need to have a few more outbursts of righteous indignation, or can I explain myself at last?

"I never intended to keep this a secret from you," David went on when Cole didn't answer. "I don't blame you for being angry, but please bear in mind that you've kept things from me, as well. Helping Naryssa was part of the bargain my mother and grandmother made back when I was very young. She refused to protect me unless they made a pact with her that said when I came of age, she could claim one favor from me. If I refused her, then she would take the life of someone close to me in exchange."

Cole groaned. "Branwen should've known better. Never deal with the fey."

"She was too proud to go to you and ask that you put yourself in the line of fire for her sake," he replied, drinking more brandy. "Though she'd never admit it."

"No," Cole agreed. "She wouldn't."

"Naryssa kept to herself, for the most part, but she knew about you. She was here during the times when you visited me but kept out of sight. She was the one who made the tea and cookies for us. In all that time, anyone could've guessed how much seeing you meant to me. When I started building my business up and doing things my own way instead of following in my father's footsteps, she asked that I provide her with sanctuary and funds so she could have a place to keep her 'children'. By then, I'd begun to suspect Naryssa was unstable. She never harmed me, but there were many times when I sensed...."

"Her violence," Cole finished for him. "Her pain, and willingness to act on it."

"That may have been it," David admitted. "I didn't know why, and it seemed like such a simple thing to give in to. After a while, though, I started to wonder. And then I started doing a little investigating. What I found out sent chills down my spine, so I had Naryssa brought to me. I demanded she leave and never come back. I threatened to cut her off. She reminded me then of the deal made between her and my mother and grandmother. She could take the life of one person close to me if I recanted on their promise, which I'd inherited when I became a man. The life she named was yours.

"So," David continued, ignoring the look on Cole's face, "I could either look the other way, or lose the only real family I had left, such as it was."

David reached up and slowly pulled off the shades covering his eyes. Cole stared across the space separating them, at the eyes his godson had inherited from him. Copper, gold, and topaz shone in the light, from both his face and the face of David Bryne, who had worn dark shades all these years to hide them. Hiding them from sight because of how many mortals were unnerved by the sight of them and because of how many blood relatives had cursed him for them. Cole looked into the eyes of the man he shared blood with because of a magical night one Samhain years and years ago, when the barriers between the worlds had thinned along with the laws of what was possible.

Cole struggled with what to say. "I'm so sorry, David. I don't know what else to say, but...."

"Don't," he cut in. "I live with my decisions. You taught me to do that, remember?"

Cole stood up, leaving his brandy on the table, and walked over to the couch where David sat. David didn't protest when Cole sat down next to him and put his arms around him. It might have been different if they'd been in one of his godson's many board meetings, surrounded by executives and such, but they were alone now. Cole held David and rocked slowly back and forth, singing an old song of wild hunts and endless colors into the man's ear. In the end, they wound up stretched out on the couch together with David resting his head on Cole's lap. Cole brushed a lock of hair from his face and gazed down curiously.

"What about the girl in the red cloak?" he asked, breaking the silence.

"I hired her," David answered simply. "The bargain my grandmother made might've prevented me from doing anything about Naryssa directly, but there are other ways out of a contract. I was monitoring Naryssa's movements, though it took careful planning to ensure she never suspected what I was up to. Once I knew where she was headed, I sent Ms. Robyn to the hospital under the guise of taking a hit out on the nightflyer. Once you two had been introduced, it was a simple matter for her to leave behind enough of a clue for you to track her back to Naryssa's place. She was on the rooftop across the street just in case something went wrong. Given that the building burnt to the ground, I'd say that was a smart idea."

"If you ignore the fact that she was the one who set fire to the place," Cole added.

David shrugged and rose up. "Nobody's perfect."

There's one other thing you should know," he added. "Naryssa swore me to secrecy, said that I would forfeit your life if I told what she was doing to anyone. The thing is, I don't think she expected me to dig deeper or to find out where her real hideout was."

Cole stood up, eyes as big as saucers. "Where?"

Before David answered, he figured it out. "Bowling Green Park," they said at the same time.

"If you knew, why'd you ask?" David wondered, frowning.

"Titania," Cole replied, already heading for the door. "I have to go, but I'll be back. If Naryssa tries anything, send a message to me. I've got to put an end to this right now."

"You'll need help!" David called out, but Cole had already gone. "Wait, you meant *the* Titania?!"

Chapter *Eleven*

THE minute the wheels on his bike rolled over onto his street, Cole knew something was wrong. Getting back to the loft seemed to take forever, even though his watch said it was less than an hour after he'd run out of David's home. The closer he got to his building, the worse he felt. Cole could smell Naryssa's glamour in the air through the thick layer of smog. When he reached the front door, Cole leaped off and ran the rest of the way up. He didn't bother picking his bike up. It was that serious.

At the top of the stairs, his worst fears were confirmed. Something had ripped the door right off its hinges. More than that, however, he could sense the tearing in the very fabric surrounding his home. Whatever was here had gotten in not just by smashing the door down, but by punching through the wards he had put in place. Which meant he should have known the moment they fell.

Unless, of course, Naryssa's glamour had been blanketing the whole building, separating him from his magic.

Cole stepped inside, feeling as though he were walking into some atrocity being committed that very second. The area was empty, but it looked as though a bomb had gone off. Furniture had not only been thrown around but literally torn in half down the middle. His couch had been trisected, and the TV was nothing but a pile of scrap metal. There were numerous holes in the kitchen cabinets and counters where something had blasted straight through them. Whatever had done that had done the same thing to his bedroom, where he could see the tattered remains of what had once been his computer.

Katalina was nowhere in sight.

Cole ran to her bedroom first. The minute he got there, he regretted it. Cole froze in his tracks, not wanting to believe what he was seeing. There, lying on the floor in a circle of her own blood, was the dead body of Katalina Weisman, her cheeks still flushed and rosy. The blood smelled fresh, which meant she had probably been dead for less than a hour.

Cole couldn't have cared less about that. The fact that she'd most likely died while he was at David's barely registered as a footnote. Falling to his knees, he threw his head back and howled at the ceiling, his rage and bitterness pouring out from his soul like a wash of poison. Cole let loose the fury of one who'd once been named among Titania's prized wolves, her hunting dogs of war. The cry was a storm of vengeance. The air in the room turned hot with it until Cole had nothing left. His voice broke, and his arms fell lifelessly to his sides with the weight of loss.

Even then, he couldn't bring himself to move, couldn't approach her just yet. She was lying there at an awkward angle, which meant her spine had most likely been damaged. Blood from her nose had dried on her face. Cole tried to be rational, to take it all in without feeling. It took all the will he could muster, which at this point didn't come to much. His chest felt raw, as though his heart had burst from it and left a bleeding, open wound there. Cole bit down on his tongue and forced himself to think.

A dead body, a murder scene, was a grisly place to be. Even humans, who rarely acknowledged anything, understood that arriving at a place immediately after someone had been killed left chills on their skin for a reason other than just the gruesomeness of it. An imprint was left, and being what he was, sometimes Cole could look past the veil of reality mortals threw up around their world and see what lay beyond it. It was what had made his skills as a police consultant invaluable when he and Corhagen had worked together before. Back then, it didn't always work, and at times it required a small push of magic. Today, however, his peering into the circumstances of Katalina's death was as natural as breathing. As he watched, tears flowed freely down his face.

She had been one of his last true ties to humanity, to a world he didn't belong to. He watched as the shapes closed in around her. None of them were familiar, but to Cole, it wouldn't have mattered. They had belonged to Naryssa, and that was enough. From the looks of things, however vague their shapes were, they'd all been injured. Katalina had put up a fight before going down. She hadn't begged for her life or pleaded to be spared; they had paid for every drop of blood she'd shed. Cole felt a small twinge of pride and satisfaction at that.

Only when they'd overwhelmed her with sheer numbers did she form the circle around her. It had been her last line of defense, a gambit in the hopes that she could hold them off until he got back. Naryssa's hit men had surrounded her then and pounded on the outside of the circle until blood had run down her face. That was where the bloody nose had come from. The stress of trying to hold them back had caused a hemorrhage. When the biggest one, who resembled the runt jack-in-irons, struck hard enough to knock her unconscious, the circle fell. That was when they'd closed in on her. Cole watched her last moments without flinching. If she could endure such a fate, he could watch it without blinking. He wouldn't dishonor her with such cowardice, not after she'd been so brave.

She'd been....

When the scene faded to black, Cole couldn't hold back anymore. His legs refused to cooperate, so he crawled over to where Katalina's dead form was and held her in his arms. He didn't know how long he sat there in her circle rocking back and forth, but time didn't seem important anymore. Things seemed to blur together, but he was aware of whispering something in her ear. Mostly, it was a stream of jumbled words in the archaic lingo of Old Faerie, empty words of how sorry he was. Of how he should have protected her better. More scenes came to his mind, and though Cole didn't want to see anything more, he didn't try to fight them back. He simply didn't have the will for it anymore.

The day when they'd first met, when a member of Katalina's coven had given her Cole's phone number. Cole had helped the woman years ago when she'd been stalked by a rather persistent will-o'-the-wisp. Katalina had been tormented for months by night terrors, murderous shadows that sucked the life from people by haunting them while they slept. She'd been on the verge of taking her own life, and her family had done nothing. It had been easy to banish the shades, and afterward, they'd kept in touch. She'd been such a tiny thing back then, but as Cole recalled through his sobbing, she'd always been small. At thirteen, however, Katalina was miniscule. When she graduated from high school, he had stood in the audience a good ways from the rest of her family. His cheers, however, had been some of the loudest. When she'd gone looking for an apartment after her first year of college, Cole had offered her a room. From that day onward, they'd laughed and cried together.

It had all seemed so perfect. And now, he couldn't even raise her body from the dead. It was still too warm, though seeing her as an empty shell with nothing but leftover memories and fragments of her persona would not make him feel any better. It didn't stop him from laying his hand over her heart and trying to will power to it. Cole had never gained the power to truly resurrect someone, though. It was not in his magic to return her to life. In that moment, he would've gladly turned all the Summerlands to dust for the chance to do so.

Something moved behind him. Cole turned and released Katalina's body just enough to draw Jabberwock. Corhagen stood in the doorway, his eyes on the barrel to the gun warily, as though Cole might fire just for the sake of it. Cole put the gun away and sat there, meeting Corhagen's eyes across the distance between them. Slowly, as though still leery of what the sidhe would do, Corhagen walked over to the circle and knelt down. His big arms encompassed both of them, and he didn't say a word as Cole leaned into him for support, letting his grief pass to someone else. It seemed selfish to hold onto it, and for once, Corhagen didn't seem to mind that they were pressing so close together. Vallimun came in next, and as he took in the scene, his face grew cold.

"Was it them?" he asked.

Cole nodded. "They were just here. I must have arrived shortly after they left."

Neither man had anything to add. "I'm going to finish this," Cole declared, setting Katalina down on the floor carefully. "Tonight. I know where she's been hiding all this time. It's time to put an end to this."

"Good," Vallimun said, nodding. "Where do we start?"

"You don't," said Cole, walking over to Katalina's destroyed computer. "She would walk through both of you like your bodies were tissue paper. I've got to do this alone."

"Right," Corhagen said sarcastically. "Like that's going to stop us."

"Listen!"

"You listen," Vallimun said sharply, getting into Cole's face. "This is our turf. They broke into your home and killed your roommate. I get that; believe me, I do. But going solo isn't going to help things."

"What do you plan on doing to her?" he wondered, moving back a little. "Lock her up? She'd tear the concrete walls apart and walk out with the guards' heads slung over her shoulder. Prisons aren't equipped to handle something like her. She's too powerful."

"Maybe," the inspector agreed. "But she has to be stopped, and it's our job to do it."

"You can't," Cole said sadly. "I respect that you want to do your sworn duty and all, but you can't. Not on your own."

"It isn't like we need your permission," Vallimun reminded Cole, warningly. "Corhagen and I are both officers of the law. You're the one stepping out of bounds here. If things are that serious, we'll think of a plan and deal with the situation, but running out into the streets half-cocked without backup is not a good idea."

"Also, no one's arguing that we need help," Corhagen added, coming up from behind. "So far, you're the only one who's tangled with the lady and walked away. Seems like bringing you along is the smart thing to do."

Cole opened his mouth to reply but was cut off as a sharp pain ran up his arm from his fingers. His left hand throbbed as power shot through him. Cole looked toward the disabled computer tower as something inside of it started to glow. Reaching into it, Cole felt his fingers close around something round and chilly. When his palm had completely enclosed it, the power grew red hot. Cole brought it out and dropped the shining sphere on the floor. Smoke rose up from it like the tendrils from a stick of incense until they joined together in mid-air and took the form of a man.

Perhaps "man" was a bit of a stretch, but the figure had definitely been a human at some point. Katalina, it seemed, hadn't put much stock in looks. Mal was squat, taller than she would've been by maybe an inch or so, with an incredibly large lose and big eyes. His clothes were like something from the Puritan age, complete with the black hat.

"Mal," said Cole, looking the figure up and down. "Katalina's boyfriend."

"She was dating a man who lived in her computer?" Corhagen wondered, then quickly shut his mouth.

"It's alright," said the oddly dressed man, looking around. "I know all about it. When the computer was smashed open, I thought I was a goner. Looks like Kitty Kat didn't come back as a ghost, after all. I was hoping, but oh well."

"How did you know?" Cole asked. "I thought…."

"She left the microphone on when she got up to check on the noise she'd heard. I overheard everything. It sucks when the woman you love dies just a few feet away and there's nothing you can do about it. When I sensed she was dead, I started to fade."

"You loved her," Cole said, looking down at the ghost. "She seemed to love you, as well."

"Well, I harbor no delusions that we'd be joined in the afterlife." Mal shuddered, looking down at the floor. "I didn't get in that book as a reward for good deeds. Mind you, that was years and years ago, and Katalina didn't seem too bothered by it. She was never one to delve into the past much. Smart too. Never had a better student."

"She loved to learn," Cole added, understanding. "I heard her say more than once that she wouldn't know what to do with herself once she was done with university study."

"What book was he talking about?" asked Corhagen. "Could you fill some of us in who aren't in the know?"

"Never you mind," Mal snapped. "I heard you three were going after the ones responsible for all this. I want to go with."

Cole looked down at the ghost thoughtfully. "Two mortals, an exiled sidhe, and a ghost," he counted off. "Sounds good to me. I'm going to take Mal with me. Katalina said that you were a sorcerer back before your spirit got put inside the book she found. Care to lend me a hand?"

"With what?" he asked. "If it's all for getting back at the bastards who killed my Kitty Kat, I'll stick my balls into the furnaces of hell without blinking."

"That makes for an interesting mental image," he replied, gathering the ghost up once more into a glowing ball of ectoplasm. "But before we get around to you doing that, I need to make a phone call. There may be one more we can add to this ragtag band of misfits."

"Who's that?" the inspector asked, but Cole had already left the room.

One small bit of good fortune was that the phone had survived the onslaught. It was left hanging limply on the wall next to a hole that looked like it'd been put there by something's fist. The cable was still connected, however, and it was making that awful racket to warn people that the receiver had been left off the hook for too long. Cole had never understood the love humans seemed to have for loud, irritating sounds. Hanging it up, he quickly punched in the number for David's private cell phone and waited.

"Pick up the phone," he growled as it rang. "Pick it up!"

"Cole," the voice on the other end said. "What's wrong?"

"Katalina is dead," he hissed out sharply. "They killed her while I was at your place. Naryssa sent her mooks here to find me but left a message instead."

The line was dead silent for a moment. "What do you need?"

"Contact Robyn," he said. "Or whatever her name is. Anyway, the girl in the red hood you sent to help me. We can't bring in regular cops. They'd be slaughtered and only get in the way. I need someone familiar with the fey and who knows how to fight them. She's got the firepower to hold her own against Naryssa's children. I'm putting an end to this before she gets her thirteenth child. She's going to pay."

"You told me about her," David said thickly. "I'd always hoped we could be introduced some day. For what it's worth, I never meant for this to happen."

"Neither did I," muttered Cole, and his voice was just as thick with emotion. "I never meant for a lot of things, but if you'd just come to me for help—"

Cole couldn't finish his sentence. "I'm...." Slowly, he breathed out in an effort to get control of himself. "I shouldn't have said that."

"Yes, you should have," David replied. "Because it's true. I've become far too used to dealing with things on my own. I like to pretend I'm not a child who needs rescuing every few minutes. It was a nasty reminder of what my family had been and how far my mother and grandmother had gone to protect me. I just wanted to get it over with and not look back. In the end, all I've managed to do is hurt you the way I thought you'd hurt me as a child by not staying with me."

Cole was quiet for a moment. "Does it make things better?"

"No," his godson said. "It doesn't. I was angry with you for years, but you never did anything to deserve this." David seemed to be getting hold of himself now. "I will get in touch with Red Robyn immediately. Where do you want to meet with her?"

"Bowling Green Park," answered Cole. "At sunset. We'll handle things from there."

"IS THIS your idea of handling things?" Mal wondered, glancing back behind them nervously.

"It is," said Cole, keeping both eyes on the street in front of them. "The plan is simple enough. We just have to follow along with it and hope everything turns out for the best."

"Easy for you to say," the ghost replied. "You're immortal. The sidhe have nothing to fear from death."

"And you're a ghost," he pointed out as they turned a corner, leading the marching troops behind them onward. "Death already came to claim you. What more have you to fear from it?"

Mal looked seriously put out then. "As old as you are, you should know better than to think spirits have nothing to fear. There are all sorts of things in this world and beyond that feed upon my ilk. I wouldn't dare wander into Faerie for anything less than to avenge Kitty Kat's death. If it weren't for that, you could shove it."

"Then don't patronize me about being immortal," Cole replied. "If there are things that threaten ghosts, then the sidhe have even more cause to fear, whether they admit it to themselves or not. Anything that is born of one world or another can die. And death isn't the only possible outcome. One of the first things you learn as a sidhe is that immortality is a very long time to be tortured. I was shown Lord Oberon's personal Citadel of Pain as a youngling. Nothing could be more terrifying than that."

"If it is," Mal said with a shudder, drawing his nonexistent coat around himself, "I'd rather not learn about it."

Onward the two marched side by side with the troops Cole had summoned following along behind them obediently. Mal kept glancing back like one of them might break formation at any moment and charge forward in an attempt to bite their heads off. The sight of such an old spirit reduced to nervous babbling might have been comical were Cole not forced to listen to it.

"Are you certain no one is going to stop us?" he tried again after a blissful moment's silence. "Surely someone will find this a little suspicious."

"This is New York," Cole answered flippantly. "These people have seen weirder, and they still deny much of the reality that goes on around them. A large platoon of the undead marching down the sidewalk at dusk isn't going to faze many. The ones that do notice us will just repeat what they saw to the tabloids. Others will assume we're doing some sort of demonstration. The ones who might actually know the truth will be inclined to stay as far away as possible. For the sake of their noses along with everything else."

Mal was quiet for a moment longer. Then: "I still say it's weird."

"You were an evil sorcerer back in the day before being hexed to spend eternity locked inside of a book," Cole retorted. "How could this possibly be weirder?"

"Never did understand that, really," Mal muttered as they came upon Bowling Green. "Why put a soul inside of a book? Seems like the clunkers in the afterlife have had more than enough experience to ply their trade in ironic punishments. Dragons think they know everything, though. 'Put the guy in a book!'"

"There you are!" Inspector Vallimun called out. Cole noted as the inspector came forward that he'd taken the time to pull his hair back into a ponytail. "You're late."

"Had to get our advance guard together," Cole replied, stepping to the left so Vallimun could see the army of undead he'd brought along with him. "They'll do a decent job, even if half of them weren't fighters in life. I got the idea from what happened in the hospital morgue the other day."

"You raided another morgue?" Corhagen gasped, eyes bulging in shock.

"Several, actually. It seemed prudent only to gather the fit ones. Also, it would look less suspicious if there were only a few dozen missing instead of their whole inventory. Then we had to stop off and get them outfitted with weapons and such. Hopefully, that will be enough."

"Where'd you get the weapons?" Corhagen asked, his face turning sour. "Cole, what did you do?"

Cole shrugged and turned away, smirking. "It might surprise you to learn just how many army surplus stores there are in the lower east side of Manhattan. Even with all of the so-called 'modern' technology available today, I still find the Yellow Pages to be very informative. Besides, it isn't as though the stuff they're wearing wasn't used already. Or worn by dead people, for that matter."

"You stole it," the inspector said flatly.

"Borrowed," he corrected. "And it'll be returned, assuming any of us survive. Are we ready to get on with it, then?"

"I am," called a familiar female voice. "I've been standing around for ages wondering whether you were going to show up."

"Robyn." Cole smiled as the diminutive, red-hooded figure stepped out of the shadows. "If you wouldn't mind, outfit the detective and inspector here with some of your better toys. We're about to jump into the lion's den, and things might get touchy."

"If they wanted guns, they should've brought their own," she grumbled but she opened her goody bag obediently. "Here, the guy with the long hair can have this spare bazooka I brought. I don't use it anymore, anyway. It's mostly just a comfort thing. Be careful with it, though, because the rockets I packed for it are a little bit stronger than what it's designed for. Also, the stovepipe is shorter than what you'd expect, so be careful of the exhaust coming out of the back, or you'll accidentally set yourself on fire."

Vallimun eyed the shoulder-launcher warily but accepted it and the ammunition regardless. "Thank you."

"For the detective," she went on, fishing through the bag's contents, "I think I put in an anti-tank rifle before I left. This one's more or less my own design. I took some liberties with this Panzerbüchse I got at a mercenary auction site and tweaked it until it gave the sort of output I needed for the time. This one packs an awful lot of kick, though. The force of the recoil could shatter your collarbone if you aren't careful. It also goes off accidentally sometimes."

"Not a word," Corhagen shouted at Cole while eyeing the rifle suspiciously. "I think," he said, swallowing, "I think I'm good."

"Take the gun," the inspector ordered. "And please don't shoot yourself with it."

"Or us," Cole added.

The Bowling Green should have been crowded. The park generally closed down after dark, but the streets were still bustling. It was, after all, right on the edge of Broadway. Tonight, however, most people seemed in a very big hurry to go somewhere else. No one was looking directly at them. A number of people gave sidelong glances as they drove past, but Cole could tell that, for the most part, it had nothing to do with them. People could sense there was something happening tonight, and the longer they stood there with the undead waiting patiently behind them as though they had all the time in the world, the more the area cleared out. Finally, there were only a couple of cars driving past every few minutes. Cole nodded at this and motioned to the circular patch of green in the center of so much concrete.

"Where are we headed?" Corhagen wondered. "You said you knew where she was hiding."

"Here," he said, pointing. "Inside the park. Or under it, rather."

"This bitch is camped out inside of Bowling Green Park?" Vallimun asked. "You're kidding, right?"

"No," Cole said. "And it's under the park, if you'd recall. At least, if my hunch is correct."

"What do you think is under the park?" asked Corhagen as he adjusted the rifle strapped to his back.

"A sithen," said Robyn, digging through her bag as something inside rattled loudly. "Oh, crap. That'll be the detonators, then. I just hope none of them were triggered when they fell over."

"What?" Corhagen and Vallimun said at the same time.

"A sithen," she repeated. "Everyone knows there's one down here. So far, it hasn't let anybody take up residence in it. If this Naryssa is the one living in it, though, that would explain a lot."

"You knew there was a sithen down there?" Cole asked, looking around.

"Of course." Robyn shrugged. "I thought everyone knew that."

"What is a sithen?" Corhagen demanded, before turning on Robyn. "And would it kill you to check inside that bag of yours to make sure we aren't about to be blown to pieces?"

"A sithen is a faerie mound," Cole explained. "Back when the Tuatha De Danann were defeated by the Milesians, the conquered lands were divided up between the two sides. The Milesians took the lands above ground, while the Tuatha De Danann were led underground into the sidhe mounds by the Dagda. Whole worlds were built inside those mounds for the sidhe to live in. When the power of the fey began to retreat from the old lands, some of it wound up being scattered over to these shores. Still, I wonder how a whole sithen got here."

"There's an underground world beneath the park we're in?" Vallimun pressed as they crossed over the threshold of Bowling Green.

"Apparently so," Cole said. "With any luck, the door won't be too difficult to find."

"Try the fountain," Robyn suggested. "The last person who spoke to me about it said the door was supposed to be hidden in the waters at the edge of the fountain in the center of the park."

Mal, who'd been decidedly quiet up until now, nodded. "I can feel it," he whispered. "It's somewhere close by. Maybe by the side over there on the left."

"Why is he whispering?" Robyn hissed back.

"Because," Cole answered for him, "we're not alone."

The park lights all around them dimmed slightly, casting dusk farther along the grass. The light from the water reflected in the fountain seemed to grow brighter, however. Cole took a step back and motioned for the others to follow as he drew out Bandersnatch. The shimmering glow seemed to congeal around the water's edge, growing stronger the closer it got to them. Cole took aim and waited as the soft light took the form of mist and rose up in front of them. From out of the fog came twin figures, ladies in white with pale, deathly faces and empty eye sockets. Their bodies were cloaked in rags that seemed to rise and fall around them as though having a life of their own. When one spoke, both Vallimun and Corhagen went slack.

"What purpose do you have here?" one crooned, wrapping her arm around the other's waist.

"Great," Robyn muttered. "More lesbians."

Cole drew out Aed Deigh and brought fire forth from the flame end. Both women hissed at the sight of it, but Cole didn't have eyes for them. Instead, with a flick of his wrist, he sent twin tongues of red-hot fire twisting through the air around behind Corhagen and Vallimun. The flames landed on their rears at the same time, and they snapped out of their ogling with loud yelps.

"Bean sidhe," he explained as they rubbed their backsides angrily. "They guard the entrance to the sithen, which means Robyn's information was right on track."

"I could've just shot them," she added, eyeing them both. "Not fatally, mind you. If they can't keep their heads on straight and out of their pants, maybe we should leave them behind. Things will only get worse once we get past these two and head underground."

"No one may enter this place," the other twin said. "Our mistress has commanded it."

"So mote it be," the other finished.

"Oh, brother," Robyn moaned. "They're doing that annoying twin thing where they finish each other's sentences. Please, can we kill them now?"

"Allow me," said Cole, taking aim.

"No weapon conceived by mortal man can harm us," one scoffed as her sister sniffed the air disdainfully. "We are a part of the sithen you stand on, therefore...."

Cole fired, cutting her off. The bullet sailed right through her, forming a hole the size of a fist in her abdomen. The mist behind her spun and twirled outward, but otherwise, there didn't seem to be any damage. There was no blood to speak of, and her eyes remained dark as ever. The bean sidhe seemed to smile for a second, as though preparing to denounce Cole once more. Then, something happened.

The bean sidhe let out a gruesome wail as she doubled over in pain. Both Corhagen and Vallimun flinched at the sound, but Cole endured it. "What have you done?" the other sister cried out.

"My guns were forged by a human," Cole explained, aiming his next shot between her eyes. "But the metal was blessed with one of the chalices of Dagda given to me by the Queen of All Faerie. These guns are anything but ordinary. Guess that means either one of you can die!"

"*Help... meeee,*" the wounded bean sidhe gasped, gazing around wildly. "*Please... sisterrr!*"

"Help her," the other demanded. "Save my sister, sidhe, or I'll—"

Cole let his finger rest over the trigger. "Open the door," he ordered her. "Let us in the sithen, or your sister dies."

Cole thought she would take longer to decide. At once, however, an opening sprung up out of the water in front of them. It was the size of a door, and water surrounded the edges, framing it. Beyond that, there was nothing but black. "Done," pronounced the bean sidhe. "Now heal my sister. I cannot lose her."

"No," Cole nodded, agreeing, "I suppose you can't."

Cole placed his left hand over the wounded sister's stomach where the hole was and channeled his will. The power from the Hand of Cold Death sprung out and wound through her, making the bean sidhe cry out again. Corhagen backed farther up, but Cole didn't stop. The hole began to shrink down until it was no bigger than a quarter. With another push of his power, it was completely gone. The two sisters looked up at him then as though looking at the face of a god.

"You saved me," she breathed. "You saved both of us."

"It's a miracle," he muttered. "We're headed below to have a word with your mistress. I suggest you find some excuse not to bother us while we're engaging her in a little chat. Otherwise, should any holes I put in you close up, I'll just add more. A lot more."

Cole turned around and motioned to the others. "Back away some," he said. "I'm going to send down our front men first. They'll clear a path for us."

The undead began falling in and marched two at a time into the doorway that remained open for them. Cole kept an eye on both sisters, expecting them to seal it at any moment, but neither seemed inclined to do so. After a moment, Corhagen came around and stood next to him.

"I thought you didn't have healing powers."

"I don't," he replied. "But the Hand of Cold Death works on all manner of long-dead things. The bean sidhe are said to be the souls of the deceased sidhe who were killed during wartime and left to guard the homes of those living in Ireland. It was just a matter of using it to sew her spirit back together."

"Her spirit?"

"Ectoplasm, if you want," he tried. "Oh, and while I'm thinking about it...."

Corhagen practically recoiled as Cole reached out to touch his face. "Just deal with it," he hissed, and the detective stiffened.

Cole placed a chaste kiss on first Corhagen's left eyelid, then the right. "So that you may truly see," he whispered. Corhagen started off stiff as a board, but as Cole moved down to his nose, he sensed a tremor pass through the man's body and into his. Cole placed a longer kiss on James's nose, and felt him breathe in sharply.

"So that you may truly smell," he said.

Another kiss was laid on the left ear. This time, Cole nibbled at the fleshy area for a moment, causing a suspicious bulge in the detective's pants. "So that you may truly hear," he breathed, letting the air from his lungs trace spirals around the spot on James's ear where he'd left his kiss.

"So that you may truly touch." With that, Cole laid a single kiss on the inside of each palm.

"So you may truly speak."

Corhagen had gone weak in the knees. Cole caught him before he could fall and leaned James back slightly in his arms. Before the detective could pull away, Cole captured his lips and kissed him deep and hard. The air around them crackled for a second, and when Cole finally rose up, the air around them had grown foggy. Inspector Vallimun was headed their way, wearing an extremely annoyed look. James flailed about helplessly at the sight of him, and Cole almost dropped him.

"Am I next?" Vallimun asked.

"Only if you want to be," Cole replied neutrally. "Thought it would help once we get down there. Sithens tend to play tricks on human minds."

"And kissing is the only way to get rid of that?" the inspector pressed, looking over at James. "Sounds fair to me."

Cole repeated the process on the inspector, who seemed keenly interested in moving right along through it to the end. When Cole leaned forward to kiss him on the mouth, and thus finish the blessing that would prevent the sithen from bespelling him Vallimun grasped him behind the neck and yanked him forward. Cole felt the inspector's tongue invade his mouth, and without thinking, he kissed back with wild abandon. When they finally disengaged, Cole became aware that they'd attracted an audience. He also wondered briefly if he'd even remembered to put the blessing on Vallimun's mouth and whether it really mattered anymore.

"No offense, kid," Mal joked, "but you're just not my type."

"You're a spirit," he chided. "I doubt the sithen will affect you much. Just keep a cool head and it should be alright."

"Maybe you should try it on them one more time," Robyn pressed, watching all three of them closely. "But take a little bit longer with the mouth-blessing thing. Oh, and wait until I get my camera out."

"Maybe later," Cole replied. "Our troops are already inside. It's time for us to move in. Do you need me to do you, as well?"

"I can manage on my own," she said, holding up a small bottle of oil. "I came prepared."

"What is that?" Corhagen squinted, his expression sour. "A bottle? How does that help her?"

"Anointing someone with oil in the same places he did will also work," she explained. "I hear that was how they'd sometimes do it in the old days."

Corhagen was not happy. "And you couldn't have told us sooner?" he demanded, eyes narrowing. "Like, before I had to make out with him?"

"I seriously doubt that was the first time you two made out with each other," Robyn bit back playfully, slipping the oil back into her goody bag. "Besides, I like his way better. It was a lot more fun to watch."

"Right," Cole said, looking toward the door and the blackness within it. "I guess we're ready to go, then. Time to go see Grandma and see if she's made us cookies."

"Over the river and through the woods," Robyn joked as she stepped forward and placed a foot through the entrance.

Vallimun grinned as he followed after her. "And out of the demon's ass."

Chapter Twelve

THE first thing that greeted Cole as he stepped through the blackness was an arm. It wasn't attached to anything, which proved not to be strange enough. The arm had belonged to one of his troops, who raced past the stairs, snatching it up off the floor, with something lumpish and hairy fast on its heels. The creature quickly found itself changing directions as the undead minion turned and raced after it, using the arm as a club to whack it over the head. Cole paused, taking in the rest of the chaos surrounding them.

The horde was having a field day. Several of them had missing limbs, though that did little to deter them. Apparently, Naryssa was aware of their presence and had sent some of her brood to the entrance. The first thing Cole's soldiers did once they were inside was find themselves under attack, and they responded accordingly. It was a good thing Cole had left them with instructions before they ever reached Bowling Green, or this could have backfired horribly. As it was, his undead were doing an acceptable job of keeping Naryssa's adopted spawn at bay, though the home team was certainly holding its own. Having seen the situation, Cole knew it was time to even the playing field.

Corhagan had already taken a post up against the wall with his new toy. "Boom! Head shot!" he cried out happily as the skull of something green and flaming exploded.

Vallimun was conserving his ammunition for the moment, given that they were in a smaller area. Cole launched himself into an attack of his own against two half-human snake goblins with Aed Deigh, freezing one while the other caught fire. His weapon worked better against weaker creatures with little magic in their veins. The half-goblins didn't immediately freeze up or burst into flame, but they were in enough pain that they reconsidered him as an opponent. Vallimun opened fire with his .357 Magnum as they turned around to retreat, dropping the both of them in two clean shots.

"Move on forward," Cole ordered, pointing toward the end of the corridor they were in. "She's just trying to stall us. Take out what you can and keep powering on through."

"Right!"

Cole fought off a few more of Naryssa's children, raising his left hand as he did so. The Hand of Cold Death throbbed, sensing the wounded among his ranks. Cole let the power flow outward from him down to the fallen lying on the ground of the sithen. It might have been Naryssa's lair, but they were inside of Faerie. The laws of their kind were much more distinct in this place, and he was a full-blooded sidhe. His magic flared, and the energy touched each and every one of his army. Bones knit, limbs reattached themselves, and eyes grew back into their sockets. His people stood up, whole once more and ready for the frontlines. Some of Naryssa's children let out screeches of horror as the undead they'd just finished tearing apart got back up again to attack them from behind. Cole grinned and enjoyed the sound for a moment before drawing out Bandersnatch and Jabberwock.

"Corhagen!" he called over his shoulder, firing. "Robyn! Let's move."

Robyn dove through the sea of bodies, twisting and turning in a blur of movement that he just barely caught. Her body moved as though she were performing some kind of complicated dance that involved kickboxing and barroom brawling. When some wouldn't go down, she opened fire with a pistol in one hand as the other sent blood splattering with a combat knife. In seconds, she was far ahead of him.

"You coming?' she snapped, looking back.

"Where's Corhagen?"

Robyn's eyes softened for a brief second. Dodging a blow aimed at her head, she leaped up over the mob and quickly swept the room, searching desperately. "I don't see him!" she called out, as she landed on the back of an overweight swamp goblin. "We've got to go now, or she'll just send more and trap us in here."

"No," Cole hissed, blowing apart a mismatched pile of arms and legs that tried to latch itself around him. "I'm not losing anyone else today. Go on ahead, and I'll catch up."

Cole didn't waste time looking back to see if she obeyed him. Sending a command out to his minions, he parted enough of the mob to push his way back toward the entrance where he'd last seen James.

Through the path made for him by the undead, Cole spotted Corhagen lying up against the wall, holding his gun feebly, trying to fend off several Doberman-sized, hungry-looking cockroach-esque creatures with the faces of human infants. Blood was coming out of a wound in his shoulder, making it hard for him to aim. The bullets kept the monsters away, but they were still emitting hungry clicking sounds that could be heard over the noise of the battle behind them. Cole stabbed one of the two nearest James in the back, watching it freeze with some satisfaction. The other caught fire at a touch of the firebrand of Aed Deigh. The remaining few scattered at the sight, racing up the walls and onto the ceiling. James watched them go, wide-eyed, as Cole lifted him up.

"You won't like this," he stated, gathering the man in his arms, "but it'll be faster. The others are already waiting."

James gave a startled yelp of pain as Cole cradled him in his arms. Keeping his gun aimed ahead of them, the detective let off a few warning shots into the crowd, causing it to split. Cole dove into it, willing his soldiers to follow after them. Shifting James slightly, he summoned power to his hand once more and healed them as they came up behind. Because there were so many, his magic was growing weaker even inside the walls of the faerie sithen, yet he refused to let up. At the end of the corridor, the hallway split into three different directions. Cole sniffed the air, hoping for some sign of the others, but it was as if the air itself was moving to keep their scents muddled.

"Which way did they go?" Corhagen asked. "Oh, and you can put me down now. I'm pretty sure I can walk."

Cole obliged, then turned toward his army. "Fan out," he commanded, raising his left hand high. "Search the place, but stay on your guard. The sithen is changing itself around, I think."

"It can do that?" James asked.

The undead moved to obey at once, but Cole remained behind as they walked past into one of the three passages. "The stories said that in the old days sithen mounds would adjust themselves according to the whims and needs of whoever commanded them. It was also a way to confuse and trap invaders. I saw Vallimun leave the hallway with Robyn heading this direction, but the air is moving around too much for me to get a clear scent. It's like a constant, swirling breeze deliberately throwing me off-track. The sithen may have changed itself after they came this way to confuse us and covered their tracks for good measure."

"So what do we do?"

Cole thought quickly as the last of his horde left them behind. "I suppose it really all depends on what the sithen wants," he admitted. "From this point on, we just pick a direction and hope it leads us to the others. If the sithen is on Naryssa's side, which at this point is highly possible, we're in a world of trouble."

"Literally," James muttered, agreeing. "Too bad Mal isn't here. Seeing as how he's a ghost, he could've walked through the walls or something."

"I lost sight of him when the battle broke out," Cole admitted. "He must be with the others. Let's try this way."

Corhagen didn't respond. "James," Cole called, turning around.

The spot where James had stood seconds before was deserted. Cole spun around in a complete circle, searching the area, but there was no sign of James anywhere. The area where he'd stood was totally undisturbed, as if he hadn't been standing there to begin with.

"Alright," he whispered, taking a step forward carefully. "You wanted to get me alone, Naryssa. I understand that much. So what now?"

If the sidhe-hag was listening, she gave no sign of it. The air around Cole shifted slightly, however, drifting off down the passageway to his right. Cole hesitated for a moment before drawing Jabberwock and stepping forward cautiously. The breeze at his back increased slightly as he moved down the dimly lit corridor, as though ushering him onward. Cole kept his guard up the whole time, but nothing made a move against him. He could smell nothing. There was no visible sign that anything was poised to attack. Nevertheless, he pressed his back to the wall and crouched down when the corridor veered sharply to the right. Peeking around, Cole saw a flight of stairs spiraling up toward a bright light.

"Interesting," he admitted, rising up. "I don't know what sort of game you're playing, Naryssa, but I'll bite. For now."

Taking the steps one at a time, Cole worked his way up, alternately keeping an eye and his gun pointed toward the entrance to the hall from where he'd come and the opening directly above. Nothing moved save a speck or two of dirt from the old, earthen walls. When he reached the top, he had to pull himself up through the small opening in the ceiling. The light disoriented him for a moment, and then suddenly, he was free.

Cole found himself standing in an expansive cavern that looked hand-carved, yet somehow more natural than anything human hands could shape. A stone table rested a few feet away, surrounded by pillars that looked vaguely like stalagmites on all four sides. Carvings in the table depicted an ancient hunt. Stags raced defiantly through brush and trees that were somehow lifelike against the brightness coming out from the very walls. Words had been inscribed around the edges, and even more on the ground. Tile was laid out as though this were a temple rather than some natural formation. Cole had to remind himself that he was still inside the sithen somewhere, most likely, and that the sithen itself had led him here. It had separated him from the others specifically to draw *him* toward this place, and no one else.

Though he was alone, he felt an urge not to break the silence. The place seemed deserted, yet Cole could feel hidden eyes watching him. Cole looked around, wondering if his observer could be viewing him from one of the shadows against the walls. As if in answer, the lights grew to illuminate the area even further. The suddenness of this made Cole blink, and he accidentally staggered backward into the table.

The stone felt warm and smelled faintly of blood. It sent shivers down his spine. Glancing up, he noticed a small altar set far away up against the northern wall. Standing there was a figure whose eyes bore into his. Rather than being alarmed, however, Cole simply rose up and met the imposing figure's gaze as though he had expected it. Though the light seemed to be coming from that direction, the figure himself was somehow concealed in shadows. It was a type of glamour Cole had seen used before, yet something inside of him whispered that this was not ordinary faerie magic. The figure motioned, and without thinking, Cole walked around the stone table toward him.

When they were but a few feet from each other, Cole fell to his knees and lowered his head nearly to the ground. "Forgive me, Father," he said breathlessly. "I did not see you."

A pair of hands, strong and calloused from years before time, touched his face, bringing the curtain of white hair back away from it. Cole felt himself drawn up into Consort's arms, the scent of autumn winds and deep wooded oak covering him like a blanket. He breathed deeply, taking it all in, as the Lord's lips pressed down into his scalp. Cole realized with a jolt that he was crying, though he couldn't remember why. Joy filled him to the point where it almost seemed like it would boil over from underneath his skin and burst out onto the floor. Dimly, he was aware of being lifted up off the ground and carried over to the table in the center of the room.

Consort laid him across it, running his hands along the length of Cole's body, and Cole realized that his clothes had somehow disappeared. It seemed so unimportant that he paid it no more mind, instead savoring the feel of the god's hands on his body, touching him through the protection of skin and bone down to his very heart and soul. It was pleasure to the point of being just slightly painful. Cole finally bowed his back up, unable to take it anymore, and he felt something being put to his lips.

"Drink," Consort whispered, holding a cup now. "My son, drink."

Cole did as he was bid, and found that the water tasted amazing. Seizing the cup with his own two hands, Cole downed the icy liquid, letting some of it splash against his naked chest. The water drifted farther down over his cock and balls and onto the table. The water became like light, spilling over onto the floor and surrounding them.

Consort took the carved wooden cup from him gently, then made him lie back down. "Lie still," said the voice that seemed to echo all around.

Cole did, not so much as twitching a finger, and waited. There was movement, though he dared not rise up to look. Suddenly, Consort was leaning over him again, holding a dagger in one hand. The other held the cup, filled with something different this time, though Cole's nose couldn't quite put a name to it.

"Choose," whispered Consort, and the one word rippled through him.

Cole reached up and carefully traced the air around the black athame. "The cup," he whispered back, swallowing.

"So be it," said Consort, before the two disappeared.

The god raised a leg up onto the stone table then, exposing himself for the first time to Cole's gaze. He was hard, impossibly so, and hung low enough that the weight of his member caused the length of it to curve downward slightly. Consort drew himself up onto the table until he was hanging just above Cole's body in a sort of odd push-up position. His beard had several braids tied into it, and they tickled across Cole's chest as he bent down low. Consort captured Cole's mouth in his own, and the world exploded around them. Cole opened up, letting the power from his Lord spill into him, causing his skin to shine like the brightest star in the sky. At that moment, Cole felt as though he could have lit up the entire Manhattan skyline.

His arms wound around Consort's neck and under the thick mat of wool-like hair that flowed down his back. Cole moaned, and in doing so, wound his legs around the god's waist. Consort moved forward a little. It was an expert move, one born out of eons of practice and bringing pleasure to others. Cole gasped, breaking the kiss, and felt Consort's cock push at the entrance down there. His body tensed involuntarily, but the Lord didn't let up. He pushed, and there was a breaking of pressure, then the white-hot flesh rod was inside.

Cole could feel everything around him: the hands that caressed his body, the stone scratching against the skin on his back, and the weight of Consort himself pushing down as he drove into him. It was like fire being born for the first time on Earth, like the wind touching the dust before rain, thunder shaking the clouds, and lightning licking through the branches of tree tops. All of that and more thrust into him, so many ancient and timeless concepts too foreign for even Cole to comprehend, for he'd lived away from Faerie too long. The sithen flexed and breathed around them, drawing itself in closer to cup the power spilling out over the side of the table. Dimly, Cole was aware of the wooden chalice being drawn to his lips. What was in there filled him from one end as the massive cock of Consort slammed in and out his ass mercilessly. Cole bucked and thrashed about around it, screaming his joy and pleasure to the ceiling for anyone to hear. None of that mattered.

He was alive. And he was reborn.

He couldn't remember when he came, or if the Consort had. The next thing Cole knew, he was waking up in a different place. Mal was leaning over him, looking very worried. "I thought maybe you were getting ready to join me," the ghost said, wiping his brow. "I've seen some freaky looking things in my day, but watching somebody rise up out of the floor like that manages to stand out."

Cole swallowed tentatively and discovered his throat was dry. "I...," he tested, finding he could still speak, if roughly. "I'm alive. How did you get here?"

"I've been here for hours," Mal replied. "At least, it feels a lot like that. You might wanna stand up and get moving, assuming you're not hurt. The others aren't doing so well, and I doubt I can hold that bitch off for much longer. She's going to break through eventually, and when that happens, it won't be pretty."

"You're holding her at bay?" Cole wondered, looking around. "How?"

"That's kind of a long story," Mal admitted, blushing a little. "Look, I know what I said to you earlier about you not being my type, but...."

"You saw Consort," he finished, standing up. "And I'm guessing 'something' happened?"

Mal looked away sheepishly. "I don't know for sure if that's who it was, but he offered me something in this wooden cup. Haven't seen one of those in a long time, a really long time. This was after all hell broke loose when we got inside and I was sucked down into the ground."

"What?"

"Yeah." Mal nodded gravely. "I thought I was a goner for sure, but then he was there, holding that cup in his hand and offering it to me. After it was, you know, all said and done, I could feel everything around me. I think whatever he did tied me to this whole place. I can feel it like it was my own body, even though I haven't had a body in centuries."

"He made you a part of the sithen." Cole nodded, understanding. "Or made it a part of you."

Quickly, Cole explained everything that had happened. "You actually went upstairs to get to the deepest level of the sithen there is," Mal repeated, wonderingly. "You know, that doesn't sound nearly as weird to me as it might have a while ago."

"I don't know how far down I was," he admitted. "But it felt pretty deep."

"You were," Mal said, looking off into the distance. "I can feel it. That's... well, I don't know how to put this precisely. Fey magic wasn't a specialty of mine, but that place is the battery of the whole sithen. You've become a part of it, too, only now it's like I can access the database and make it do what I want."

"Then I grant you permission to use the sithen however you need to in order to help us fight Naryssa," he stated flatly. After a moment's hesitation, Cole added, "Did that work?"

Mal blinked, then nodded quickly. "Oh, yeah."

"Good," Cole breathed. "I don't know about any of this, but it seemed like it was worth a shot. Can you get me to where the others are fighting?"

"I think so." Mal closed his eyes, and a second later, a brown door appeared off to the side. "Head through there," he said, pointing. "It'll take you straight to the battle."

"Thanks," said Cole. "Come with me. Let's get that bitch together. For Katalina."

Mal stood proudly and saluted, which Cole couldn't help but chortle at. "As you command, mon capitaine," he declared. "Lead the way."

Cole did, and he found himself standing in another corridor, different from the ones he'd seen before. This one was much darker, covered in black-and-gray tiles all along the walls and floor. There were torches hung on the walls that gave off light but no heat. Matching pillars spaced every few feet lined each side, meeting in archways overhead. The archways looked like oak branches knotted together to form faces screaming in pain. Apparently, this was one region of the sithen still under Naryssa's control.

"I thought they were here," he asked, looking around for Mal.

"So did I," the spirit confessed, appearing suddenly beside him. "That bitch must've intercepted me. She still has control over certain areas."

"And you have control over the rest?" he pressed, thinking quickly. "How does that work?"

"The sithen took in Naryssa simply because there were no other fey left to occupy it," Mal stated, as though reading from something. "It needed something to live here, but I'm not entirely sure why. I do know that the place you were in earlier is meant to be some type of temple. When you came, it sensed you were powerful enough to take control away from her. That's why it brought me here. I could communicate with you better, and act as a sort of interface."

"You're just now learning all of this?"

"It's a work in progress," Mal admitted, shrugging. "I'm still figuring stuff out myself. But the part of me that's connected to the sithen…. It's more like the sithen became my new body. I'm here now talking to you because I need to be, but this isn't my real form anymore. The part of me that's the sithen is spreading out into it like a virus, only it's more like Naryssa is a contaminant, and she's being purged."

"You could throw her out, then?"

"Maybe," said Mal as he screwed up his face in concentration. "The bitch is losing ground fast. With a little bit of effort, and maybe a boost of power from you, we can force her back up to the surface. Care to lend me a hand?"

Cole reached out, but before he could touch Mal's ghostly body, the floor in front of him broke apart. The gray-and-black tiles shifted around, back and forth, until there was a small opening there with wind whistling up through it. A glass ball the size of his head rose up. Inside of it was a vortex as blue as a summer sky.

"Touch it," Mal instructed. "It will allow you to channel your power directly into the sithen."

"What is it?" Cole asked.

"No time to explain," Mal replied. "Just get ready. Oh, and you might want to hold on to anything of yours that isn't attached. Once this gets going, you probably won't like the trip."

"What do you mean?"

Chapter Thirteen

COLE sputtered, gasping as water dripped out of his nose. The air all around him was rank with the scent of rotten flesh soaked to the bone in a flood. In the distance, he heard Corhagen cussing angrily as Vallimun called out his name. Robyn was with them; he could hear her muttering something about ruined C-4. His undead minions were scattered all around, as well as the legion of mixed fey under Naryssa's command. The sidhe-hag was nowhere in sight, but that didn't bother him. He would deal with her just as soon as he had sneezed out the remaining moisture from his nose and could stand up again. Before, Cole had thought of only the rubber-tube sense of being summoned and the years spent under Oberon's rule as the most unpleasant experiences of his life, not including being banished, of course. Mal's actions had added what felt like being flushed down a toilet and spat out by an erupting geyser to the list. The newly appointed spirit of the sithen had certainly brought the battle back up to street level.

And put water in his ears in the process.

Cole tilted his head to allow the liquid room to flow out properly and checked around for signs of Naryssa. The other fey were already getting to their feet, some of them looking a little the worse for wear. Before Mal had performed his little stunt, the tide of battle had apparently shifted in Naryssa's favor. The undead soldiers at Cole's command were barely holding themselves together. From where he stood, Vallimun and Corhagen looked to have been put through the wringer. Only Robyn was unscathed, and even she had been winded by the fight.

It was up to him now. Although being inside the sithen greatly increased his magic, the same was true of Naryssa and her children. Cole had to shift the balance back in his favor, and that meant taking them all back to mortal soil. Had any humans been around at this point, they'd no doubt have been flabbergasted. He supposed Consort and Goddess were to be thanked for small favors.

With Aed Deigh at the ready, Cole walked a circle around the fountain, waiting for the smallest movement. Mal had bought him a brief reprieve, since no one had been expecting the entire sithen to simply up and belch them back out into the park. Cole certainly hadn't, but he wasn't about to let the opportunity slide past without taking full advantage of it.

The Hand of Cold Death flared to life, and Cole cast his power out into his remaining troops, those still in more or less one piece. "Naryssa!" he cried, his voice carrying out past the borders of the park and between the buildings beyond. "Is this all that remains of you and your ilk? I expected more from someone of such reputed power. Come and face me, face the vengeance that awaits you for the murder of Katalina, or do you want your children to see you as the coward you really are?"

Silence and then: "I am here, Tuulois," she said softly from behind him. "Here, and waiting. Not a coward, and not hiding from my so-called fate."

Cole turned around and faced her. Naryssa's eyes glowed brightly, as did his. Some of the other fey rose up, preparing to charge him, but Naryssa sent them back with a glance. "This is between myself and the fallen wolf of Titania's," she declared, her eyes never leaving Cole's. "Anyone who interferes now faces my unhappiness."

"This could have stayed between us," Cole said, stroking Aed Deigh's hilt unconsciously. "I would've fought you on equal terms, but you dragged a protected human into this. Even by the standards held among the exiled and the lost, that was reprehensible. In the lands of Faerie, you'd be executed at once without fail."

"The old ways are gone," Naryssa dismissed with a wave. "Those that cling to such codes are fools."

"The Old Ways are only abandoned when there are none left who remember them," Cole replied, stepping forward. "You never knew that, did you?"

Naryssa cocked her head slightly and studied Cole as he stood in front of her, directly in the path of the lamplight. "Something has changed about you," she noted carefully. "What has made you so interesting? You were never quite this bold before."

"I have seen the face of our Lord," he answered with a serene smile. "I have felt his touch, and his grace. You stand on land once consecrated in his name, for the purpose of sharing his power with the world around it, and you never realized what it was. It should have been obvious, yet you've ignored it all this time, choosing to see only what it could do for you and yours. Now the land has rejected you and cast us from it. Only one may enter and stand in its bowels again after this night. I intend that it should be me."

"Why you?" she challenged. "Why in hell's chambers would Consort choose you, a man who wasn't worthy to stand among the ranks of the queen's horde and hunt throughout the nights?"

Cole shrugged. "I guess he just has good taste."

Aed Deigh flared to life at both ends. Cole gave the weapon an expert swing with his wrist as he lowered himself slightly in a fighting stance. "Come." He beckoned with the other hand. "Let us put an end to this. For the lives that you've taken, and for the life of Katalina, I intend to snuff yours before dawn breaks over the skyline."

Naryssa stepped forward to meet his challenge, wearing a smug grin and holding her right hand out. "I find your obsession with the death of one lone mortal intriguing," she mocked, drawing power into her hand. Somewhere overhead, Cole thought he heard thunder rumbling. "What was she to you? I thought the mortal detective held your fancy."

"She lived with me," Cole replied very curtly, not allowing himself to be distracted. "She was a friend and under my protection. And I loved her, if that means anything to you."

"Ah, of course," she said, as what looked like electricity jumped between her clawed fingers. "For want of it, sidhe and mortals alike are willing to make fools of themselves. I have always found such trivialities meaningless except for when it comes to my children, of course. For them, I would do anything."

"Including take the lives of others."

"I have done far worse than that for their sakes," Naryssa responded as the air around them shifted and grew heavier. "And I would do it again. Now, however, I think that I would like you to witness something extraordinary. You, who were raised among the courts, with their bright, glittering lands and hallowed hills, might find it interesting that I possess a Hand of Power myself."

"You are half-sidhe," he said, keeping both eyes on her. "How is that so unusual?"

"My Hand of Power," Naryssa answered smugly, "is the Hand of Storms."

Naryssa thrust her hand skyward. Overhead, an arc of lightning jumped from one cloud to the next before landing in her fingers. The sky had been clear before now, Cole thought, yet Naryssa's magic had summoned a storm to her in a matter of seconds. The lightning jumped again, this time from her hand to the ground between them. Smoke rose up from the grass, and the wind suddenly kicked into high gear.

Then all hell broke loose.

Cole sent out a command to his undead, then ducked low to the ground as wind cut the air above him like knives. The high-pressure system met with the low. Heat and cold slammed into one another like fists, then rose up in a tangle. A twister now blocked the space separating Cole from Naryssa, and her mad cackling could be heard over the howling wind.

"My power is to command the skies and the winds," she crowed joyously. "The rains, the thunder, and the lightning all rest in the palm of my hand. You, who can summon the long-dead, what can you do against such a power? How does one mighty sidhe stand a chance against a lowly, gutter-blooded half-hag like myself?"

Behind Cole, his minions had jumped on top of Robyn, Corhagen, and Vallimun, keeping them down and out of harm's way. The extra weight ensured none of them would be blown away. Naryssa was still laughing madly even as some of her own children were thrown into the trees.

"What now, sidhe?" she screamed, as the twister gained in speed and strength. "What now, I ask you?"

"Now?" Cole muttered, bringing up the fiery point of Aed Deigh. "Now this, I suppose."

Fire exploded out from the blade, leaping across the windy air into the root of the whirlwind. Cole focused his power, letting the spirit of summer flow out of his core into the blade, powering it up so that it brought the flames almost to a full white heat. The storm seemed to hesitate for a moment and sway slightly, as though off-balance. Cole didn't let up, keeping the blade pointed even as he felt the drain begin. The air grew hot, and as the heat intensified, Naryssa let out a shrill cry. Thrusting her hand forward, she threw more power into the twister, forcing it back under her control. Cole had already gained a foothold, however, and he kept it. There was a flash that ran up the length of the wind funnel, and the air grew suddenly still as the twister dissipated. Cole heard something metallic fall into place behind him, followed by what could have been the scraping of a body over grass.

"Basic meteorology knowledge," he breathed. "Tornadoes are formed when low pressure drags a formed mesocyclone down. Adding heat to the low pressure causes it to rise. In the case of such a small twister, it dissipates once it drifts up toward the atmosphere and out of range. The lightning bolt was a nice touch, but it really was just for show."

Cole bowed, keeping his eyes forward the whole time. "And I would like to thank Wikipedia for providing me with such life-saving knowledge when I was bored and low on porn to watch. You see, Naryssa, the School House Rock lesson of the night is that power is useless without the knowledge to use it. And just so you know, I'm saying this strictly to rub it in your face."

"Why is that?" she snarled, bringing her claws forward.

"Because it pisses you off to no end," he said, grinning. "And also because it provides Vallimun with a long enough distraction."

Aed Deigh's blades snapped back into the hilt as Cole threw himself flat onto the ground. A deafening roar echoed behind him, followed by a rocket whizzing over his head. The projectile landed squarely in Naryssa's stomach and exploded on impact. The sidhe-hag was thrown clear off her feet in the blinding blast as a hole bigger than a basket ball appeared in her abdomen. With a sickening thud, her body landed on the ground several feet away and continued to roll past the stunned faces of her children. When it came to a stop, the charred remains lay smoldering in the grass near a row of bushes.

Cole knew she was still breathing. Even after that, Naryssa wouldn't die.

"*Mother!*"

It was Raywing who screamed as she came swooping down from overhead. More of Naryssa's children joined her in her cries as they gathered around the still form up ahead. Cole watched them, and for a moment, he felt the barest sting of pity. Then, Katalina's face passed before his mind's eye, and he sneered in disgust.

"He hurt her!" Raywing screeched. "He hurt Mother!"

"Tear the bastard and his companions apart," Spinner's voice shouted out somewhere behind them.

Cole joined the others as his minions obediently rose up and began walking toward the approaching lynch mob. "I don't suppose you have another one of those?" he asked Vallimun, who was able to stand up now that he wasn't buried under a pile of dead bodies. "Or three? Or even ten!"

"Lost all the ammo when we were spat out of that place," he grunted. "That was the only shot I had."

"I've still got the gun she loaned me," said James, standing up next to Robyn. "Only I don't think it's working."

"We're probably doomed," Robyn noted, watching as the fey came closer, past the line of guards shielding them. "I'm all for running away, only it looks like a lot of them would be able to catch up to us before we got very far from the park."

"Maybe we could call a taxi?" James suggested.

"Or maybe," Vallimun said, pointing, "someone could call the cops."

Flashing lights were approaching in the distance. The sight of them made every last one of Naryssa's children stop dead in their tracks. As what looked like twenty or so police cars approached, Raywing gave one final wail of desperate rage before flying off into the darkness. Spinner watcher her go, then gave Cole a look of pure contempt.

"Another time," she promised, shifting forms.

"Collect Mother and spread out," she commanded to her siblings. "We'll meet up at the cabin later."

The cop cars were just pulling up as the horde began to disperse in groups. Beyond the trees, Cole heard car doors slamming shut and the shouts of angry policemen as they ordered the retreating figures to halt. There was no doubt in his mind that none of them would be caught tonight. He hadn't slain Naryssa like he'd sworn, but Cole let his quest for revenge drop for now. From the looks of things, it was going to be a long day, and he'd used up enough strength to make him want nothing more than a long shower, a cup of hot chocolate, and a sound day's sleep. None of that was going to happen soon, though, if the angry looks on some of the policemen's faces were any indication. The sight of so many dead bodies just lying around caused one officer to promptly lose his lunch. Cole guessed he was a rookie. However, the others didn't look well, either.

As one of them approached, Vallimun quickly drew out his badge and flashed it for them to see. "Inspector Joss Vallimun," he proclaimed, waving it around. "NYPD. They're with me, boys."

"Joss?" Cole wondered aloud.

"We got reports of a fifty-foot geyser coming out of the park earlier," one of the uniforms said, looking over the inspector's credentials. "Then the precinct got an emergency bulletin. Someone claimed they'd seen a tornado over this very same spot. If we hadn't gotten in about a hundred phone calls all at once, I'd have said it was a crank call."

"I guess a geyser and a small weather anomaly are the two things New Yorkers just can't ignore," Robyn commented, shrugging.

James looked stunned. "You thought that was small?"

"It's been a long evening for us, officers," Vallimun explained. "Would you and your men mind coming with me? I'll explain everything, but the others could use a little down time. You have my word that they won't be going anywhere."

"That's what he thinks," Robyn muttered, as Vallimun managed to persuade everyone to walk back toward the parked cars. "I don't know about you, but getting caught with enough armaments to start another Korean Conflict isn't on my to-do list. I'll take my rifle and bazooka back now and be on my way, if neither of you minds."

Cole didn't bother protesting. After Robyn had collected her treasured items, Cole watched her leap down across the grassy knoll out of sight and into the darkness of the city, which welcomed her with open arms. "That girl is completely psycho," he noted.

"I don't ever want to hear you criticizing my taste in women again," James replied, looking at the spot where she'd disappeared. "She was running around inside that place like a lunatic, laughing and giggling the whole time like it was her first trip to Disney World. I thought I was going to lose my mind, and she was having the time of her life."

"Different strokes for different folks," Cole commented. "You should know that by now."

Corhagen ignored that remark. "I don't know what I'm going to tell my superiors now that this is over with," he said, sighing. "None of them are going to want to hear this, but I hate lying on police reports."

"It's not over," Cole informed him. "Naryssa was still alive when they took her body away. It'll be a while before we hear from her again, but make no mistake. Once she's healed, this will have been the preliminary round before the main event. She's going to want revenge, just like I do."

Corhagen didn't say anything for a moment. Then he said, "Did you ever find out why I turned into a sidhe that time in the hospital?"

Cole blinked. "Why are you asking now?"

James shrugged, then wiped his hands off on his jacket. "I don't know," he replied, evasively. "Maybe it's just that so little of this made sense to me. I was hoping something that'd happened over these last couple of days might become clearer." He took his time before continuing. "So, did you ever find out?"

Cole sighed. "If you want things to become clearer, you have to be willing to accept things for what they are," he explained, picking over each word carefully. "There's no point in me telling you anything if you aren't willing to accept unpleasant truths. They might not be what you wanted to hear, but you must open yourself up to them if you want to understand anything."

Corhagen frowned. "I'm not good with uncomfortable truths," he admitted.

"I never noticed," Cole replied sarcastically. "And I won't say anything more on the subject, except that maybe you didn't really become sidhe. Maybe I somehow made you look like one, and feel like one, because you secretly wanted it. If you were sidhe, a lot of obstacles in your life wouldn't be a problem anymore. Am I right?"

"I'd rather not think about that." Corhagen winced as Cole placed a hand gently on his shoulder. "At all."

Cole took in a deep breath and let it out slowly, letting his hand slide away. "I can't change what I am," he informed James, moving away. "Any more than you can."

"No, you can't," James said. "But maybe I'm not what you want me to be. Maybe we're both too different."

"We're not," he stated, looking off toward the fountain. "We're too much alike. That's always been the problem between us. With me around, you can't become what you'd like to be for the rest of the world."

He could practically hear James stiffen. "You're right," James whispered softly. "I can't, but I need to be. For my kids."

When James walked away, Cole didn't make a move to stop him. Instead, he kept both eyes squarely on the fountain in front of him and on what lay directly beneath it. Only when James's footsteps faded out of earshot did the tears fall down his cheeks. Cole stood there proudly, refusing to wipe them away. Some landed on the surface of the water, causing ripples. In response, the water surged up and formed a door leading back down into the sithen. Cole breathed the night air into his lungs, then stepped forward into the darkened opening that somehow managed to stand out even in the dead of night. The moment he entered, Cole instantly felt more relaxed. Power was easing into him through his pores, and he gave a slight wave back the way he'd come. At once, the door vanished.

Mal was waiting for him. "Tuulois MacColewyn," he said, as though announcing his presence at a ball. "Welcome home."

THE next few weeks went by quickly, save for a couple of spots here and there. Cole had gone back to his loft to retrieve his stuff and inform the landlord that he was moving out. The man had taken it well, all things considered, and only threatened to sue him for everything he was worth twice. Cole made his exit with quiet dignity and tried not to think about the loft that'd been home to him for several years now. It was why he'd tried not to get too attached to a place for very long. Eventually, he had to move far enough away that people wouldn't recognize him on sight. The landlord was not likely to forget Cole's face on account of the damage Naryssa's brats had done. This time, however, Cole wasn't worried about someone finding him. It was unlikely he'd be located soon, given his new address.

No, it was thinking about what the loft had meant to him and remembering Katalina's presence there that was so unbearable. The whole time he'd gathered up his things—what had survived the onslaught, anyway—he'd been tortured with images of her moving around the place like she was still alive. It wasn't her ghost, just Cole's mind refusing to accept her death.

Thankfully, perhaps, there was still plenty going on to keep his mind occupied. A fat check from the city of New York arrived in his new post office box a few days afterward, enough that Cole felt obligated to spoil himself by going out to a Broadway play one evening. These days, it wasn't such a chore getting there.

The play was good, and he made the acquaintance of a lovely young woman who'd been dragged along by her friends. It turned out they shared a few things in common. She too had lost a loved one recently, and she attended classes at the same college Katalina had. The evening turned into a night spent sharing the pleasure of one another's company. In the morning, Cole left her apartment complex feeling considerably lighter than he had in a few days, his skin still giving off a slight glow even several hours after lovemaking.

There had been questions, of course. Given the publicity surrounding the mysterious events at Bowling Green that night, the chief of police wasn't going to simply accept the story Inspector

Vallimun handed to him in his report. The tabloids were having a field day with it, but Cole suspected that was for the best. There was little chance, if any, that they'd discover the sithen. So long as the gossip-mongers had something to talk about, people would be sufficiently distracted. Nothing concerning the murders had been leaked to the press just yet, so Cole felt Corhagen's superiors should be grateful for their luck and let it go.

As for James, Cole had not laid eyes on him since the night of the battle. James had been carted off to the nearest hospital once Vallimun had managed to smooth things over. It turned out he'd endured a couple of moderate wounds during the battle, though it was nothing too serious. Cole had tried to visit him the next day but was cut off at the pass by an enraged Sarah, who threatened to call for security. James's kids had been there, and the more she'd yelled, the more it looked like they would start crying. In the end, Cole had walked away without being escorted out. Sarah had screamed the whole time and even chased him to the elevator. He was sure James had known of his visit, but the detective didn't try to call or contact him in any way afterward. Cole guessed he was still trying to make a go of his marriage, for whatever reason. In the end, it was just one more kick to his balls, yet he knew it was time to let things go.

It didn't do any good to try to hold onto something as it slid impossibly through your fingers.

Sarah wouldn't have stood a chance against him, but Cole knew he had no hope of winning James's heart when pitted against the eyes of a child.

These days, his primary companion was Mal. The former sorcerer was having quite a time learning his newfound powers as the brain of the sithen. The ghost could no longer leave the hidden faerie mound. Something about him was tied to it inexorably. Cole had felt bad for him, but Mal seemed to take it well. Overall, as he'd pointed out, the sithen was a much better prison than a book or a computer. Though he missed surfing the web, the sithen was still compatible with Wi-Fi. It seemed the place adjusted to modern conveniences quite nicely when handled by someone with experience in such matters. It was because of this that Cole received an unexpected e-mail requesting his attendance at a local bar. When Cole arrived in the pouring rain, Vallimun was already waiting for him by the window.

"I thought you might've drowned," the inspector teased as Cole pulled up a chair.

"Sidhe warriors do not drown," Cole informed him, shaking some of the water off. "I got your e-mail. You made it sound like it was urgent."

"It is," the inspector replied evasively. "First, though, have some nachos. They'll warm you up."

Cole wasn't chilled, despite the rain, but he accepted one anyway.

"I've got a proposition for you," Vallimun began as Cole chewed quietly. "Things have been getting hairy among the brass since the homicide investigation was officially closed. Even if the boys upstairs don't know what to make of my story, they're willing to believe that Naryssa is still out there. No one wants her to start up again, and I've been talking to some folks who owe me favors about what could be done to prevent that very thing from happening."

Cole didn't answer and instead munched on another nacho while waiting for the inspector to continue. "James has a few contacts," Vallimun said. "I know some men that need time away from vice squad, so we're trying to put together a new squad with the support of the chief. He's not happy with it, but word from above says he hasn't got much say in the matter."

"What's this got to do with me?" Cole asked, swallowing.

Vallimun reached into his coat pocket and pulled something out. When he laid it on the table, Cole saw that it was a badge—an NYPD police badge for a Special Detective, Tuulois MacColewyn. "I asked Corhagen for your full name," he explained, dipping a nacho into the mound of sour cream in the center. "We're going to try and bring back Section Thirteen. The two stipulations the brass had was that our reports not sound like a bad LSD trip, and to locate the missing children. That was something the tabloids picked up on, and now the politicians can't afford to let it go. I don't know if we'll be able to hold our end of the bargain when it comes to writing reports, but it's worth a try."

Cole hadn't taken his eyes off the badge the whole time. "What do you say?" the inspector asked, eyeing him closely.

Cole didn't look up. "You want me," he began, as though grasping at a concept too alien to comprehend, "to become a cop? Are you out of your mind, or is this some sort of early April Fool's Day prank?"

"The pay is shit," Vallimun admitted. "And the benefits are a joke, but we need you. Otherwise, it'll be just like tossing lambs to the slaughter."

"You've got that one right," Cole muttered, looking away.

"I have one other incentive for you joining up," he added, glancing off to the side to make sure no one else was listening. "That is, if you're willing to hear me out."

Cole waited, and the inspector quietly moved the badge past the nacho plate and over toward Cole. As he drew his hand away, Vallimun lightly brushed his fingers along the back of Cole's hand. The contact was brief and went unnoticed by the bar's other patrons. Cole felt his breath quicken as he met the inspector's heated gaze. When he didn't move away, Vallimun stroked the length of Cole's palm and licked his lips.

"So," Vallimun whispered huskily, "what do you say?"

J.L. O'FAOLAIN was born the youngest, with four older sisters, in the backwoods of the Deep South. Those that've braved getting to know him have attributed this to being the root of his growing insanity. A teased bibliophile in his youth, O'Faolain spent his years prior to getting published as a cook, laundry man, delivery boy, grease monkey, and retail stocker. He has a plethora of skills and abilities, none of which would work well on a job application. In his spare time, O'Faolain enjoys weightlifting, philosophy, reading, writing, porn, and the Internet in general. Aside from becoming a successfully published author, he would very much like to pilot a giant robot while Two-Mix's "Rhythm Emotion" is playing in the background. This past year, he celebrated his thirtieth birthday and is very much looking forward to the rest of his life without slowing down for one second.

Fantasy Romance from DREAMSPINNER PRESS